The Work of the Kabbalist

By the same author

Adam and the Kabbalistic Tree
Kabbalah and Exodus
A Kabbalistic Universe
Psychology and Kabbalah
School of the Soul (School of Kabbalah)
Tree of Life: Introduction to the Cabala
The Way of Kabbalah

Z'ev ben Shimon Halevi

the work of the Kabbalist

SAMUEL WEISER, INC.

York Beach, Maine

First American edition published in 1986 by
Samuel Weiser, Inc.
Box 612
York Beach, Maine 03910-0612

99 98 97 96 95
11 10 9 8 7 6 5

Library of Congress Catalog Card Number: 85-51910

ISBN 0-87728-637-X
BJ

Cover illustration is titled "Aaron the High Priest filling the Menorah." Reproduced here by kind permission of the British Library, London.

Printed in the United States of America

The paper used in this publication meets the minimum requirements of the American National Standard for Permanence of Paper for Printed Library Materials Z39.48-1984.

For

Moses Cordovero

1. **THE WORK OF THE KABBALIST**
Standing amid the four elements with the mineral, vegetable and animal realms on the left, and the works of mankind on the right, the Kabbalist, dressed in garments of the soul and spirit, raises the hands in a receiving and imparting gesture, while occupying the Kingdom position of a Tree made up of the moon, sun and planets. Above the canopy of stars, the angelic and archangelic worlds headed by Metatron, hovers the radiance of the Divine.

Contents

Illustrations

Preface

To be acquainted with Kabbalah is one matter, but to do its Work quite another. Many who begin to walk the path soon tire or turn away when the novelty has gone, and some even double back after great progress when they see there is nothing for them. Only those who do the Work for its own sake are initiated. Only the individual who wants to make manifest what Kabbalah reveals can be an initiate. This process is nothing less than to integrate the body, soul and spirit, and so become a finer instrument whereby the inner and outer worlds can come into communion. Each time this is done, the Divine is known by Adam upon the Earth. By such a labour of love, the Universe comes increasingly into focus as a reflection of the Absolute. When the human image of the Divine realises upon whom it gazes, then God perceives God, and the cycle is complete. To assist the Holy One in this aim is the Work of the Kabbalist.

Winter 5742

2. **JACOB'S DREAM**
As the spiritually unawakened Adam lies asleep the angelic beings go up and down the great path that stretches between Heaven and Earth. This state of consciousness is the normal condition of most people, until one day they wake up, if only for a moment, to say in awe like Jacob, "The Lord is in this Place and I knew it not". This is the first rung for the Kabbalist on the Ladder of Realisation.

Introduction

The kabbalistic method is the practical art of entering into and participating in the higher worlds. Whether it be by action, devotion, or contemplation, its aim is always to serve God and aid in the great Work of Unification. This work is the perfection of mankind so that Adam, the image of the Divine, may realise that the exterior and interior universe is the reflection of God beholding God.

Prior to this penultimate state of being, before total union with the Absolute, the universe and mankind have to pass through many stages. According to one view the human race as a whole is less than half way in its development. Indeed history and the events of the present century indicate that the vast majority of human souls on the Earth are somewhere between childhood and youth. After two global wars the possibility of a third remains quite real as the so-called advanced nations still react like adolescent gangs over territory, while the rest squabble amongst themselves for the marbles of power and wealth. Fortunately, there has always been a proportion of the human race that is more mature, even as there is a minority of childish souls in every society that is still primitive in its outlook. This evolved spearhead of mankind occurs all over the world, and at every point in history. It may be seen embodied in Messianic figures, great prophets and teachers, or in traditions of high spiritual development. Its indirect influence may be witnessed in the living religions of mankind, and in periods of advanced culture when the creative impulse of cosmic influx has been married into a moment of flowering in a society to produce a civilisation such as early Islam or ancient China. These great epochs, like the period of the cathedral master builders in the Middle Ages, could not have arisen without the presence of people who not only knew about the upper worlds, but had the ability to draw down their substance and power, and focus it upon the activities of the Earth. Like other spiritual traditions, this is the Work of Kabbalah. However, before such a task can be undertaken by an individual, group or school, there is a whole process of training and understanding of what is involved. This must be, or the operation of unifying will become no more than a magical exercise concerned with personal inflation and private interests, which are the very opposite to the aim of the Work of Unification, as Kabbalah is sometimes called.

Kabbalah is one of many traditions involved with such activities. If we look at its ancient line it will be seen that Kabbalah, although it was not always known by this name, was practised in many of the great cultural centres of the Middle East and the West. It was to be found in pre-exile Israel, Babylon, Hellenistic Egypt, and in Roman-occupied Judea. It was present in Islamic Mesapotamia before it transferred to Provence and Spain in the Middle Ages, and was practised in Flanders and Bohemia, as well as in Poland, Italy and Elizabethan England, where Shakespeare no doubt knew secret Jews then living in London. Kabbalah was studied in 17th century Holland, and in 18th century Germany, as well as Victorian England, although the system practised by this time was several removes from the Jewish line that had continued on in Eastern Europe and Western Asia.

As may be realised, mere contact with the theory of a spiritual tradition is not enough to transform an individual, let alone a society. Action has to be taken in accordance with the sequence of the four levels of existence. To will, conceive, form and carry out a spiritual project, or transmit a cosmic influence, requires not only a comprehension of esoteric principles, but skill to implement them. This book endeavours to set out the process of acquiring such knowledge and the techniques of how to use it for different purposes and at various levels. It will draw upon traditional material designed to meet contemporary conditions, because Kabbalah has always adapted itself to the present. If this had not been so, then the line would have died long ago in ancient Israel, instead of still being alive and practised all around the world in forms appropriate to each period and place. And so we begin with the Eternal and translate it into our own time.

1. Origin of the Work

The root of all practical kabbalistic work goes back to the source of everything that exists. Indeed, the whole process of coming into being, carrying out one's destiny and returning to that point of origin is the essence of the Work of Unification. Everything begins with the Most High Name of God: I AM THAT I AM. This Holy appellation is associated with the Crown of Crowns at the head of the Great Ladder of Jacob which describes, in its four interlocking worlds, all the levels of existence from its highest manifestation of pure consciousness to the lowest and densest concretation of matter.

The Divine Name I AM THAT I AM was given to Moses as he stood before the burning bush upon the Holy Mountain. It was in answer to his question (Exodus III.13) as to what should he say to the Children of Israel when they asked who had sent him. *EHYEH ASHER EHEYEH* was the reply, and then, "*EHEYEH shelachan: alaychem*"—"I AM has sent me unto you". This was followed by the better known Divine Name *YAHVEH*, which came to be the title by which the Holy One was to be remembered and honoured in the exoteric tradition. Here we have the differentiation between aspects of Divinity as it enters into manifestation and multiplicity.

If one contemplates the first Name that was given, and its significance, then an awesome depth of meaning is revealed, for it speaks of what was, that which is, and which shall be. This is a statement of intent, as well as a cycle of being. When associated with the Crown of Crowns, I AM THAT I AM sets out the Absolute's Will with succinct precision, as God calls forth existence from the midst of non-existence. In the utterance of *EHEYEH*, the hidden Holiness appears as manifest Divinity. This is symbolised in Kabbalah as Light emerging out of the darkness of a void. However, the process does not stop there, in that Divinity extends itself in order, as said, to behold Itself in reflection. Thus the Divine proceeds into *ASHER* or THAT before resolving into *EHEYEH*, or I AM again. Here is the plan for all existence. Everything to come into manifestation is contained in this Name of Names.

3. **NAME**

AHYEH ASHER AHYEH: I AM THAT I AM is the highest Holy Name at the Crown of Crowns. It is the first and the last Name that every being called forth, created, formed and made speaks, as it comes into and passes out of Existence. In its utterance the Divine perceives, and is perceived, as the source of Light, and its reflection in Existence.

The implication of this gives us a key to why the universe and its inhabitants exist, in that everything held between the poles of unity above and multiplicity below is part of a great precession of realisation. This process will be terminated when the mirror of the macrocosm reflects the name I AM back as a fully conscious image to its Divine origin. Such a moment can only happen when everything in existence has reached its full capacity of self-realisation. This will take the complete round of a great *Shemmitah* or cosmic cycle in which all creatures will evolve through experience into knowledge of Divinity.

According to tradition, each being calls out "I AM THAT I AM" as it comes forth into and departs from existence. Between these two instants of self-realisation lies the long loop of destiny. Some beings shorten their time out of total union with the Divine by working consciously upon themselves. This does not exempt them from the particular task for which they were called, created, formed and made, but indeed obligates and equips them all the more to assist in the Work of unification. Spiritual traditions are designed to help such people, because to overcome the forces of nature, rise above fatal patterns, avoid the tricks of tempters, and tactfully move among the angels on the ascent of Jacob's Ladder, is no easy matter. Kabbalah is one of many disciplines concerned with spiritual evolution. Its system and methods are designed to help those who wish consciously to return to the Light and serve the Holy One. However, before access to the upper worlds is allowed, a series of trials has to be undergone, because it is necessary to find out whether a person is fit to take up a place in the Work. Many people wish to climb Jacob's Ladder in order to escape the lessons of the lower worlds, and not a few seek the path of higher knowledge for glamour and power.

The point when the descent into matter turns back up towards the Light is a crucial period. So too is the stage when a second descent occurs in order to impart to those below what has been received. All this requires delicate monitoring by spiritual mentors, until ultimately one relates directly to the highest of Names and resonates Its sound in one's life on Earth. When this operation is brought to perfection, then I AM THAT I AM becomes fully manifest in the microcosm of the individual. This conscious reflection of the image of God back to its point of origin meets and completes the Divine intention to behold Itself, and precipitates the fourth and final journey home to the Holy One. Before this ultimate state can occur, however, much has to be gone through. An ordered first ascent begins with training which starts in this tradition with the outline of the theory of existence, the background of the four journeys of body, soul, spirit and Divinity.

2. Ladder and Descent

According to tradition, existence emerged out of a void that had been willed in the midst of the Absolute. Within this space, in the middle of nothingness, a series of Divine Lights, some say sounds, caused the manifestation of the Ten *Sefirot* or radiant attributes of God. These numbers, or vessels, or instruments, as they have been variously described, were ordered into a pattern of Laws that would govern the universe while still retaining a simple unity. Some Kabbalists have seen the *Sefirot* as a downward growing tree with its roots in negative existence, as the void is sometimes called, while others see the configuration of *Sefirot* as a great Man—Adam Kadmon, the primordial human being, from whom the whole of mankind everywhere in the universe has descended.

Tradition further states that each person contains a spark of this original Adam deep within, and that the pursuit of completion arising from the sense of separation that everyone feels is the impulse of this spark seeking to return and become one with Adam Kadmon, who is the perfection of human possibility. We are in effect atoms of this great Image of God, and contain in miniature all the qualities and attributes of our ultimate ancestor and descendant, because at some point in the distant future, we shall be united as evolved atoms, to become cells of the organs and limbs of this Divine Being, who lives in that Eternal and unchanging realm of Light.

Now it is because Adam Kadmon exists in this most pristine of worlds that God brings forth the necessity for movement. In the eternal world of Emanation there is no time, for it contains past, present and future and therefore there is no flow of development, because everything just is. We are told, however, it is not God's intention to call forth a being to mirror the Divine that cannot exercise its attributes and free will, for it is these very qualities that make Adam quite different from all other creatures who were to come into existence in the three lower and separate worlds to be called forth, created, formed and made later. Adam Kadmon at this

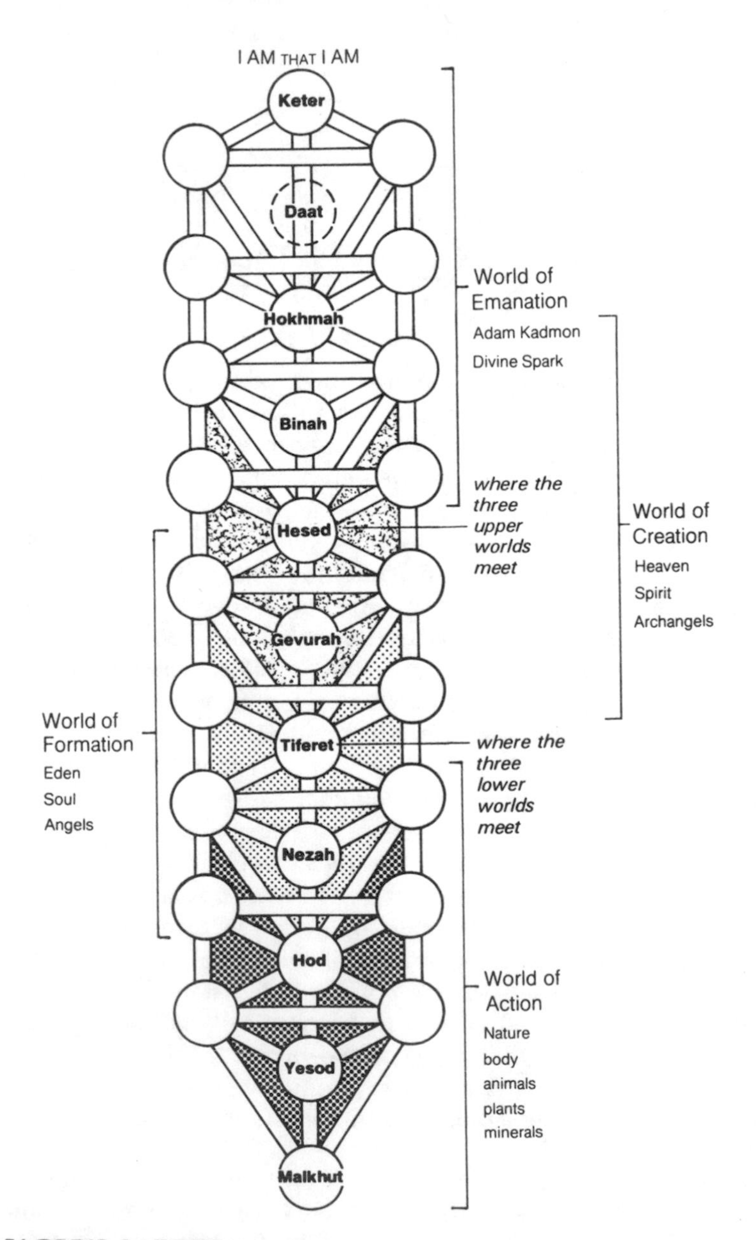

4. JACOB'S LADDER

As the Divine Attributes descend the central column of the great Tree of Existence, so all the four worlds come into being. The first world is of pure Light, while the lower worlds manifest energy, form and matter. Thus time and space emerge to contain the unfolding of Creation in its various levels of materiality, and their inhabitants. Of all creatures only mankind has access to every world.

point is entirely innocent. Experience begins with the first seven Days of Creation that initiate the process that will only finish at the end of Days, when everything in the universe is drawn back up and merges into the body, soul and spirit of a now mature Adam Kadmon again.

The difference between the Adam of Innocence and the Adam of Experience is the reason for the four journeys down and up the ladder of worlds. But first let us briefly set up the terrain of these descents and ascents. Out of the radiant world of *Azilut* or Emanation emerges creation. Here the realm of Spirit divides into seven levels, or halls, with many chambers to each side filled with wondrous forces and beings, some good and some bad, for with the separation from perfection came imperfection and its deviations. Genesis opens its text with the Creative world. Only the oral tradition, touched upon in the rabbinic and Kabbalistic tradition, speaks about what happened before creation. After the Heavenly world of *Beriah* came the world of *Yetzirah* or Formation, known as the Garden of Eden in the Bible. This became the world of the Chariot below that of the Throne in which sat the Divine Man of the vision of Ezekiel. The realm of Formation, as the name suggests, is concerned with the ever changing configuration of forces flowing out of the creative world under the direction of the Divine Will emanating from *Azilut*. The lowest world of action and elements, or energy and matter, is the one with which we are most familiar. Its mineral, vegetable, animal and human levels echo the four worlds in the physical universe. Kabbalistic work consists of becoming acquainted with all the worlds and working in and with them, so as to assist in Adam Kadmon's education.

Tradition goes on to say that, as atoms of Adam Kadmon, we descend into the lower worlds in order that Adam may know what it is to walk upon the Earth, experience all the pleasures and pains of the flesh, explore the realm of the psyche and Worlds of Angels, before returning with our cup of experience to the kingdom of the Spirit. From there we carry out our destiny, that is, our contribution up to Adam Kadmon. The *Zohar*, the great classic of Kabbalistic literature, describes how each of us is called before the Almighty, prior to being sent down into the lower worlds, and how we all decline to go, preferring Eden to the Earth. But go we must, and so we pass out of Paradise and into the flesh, because this is what we were called forth, created and made for. So that Adam Kadmon might experience every level.

Thus the cycle unfolds. First we are separated from that sublime state of union with the Divine by entering into the world of Creation where we are given the dynamic of a spirit for a vehicle. This enables us to traverse time and space, so that we may view the universe from one end to the other. However, tradition says, the spiritual power we are endowed with overlays the Light that is at our centre. Fortunately, it is not enough to dim the memory of whence we come. After this, we are brought down by the archangels into the world of Formation where the angels responsible for such things enclothe us in a form that corresponds to our particular soul, which is determined by the course of destiny given to us when we come before the Throne of Heaven. Here we reside in what is called the Treasure House of Souls until it is time to descend to the Earth and appear in the natural world encased in matter. This process ends the first journey of which we remember but little, except as young children, or as flashes in rare moments of reflection or recognition as we begin the second journey up through the worlds, back towards the great Light of which we are a spark encompassed by body, psyche and spirit. This situation is at the root of our sense of isolation and separateness. It is also the impulse behind the yearning to go home and be one with our Creator.

3. General Evolution

The process of evolution, like all sequences of development, follows the pattern of the Sefirotic Tree. This accords with the Law that every complete world, level, organism, or situation, is modelled upon the Divine principles of Emanation. For those not familiar with this, the Sefirotic Tree is the schematic arrangement of the Holy attributes according to the prime set of laws that govern existence. These briefly are as follows.

The Crown of the Tree, called *Keter,* represents the origin and unity of the whole. It is the place of the Will, while the two sefirot immediately below and to the right and left are *Hokhmah,* or Wisdom, and *Binah,* or Understanding. These head the two outer columns of Mercy and Severity which represent the expansive and contractive poles that may also be seen as masculine and feminine, or energy and form, respectively. The universe is balanced between these positive and negative pillars on the fulcrum of the central column of Grace, or Equilibrium. Here we have the laws of unity, duality and triplicity.

The dotted non-sefirah of *Daat,* or Knowledge, which is the child of the supernal trinity above, is also called the Abyss. This is because it is the access and exit point into manifest existence of that which lies above. It is the space through which higher influences can have direct contact with the seven sefirot of Construction, as they are known below, and the place where anything beneath may contact that which is above. The two sefirot of *Hesed,* or Mercy, and *Gevurah,* or Judgement, represent the emotional poles, as against the intellectual functions of the two side sefirot above, while the two sefirot of *Netzah,* or Eternity, and *Hod,* or Reverberation, below perform as the sefirot of action. Thus, we have the three functional side pairs of the Divine mind, heart and action, saddling a central column of will, knowledge and three lower levels of consciousness represented by *Tiferet,* or Beauty, which is the pivotal overseer of the scheme; *Yesod,* the Foundation, which acts as the surveyor of details, and *Malkhut,* which is sometimes considered as the Divine

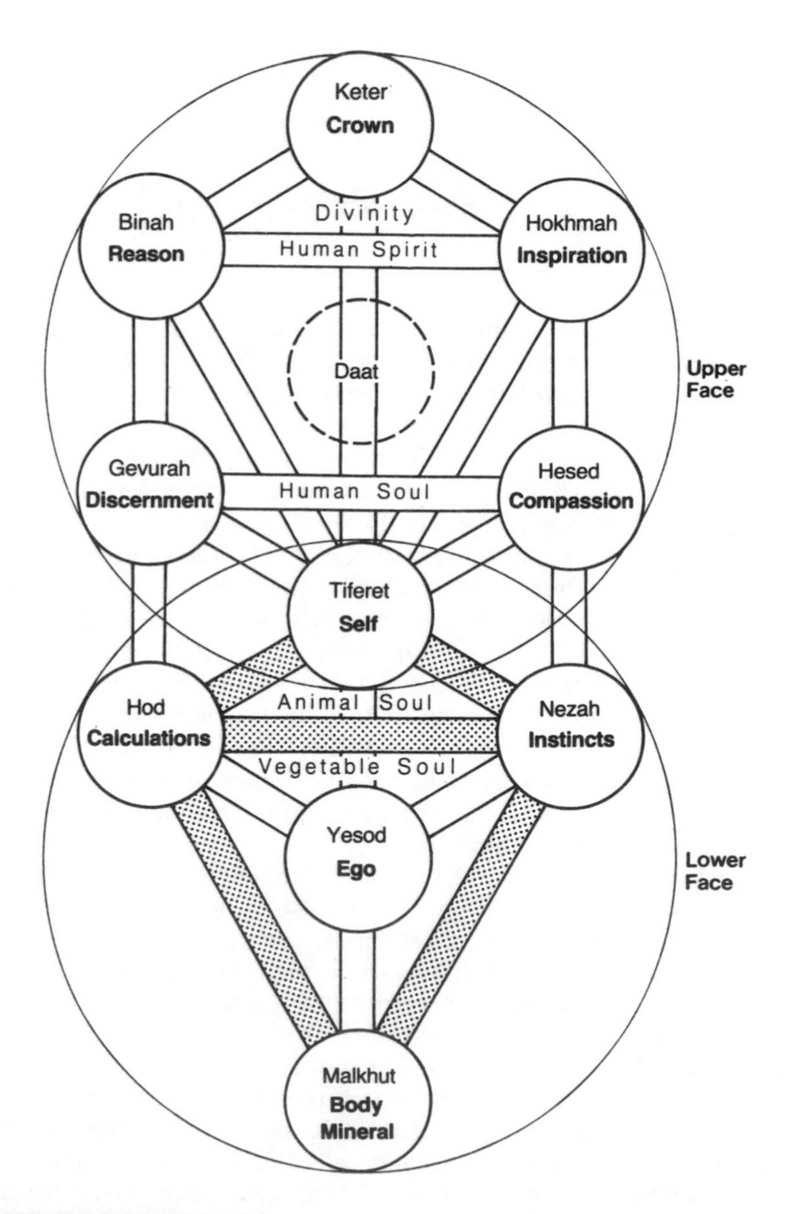

5. LEVELS WITHIN MAN

Human beings are modelled upon the Divine. When incarnate they are in contact with all the worlds. The body is made up of the four elements and possesses a vegetable and an animal intelligence. The higher levels manifest as soul and spirit which relate to the Worlds of Formation and Creation. The Crown centre maintains the Divine connection.

Body in that it has, at this lowest point, the most contact with the material worlds.

The paths and triads that are generated by this arrangement are based upon a definite sequence that flows from the Crown to the top of the right hand column, and across to the left and then on down in a primary zig-zag line before reaching the bottom. The process of ascent is in reverse up the track of this Lightning Flash, as it is traditionally called. There are many other details such as letters ascribed to the twenty-two paths and names to the triads, but in this book we shall only refer to those relevant to our subject. The less informed student should consult earlier books for a detailed account of the Tree and Jacob's Ladder.†

As we have seen, the process of evolution or return to the Light, as against that of creation or descent into matter, follows the path of the Lightning Flash, but in reverse. Thus taking the macrocosmic aspect first, the planet Earth having emerged out of the finest of the atomic and molecular levels of existence has become a dense and substantial ball of elemental matter. This sphere is composed of a metallic core with a mineral coat of rock. Above this floats a liquid sea and a gaseous mantle surrounded by a flamelike belt of subtle radiation that extends far out into space. Here we have the base of the four elements. Moreover, if we take metal and mineral as the upper and lower Earth elements, the same interpenetrating principle is seen between the land, the oceans, the clouds and radiation, as the watery, airy and fiery elements merge into one another. This is the *Malkhut*, or kingdom of the physical world.

The next stage is the level of the vegetable kingdom, that is of organic life, as against the inorganic consciousness of the elements. This vitality relates to the sefirot of *Yesod*, or Formation, and *Hod* and *Netzah*, that compose the great lower triad, which holds the yesodic level of moment by moment consciousness in a rhythmic interaction of cycle and reverberation. *Netzah*, or Eternity, means to endlessly repeat, while the root of the Hebrew word *Hod*, sometimes translated Glory, is to 'resound'. Thus, this great triad contains the repetition and vibration which maintain, and yet allow fluctuations to occur, that is the characteristic of the vegetable world in its daily and seasonal round. Such a process is

†*Tree of Life* (Introduction); *Adam and the Kabbalistic Tree* (Man); *A Kabbalistic Universe* (Macrocosm).

quite different from the higher animal triad of *Hod, Netzah* and *Tiferet*, which perceives and acts with a greater degree of consciousness, because of the connection with the Seat of Solomon at the centre of the Tree. Here we have responsive will, mobility, relationship and all the instincts of the herd.

The human parallel of this is that while mankind contains the elemental, vegetable and animal levels, it has the capacity to develop further. However, as noted earlier, the majority of the human race is still centred in the *Yesod*, or ego level of consciousness, and this makes it come under the laws of the vegetable kingdom, that is, it is principally preoccupied with having an elemental place to live, with enough water, air and light so that the next generation can be propagated and fed until mature enough to flower, be fertilized, and bear the following generation before withering and dying itself. This fact is not a judgement, but a simple observation of how life is for most people. There are also the animal members of the human species. These are the dominators of history. They can range from Attila the Hun, to the dictatorial foreman on the shop floor, or the overbearing headmistress to the pop star and politician. Their chief characteristic is to be ruler of a group of people, be it an international corporation or a village sewing circle.

At the level of the individual, where personal development begins, the process starts to take one out of the domain of these lower triads as contact with *Tiferet*, or the place of the Self, is made. This is where our study begins, because it is the entrance to the Way and the area where kabbalistic Work is carried out. However, before this can be done certain requirements have to be met.

4. Individual Development

To be an individual requires many qualities. A person has to be able to support him or herself, that is manage the elemental problems of life, like finding a tolerable place in which to live, with, for example, a good climate and stable economic and social conditions. This should allow him or her to earn a living and maintain a contact with the ordinary world that many seekers of the path try to avoid. In Kabbalah, this ordinary life contact is vital, or there is no possibility of earthing whatever may be drawn down from the higher worlds. Such individuals must also be able to feed and clothe themselves by their own labour, and have the capacity to relate to their society in a balanced way, seeing it, whatever its current state of reaction, revolution, or equilibrium. This is how conditions are at the moment as Creation unfolds. This requires a vision over and above so-called informed opinion, which is often no more than pragmatism, or propaganda, to be disregarded as most egocentric views are, with changing conditions. The individual must be aware of Eternal laws, even if they are only dimly perceived. This is what marks the individual out, and gives that objectivity to the Work.

Such people are usually regarded as odd by their peers, and indeed, often remain isolated for years until they make contact with others like themselves, when the time is ripe. This can only occur when the tests of courage and integrity have been passed, and they make a committed shift from the vegetable state of consciousness which is preoccupied with survival, through the animal level concerned with ambition, to that place which wants more than just to live comfortably, or be top dog in whatever field of activity is being practised. To recognise that vegetable existence ends in death and that an animal-based reputation is a fragile bubble, is to open the question as to what is ephemeral and what is Eternal.

When a person reaches this place of the soul many things become possible. In some cases such a moment of truth is too much. Some people cannot face the notion of their own physical extinction, or the loss of, in their own estimation, their hard won position. They back away and try to drown their realisation in greater or lesser activity. Many succeed only to be repeatedly disappointed by having too much of this, or desperate because they have too little of that. Either way they find no satisfaction until the day they die, or even beyond. For those who face such a moment of realisation, which may come in flashes rather than a great illumination, the opportunity offers the chance to enter the upper worlds, and so glimpse a higher form of existence. Such experiences come by Grace from above and can change a whole attitude of life. Again, such insights into another reality can cause a person to back away, if they have not the balance and the stamina to hold the Gift of Heaven. This is why traditionally Kabbalists have to have a degree of maturity and stability.

In kabbalistic terms, the individual who has reached this far has a measure of command over the elements of *Malkhut*, recognises the ego level of the Yesodic consciousness, suspects that the cleverness of *Hod* is not real thinking, and knows the power of Netzahian passion is not emotion. At such a point people often recognise their imbalance and seek to solve the apparent problem that they are not like everyone else, in that no one seems to be bothered by the things that disturb them. Often they will look at this or that therapy, method of meditation, or spiritual training. Most of these will be found to be superficial, incomplete, and sometimes even sinister. Occasionally, a discipline will offer some promise, only to become disappointing because it does not go beyond a certain point, or is not the right way for the aspirant. These are all preparations in discrimination set on the path to the particular tradition that is correct for that individual.

When the time is ripe the individual, often at a point of despair, meets someone to whom he can relate. It may be at a lecture or on a train; it could be at a party or even at home when someone who has a certain inner quality suddenly speaks quite out of character about the things of which he wishes to know. Such a connection may be made with an ancient line such as the Sufis, or with a group that is only a generation old. If it is a true manifestation of the Spirit on Earth, it will have a distinct integrity about it. This is the hallmark of a real working group. Such a quality will reveal its Way in its dealings with the individual. It will apply no force or persuasion. Indeed, such groups rarely issue an invitation, but merely leave the door open for the individual to enter if he or she chooses.

When that threshhold is passed then the situation changes radically, often altering the life of the person beyond recognition. This is why no one is lured or pressured into a school of esoteric study. They must enter because they wish to, despite the hazards and the labour of the inner ascent. As one Kabbalist said, "One cannot begin this Work lightly for there is no turning back, except with great peril".

The journey from this moment on is taken in many stages. At first there is the probationary period where there are only a few obligations. Then comes the initiation, which is the real beginning, long after the honeymoon period is over. From here on the Work is primarily upon the person himself as he acquires the theory of the tradition and does its practices. Later, group work is done, as the individual learns to merge into a disciplined association with others on the Path. Later still, individuals become aware not only of other groups, but the school they are part of, as their development takes them up through the various inner levels to contact the upper regions of the spiritual company of mankind.

On reaching a certain point of ascent in this or some future life, the privilege of just receiving is ended and the third major phase of imparting begins. Here is the third journey of redescent, or obligation of service. This not only means assisting those above and helping those below, but direct involvement in the Work of Unification, as Kabbalah is sometimes called so as to bring the inner and outer worlds, and the upper and lower levels of existence together in consciousness. As can be appreciated, this view is totally different to that of the mundane universe that science presents. In these higher dimensions, time and space are quite beyond most people, although Grace-given glimpses are seen in moments of illumination. In a kabbalistic group which has techniques to raise the level of those present, it is possible to experience and even perceive higher worlds and their interplay of energy and substance at will, but this requires special knowledge and skill.

The training in the application of such techniques is one of the tasks of Kabbalah. What follows is only a fraction of the repertoire used. However, it is hoped that this little might convey something of what is involved and give guidelines to anyone who can make use of what is written about individual and group techniques. The fourth journey and ultimate ascent occurs when an individual's destiny is complete, and the incarnated speck of Divinity returns to its origin. Such a process is quite different from all other work, because it means entering the world of Emanation and passing through the Abyss into total union with the Godhead. No one has seen the face of God and returned, and so we are without a report on this final phase of realisation.

For those still standing on Jacob's Ladder, let us continue to examine the general situation, and principles behind individual and group work, so as to put them in a setting. Here it must be repated that what is described is one particular form of Kabbalah. It should not be taken as the sole approach, for while the essence of the Teaching remains the same, its manifestations change according to inner and outer conditions.

5. Different Worlds

Nearly all kabbalistic work is based upon the model of the Sefirotic Tree or Jacob's Ladder. This is because in order to be effective any operation must not only conform to the structure of the universe, but resonate with the various levels of energy inherent in it. If an enterprise is not related to the laws of Existence it simply will not follow the desired course, and so obtain its objective: an aircraft cannot fly if its wings are not the right shape, no matter how powerful its engine may be. The correct relationship between form and force has to be set up. It is the same with kabbalistic work where the dynamic and the configuration of an operation have to be taken into account.

The difficulty with esoteric operations is that unlike the elemental principles of aerodynamics and metallurgy, the worlds in which they are set cannot be directly observed or measured. The marvels of modern technology are possible because the theory and practice of science has reached a point where the qualities, properties and characteristics of physical energy and matter are well understood. This has taken several thousand years to accomplish. For example the principle of the steam engine was known in ancient Alexandria, but never put to practical use because there was not sufficient practical knowledge of other techniques to build complex machines. Ironically, in the case of esoteric knowledge it was the reverse, more was known in ancient Egypt about magic or the art of psychic manipulation than is known today.

Since very early times it has been known that certain actions when applied at a particular time and in a special way generated specific effects, either in the state of an individual, or within a given situation. So-called primitive shamans could cause rain to fall at will, and some of the early sorcerers perceived and conversed with nature spirits after altering their perception by drugs or ritual. In later and more refined societies, priests contacted the lower angelic powers that were drawn to temples dedicated to them. They even negotiated favours in exchange for worship. The priests who acted as communicators between the gods and human beings amassed, over many centuries, much empirical knowledge about the ebb and flow of natural forces, the influence of the heavens and the characteristics of the intelligences that lived in the unseen realms close to the Earth level. Some traditions built up elaborate schemes based upon observation of the hierarchy of powers and the relationship between levels and different forces at work within one stratum. The cosmologies of the ancient worlds are full of such systems, and although there are many differences between cultures, there are quite recognisable common denominators in their various pantheons of gods. The warlike qualities of the planet Mars appear, for example, in many cultures, as do the image and attributes of Mother Nature.

Besides the body of collected knowledge, there is the innermost part of any spiritual teaching that has been acquired by revelation or illumination. This is the result of the interior work of a group, or of individuals who have actually changed their normal state of consciousness and risen up out of sense perception and ordinary psychological appreciation of the world to enter the supernatural realms. By definition, supernatural means above nature, and so it is, in that the group or person perceives the higher world and its inhabitants directly. Such an experience is likely to shake the individual psyche profoundly, and so generally there is a period of training under discipline for aspirants before they are allowed such experiences. We find this the pattern of both ancient and modern esoteric schools.

In the Bible the Egyptians were considered masters of many such techniques, and indeed the training of a priest was long and complex. There were also master magicians like Balaam who not only had skill in prophecy, but the power to bless or curse, within certain limits. However, there is also a level beyond which skill in the magical arts of subtle manipulation cannot be effective. The contest between Moses and the Egyptian priests with his rod-snake swallowing up all the Egyptian snakes is a symbol of the miraculous being superior to the magical. In terms of Kabbalah, this indicates how the spiritual power of the Creative world of *Beriah* can contain and override the psychological constructions of the World of Yetziratic Forms.

From time to time in history there has appeared in the world a person or a school of the highest order that has imparted what had been received either from an incarnate master or even higher intelligence. Although usually in the guise of a great religious teacher or prophet who spoke about such matters obliquely, such esoteric teachings are often only given to a select circle of prepared people who could make good use of them at that point in time to forward the development of mankind. We see this in the hidden knowledge behind Islam, Buddhism and Christianity. Kabbalah is the esoteric teaching of Judaism. Such a body of knowledge is always based on material that has been revealed orally, rather than those things that have been written down in books, because it cannot be communicated in any other way. Although books can outline the principles, such knowledge can only be taught when there is a rising up from below to the place of inner comprehension. This takes place in that zone between Heaven and Earth, where the soul hovers between the body and the spirit.

Thus we begin to see how the inner and the outer worlds are intimately related in kabbalistic work. The microcosm of a human being, because it is designed on the same principles as the macrocosm of the universe, is the instrument by which one can consciously enter the greater worlds. This means, however, that the cosmic realms not only greatly affect, but are in proportion influenced by, a person sensitive to them. The man who is concerned only with his job will not be directly touched by or modify planetary situations, nor will the woman who just sees her own family; while individuals who have begun to resonate with the cosmos will be affected to such a degree that they will respond to the tensions between the planets. Simultaneously their reaction can alter the terrestrial and celestial balance to a greater or lesser degree, depending on their level. For example, such persons might suddenly change their role in society and alter its values as Buddha did, or just do something unconventional like turn down a top job, which in the long run proves to be a killer and doing something more useful. This is one of the reasons why transformation occurs in people when they begin spiritual work. They begin to live under the selective law of individual fate and not the general laws of social and mass behaviour.

The advantages and disadvantages of kabbalistic work now begin to become apparent. To gain access to the higher worlds and acquire knowledge of how to work in them requires great responsibility; for there are the dangers of excess, inability, temptation, inflation, and many other hazards unknown to mortals who do not seek the door to immortality. However, once the commitment is made and the training is initiated, the student begins to become involved in a vast cosmic game into which one is introduced by degrees. The second stage of kabbalistic induction is to apply metaphysical theory to a known reality, and so we shall continue with a brief account of the lower part of Jacob's Ladder which involves the natural and psychological worlds. If the principles at work at these levels can be perceived, then the reality of the other worlds may come a little closer. With the practice of the exercises later they may actually be experienced. This to many people's surprise often confirms what they already knew, but had somehow forgotten on being born, which leads us on to the first stage of study, that is to become familiar with the different worlds of our body and psyche, and how they interact, as set out in the diagram.

6. Different Bodies

Tradition tells us that Adam is made in the image of the Divine, and that all human beings are constructed in the image of Adam. Therefore, each individual has will, intellect, emotion and action as part of their nature. We are told, moreover, that the Adams of Emanation and Creation are androgynous, that is both male and female. This is to say that the Divine Man and the Adam of the Spirit are integrated to a greater degree than the lower manifestations of humanity, which are separated out into Adam and Eve at the level of the psyche, and physically divided into two sexes by the body. This increasing division and sub-division is the result of the multiplicity of laws as one moves down and away from the perfection of the Divine World. Thus, by the time we incarnate on the Earth, we have acquired four distinct bodies, one for each world, which act as vehicles for consciousness and work at their own levels.

The first vehicle is the physical body which is composed of four sub-levels of mechanical, chemical, electronic and consciousness. These are held by the mineral, vegetable and animal life principles between the pillars of energy and matter. At the *Tiferet* of the Tree of the body is the central nervous system that watches, like the self of the psychological Tree, over the adjacent sefirot, triads and paths that flow into and out of its sphere of influence. As will be seen in the body diagram there are many sub-divisions within the Tree, and an infinite number of finer sub-sub divisions down to the frontier of the physical world where the particles of matter and the impulses of energy are interchangeable. From the point of view of Kabbalah the study of the body can be very useful, because it enables one to see the same processes at work as in the psyche, or the spiritual Tree, but at a coarser level of reality.

In diagram 6 we can see how the Tree of the psyche interpenetrates the body so that the upper half of the physical world percolates and influences the lower portion of the psyche and *vice versa*. This is directly observable in everyday life, and

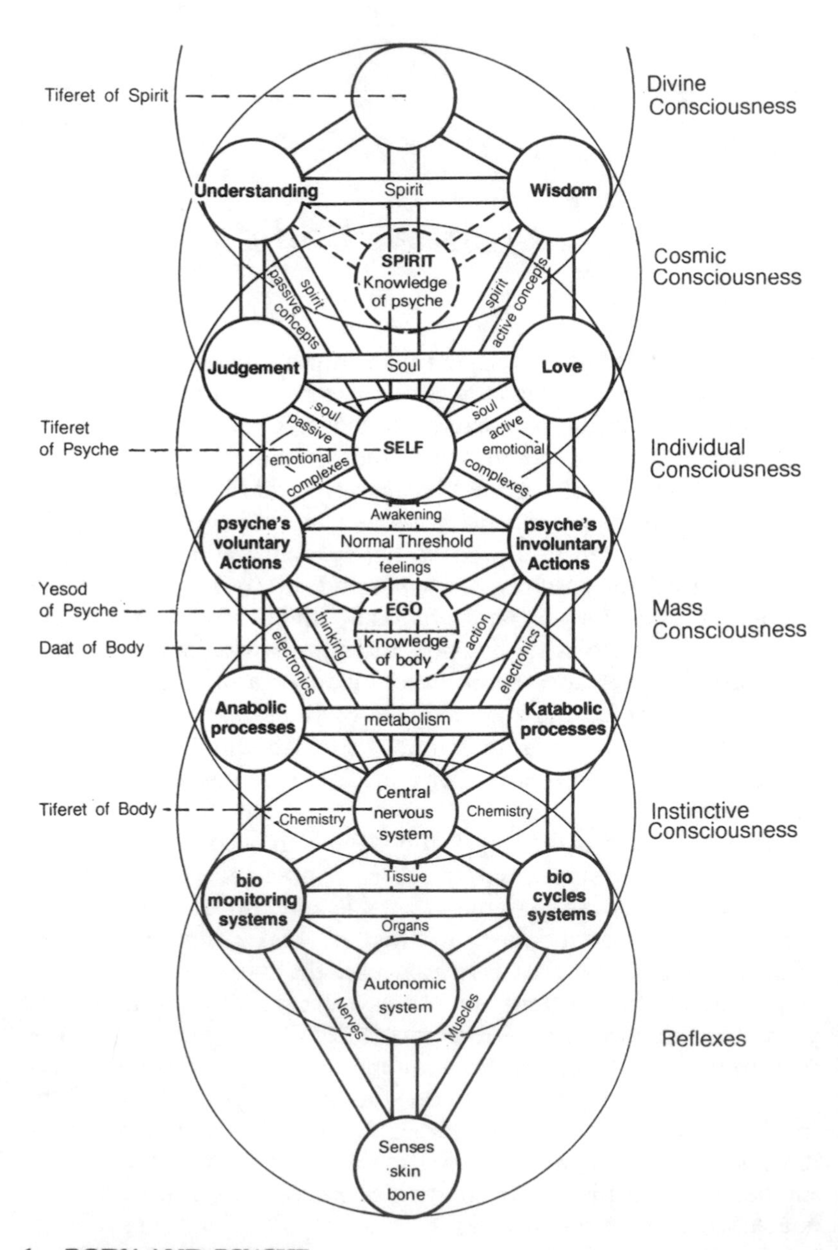

6. BODY AND PSYCHE

The physical and psychological bodies interpenetrate each other at the place where the coarsest psychic level matches the finest material level. The same occurs in the zone between the upper psyche and the lower spiritual level. The circles show the various ranges of appreciation and action experienced by the different centres of consciousness.

should be remembered as an important principle when considering or working at the points of interchange between the higher worlds.

The psyche, like the body, is divided between consciousness and function. That is, the central column carries different degrees of awareness, while the side pillars and triads perform as balances of action, emotion and intellect. In the early part of a Kabbalist's training this division must be clearly established. You are not your actions, emotions, or intellect; they are the manifestations of consciousness like, as traditional Kabbalah says, the arms and legs. Consciousness means to 'know'. However, when a person is only conscious of his body, his knowledge extends just to the orbit of influence of his central nervous system. Likewise, someone who lives primarily in the ego is indeed egocentric. This is the normal condition of most people, and as the diagram shows, their radius of consciousness is confined to routine thoughts, feelings and actions, with an occasional contact with the self when the repertoire of mental reflexes cannot cope with a new situation.

Under average life conditions, a crisis can generate a direct contact with the higher and deeper aspect of the self, but it usually fades once the crisis is passed, as the watcher in oneself again becomes part of the unconscious, only being able to influence indirectly in dreams, moods, or flashes of truth. The Kabbalist seeks consciously to establish a permanent connection with the *Tiferet* of his psyche and expand his self-knowledge into the triads of emotional complexes and concepts, as well as extend up the central column and so enter the realm of the soul and the world of the Spirit. This is done by constant observation of actions, emotions and intellect. By this is meant to perceive impartially the way those functions operate, and to seek to correct and perfect their performance so as to become a balanced instrument for kabbalistic work; for a major defect in the psyche can not only mar an operation, but expose some psychological malfunction to enormous stress with dire results.

The study of the Soul is not something that can be easily written about. Indeed, it is perfectly correct to repeat that Kabbalah cannot be transmitted by a book, but only through the intimate relationship between student and instructor. However, one has to begin somewhere, which is why Kabbalists have written manuals on inner work over the centuries despite the fact that only a shadow of what is involved can be conveyed.

The soul when set out on the Tree of the psyche looks quite

simple in its nature, but if one observes its connections to everything around it, it will be seen to occupy a crucial position. It is the bridge and the barrier between the upper and lower worlds in the individual. It has access to all the ideas and emotional memories of that person which colour and pressure the material passing through the soul, whether it is being given by Grace from above or being received externally from below. The soul is the place where all the individual experiences are processed in the light of conscience which is the synthesis of the three sefirot of Judgement, Mercy and Beauty, that can also be seen as the Sefirah of Truth. The soul is the gateway into the Spirit which, it will be noted, matches the lower face, as it is called, of the world of Creation in the same way as the lower psyche interpenetrates the upper face of the body Tree.

The realm of the Spirit begins at the place of the self, which simultaneously contains the Crown of the body Tree and the central sefirah of the psyche. Thus, we have three levels of reality concentrated in one place. In kabbalistic work this is the initial access point to the higher worlds and the first of the seven great halls of Heaven. However, before these can be entered the seven lesser halls have to be passed through, although occasionally one is allowed a glimpse of the celestial chambers. There are those who have broken into these vast cosmic palaces by means of drugs, but they tend to get a very distorted view of them because of their own psychological imperfections and impurities, and often this is enough to frighten them away from any real possibility of a proper and balanced entry into the Kingdom of Heaven. Preparation in Kabbalah is a long and slow process for this reason, for the sights and sounds of the upper worlds are extremely disturbing, if one is ungrounded, unstable and ill prepared; that is, one's physical and psychological bodies are not in a healthy condition, or are ill matched.

In order to be able to enter the upper worlds safely, one should have these lower organisms healed and trained by an experienced instructor within the context of a group, which is part of a larger school in direct contact with those concerned with the spiritual life of humanity. Therefore, let us now look at such a group, so as to see how and why it is organised as it is.†

†For greater detail of body, psyche and spirit see the author's *Adam and the Kabbalistic Tree*.

7. School

In this outline of the setting of Kabbalistic work we will follow the sequence of the Tree to show the anatomy of a school. While the source of the line must come from the Crown with its contact with the lowest sefirah of the Divine World, the Work begins at the bottom at the *Malkhut* or Kingdom of a Tree that corresponds to the Yetziratic world, or the psychological Tree.

The *Malkhut* of a group is the place where they meet. This can be a room or house. Such meetings should be daily or weekly; any less frequent use will not build up an energy field, and no subtle charge will remain in the place while the group is absent. Over the months and years the *Bet Midrash*, or House of Study, will become saturated with the dynamic and substance drawn down from the higher worlds through the being of the group. People entering such a place for the first time often sense a clear strong presence in the atmosphere. Such a quality is to be noted in any place where sacred work is done. This is because the energy and matter of a higher order has permeated, then saturated, the physical fabric of the building to form a reservoir and transform the elemental aspect of the school to put it on a level above that of an ordinary building.

The ideal place should provide enough room for the rituals, devotions, and contemplation of the group, that is for group enactments, meditations and discussion. It can be a space in which little decoration is to be seen, so that whatever is done is projected in an abstracted form by imagination, or it may be physically laid out according to a definite plan, ranging from a simple altar table and chairs to a room full of Kabbalistic images to evoke a heightened state as soon as one enters the chamber. The particular formula used will depend upon the particular line of the tradition, the type of instructor in charge, and the kind of students who are drawn to that way of working.

The members of a Kabbalah group may vary enormously. In the orthodox tradition, they will nearly always be mature men who have studied the Torah in its original Hebrew and are familiar with

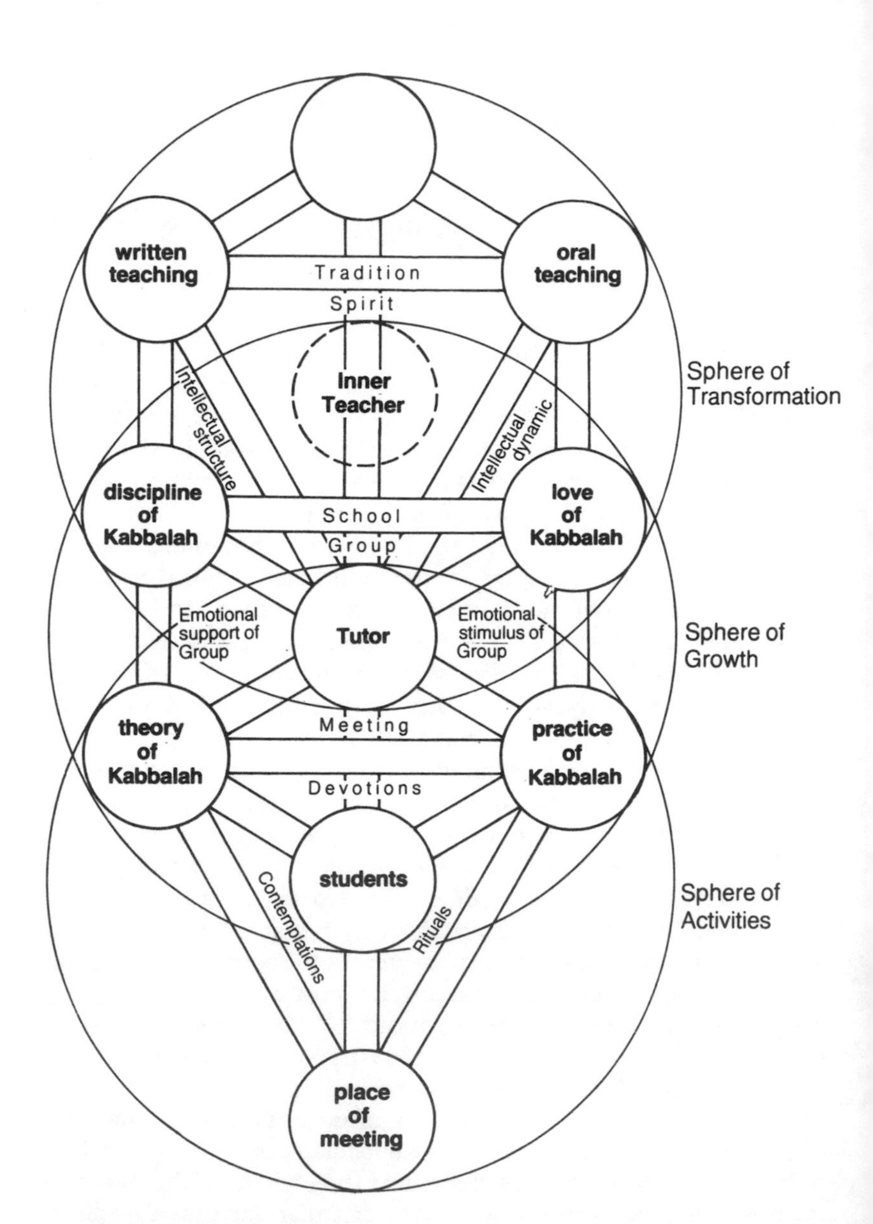

7. KABBALISTIC SCHOOL

A group is a vehicle for development. Therefore it follows the principles of the Tree in that it has its various spheres and their dynamics. While only the lower and outer part of the school may be visible, the interior levels are discernible according to the level of its members. Only those in the tutor's state would realise there was an Inner Teacher.

the rabbinical commentaries of the Talmud. However, times change and so does Kabbalah. Kabbalists no longer live, as many religious Jews do, in a ghetto of orthodoxy. This is not to say that the old ways do not have value, but that in order to continue the living tradition, Kabbalah moves as it has always done, with the needs of each generation. Thus, in our western emancipated society, we might find groups composed of women as well as men, who may not read or speak Hebrew, and who indeed, may not even be Jewish, but who nevertheless, wish to work in the Way of Kabbalah. In this manner the biblical injunction "to be a Light unto the Nations" is fulfilled.

After the entry into such a group, the initial training is to study the theory of Kabbalah and to do the routine practices given out by the instructor. These will include becoming familiar with the Tree and carrying out such operations as perhaps meditating three times a day. Weekly exercises will be of a progressive nature, in that each topic to be considered or acted upon, is held for that week in the forefront of consciousness and reported upon to the group at the next meeting. An example of this is to examine one's habits and see how they stop any possibility of self-knowledge. Out of this will come an exercise for dealing with a useless tendency and observing how another habit will compensate for it. This is a continuous process of discipline in the pursuit of making one's inner Tree balanced. On a larger scale the subject being examined may extend over a whole term of three months to draw out, for example, the implications of the workings of fate and how our lives are governed by gentle but quite compulsive trends. This study may lead into a year's project of learning about the laws of destiny and why so many opportunities to find real fulfilment of our potential are lost or missed in life.

The exercises of rituals, devotion and contemplation are the three methods of the sphere of action on the Tree of the group, while the triad of awakening is where the meeting takes place. It is here that the group gathers before the instructor who occupies the place of the Teacher at the *Tiferet* centre of the Tree. This Seat of Solomon may be filled by a senior group member who does no more than perform as the chairperson from which standard instructions are given out, if he or she has no personal experience, or a gifted teacher with an inner connection to the tradition. The latter is rare because to work with someone directly in contact with the higher levels means that the group has reached a relatively advanced state itself. Generally groups are run by people who have enough knowledge to be able to act as the Elder or *Zakan* of the group.

The heart of the group lies in the triad of the soul, between the sefirot of *Tiferet* or Truth, *Gevurah* or Discipline, and *Hesed* or Love. In a junior group not all the people taking part in the meetings will necessarily be members of the group. They can be visitors, probationary students or people passing through. At a more subtle level the people present may, at any time, enter or leave the state of inner contact with the soul of the group. This can include the leader of the group, when the attention wanders or ego intervenes, as in the case of a power trip. Such things do happen. The senior or inner group may only have a few members at any one time, or it can, for a moment of Grace, include all who are present, even the stranger who has just been invited to observe. Such visitors of course are carefully selected, because by the nature of the Work, not every person who wants to know about Kabbalah is a suitable candidate.

The school to which the group belongs may or may not be discernible to most of its members. However, those who have begun to move into a condition of interior development with its implications and responsibilities, will slowly become aware of other spiritual lines. This contact may be direct, in that they meet other students through their leader's connection with other fraternal instructors, or they may detect intuitively during the meetings the scale of a wider scope that involves other 'Companions of the Light' working at the same level. The association with other groups may be intimate or distant; they can be in close proximity within the same city or oceans away, for beyond a certain level distance does not matter when the group's work is with the higher worlds where time and space are quite different.

A cohesive collection of groups constitutes a school. This sometimes has an obvious guiding teacher or group of senior people, who see the over-view and direct its particular aim. Here it must be said that while there is a spiritual hierarchy it is not always apparent. The real core of a school, for example may sometimes be hidden in amongst the tutors or students, so that only someone of perception can identify it. A school is an organism dedicated to certain objectives. These might be perpetuation of knowledge, revival of religion, esoteric science, art or social questions. A school can be a loose association of groups or a tightly woven organisation with a physical headquarters. On the other hand, it might not have any home on Earth and even be located somewhere else in time. As said, at these levels ordinary laws and logic do not apply.

A tradition is the sum total of all the lines, schools, groups and individuals involved in that way of operation. The root of this tradition, in our case, goes back to Kabbalah, which is represented by many hundreds of schools down the ages. Most of these are Jewish, but some are Christian and occult in form. However, all have their origin in the knowledge that lies behind the Bible that was revealed to Solomon, given to Moses, and passed onto Abraham by Malchizedek. Beyond this point, it becomes the pure teaching as handed down from the first fully realised man called, Enoch, whose name means the "Initiated". He became *Metatron*, the great Instructor of Mankind. At this level we perceive the source of the various roots of spirituality that run through human history, which have become the great esoteric traditions of the world.

The initial training of Kabbalah is to help raise the individual to a place where he or she can work harmoniously with a group which has a greater capacity to receive higher knowledge, in the early stages, than any one person. This operating in concert enhances the group's capability within the larger context of its school which in turn is related to the wider field of the tradition. The tradition is a stem that carries the various schools like blossoms. Such blooms, if pollinated by the Spirit, will turn into fruits that may feed many, over hundreds of years. We see this pattern in the Hassidic and monastic movements. Like fruit, these spiritual impulses decay and then fall. The seed they scatter is then sown into the ground for the next phase of general development. Fructifying these seeds is one of the main tasks of a tradition, so that each generation has the spiritual capability to take up the work.†

The training of individuals is also an important function of esoteric schools, for it is through them that a group can become a finer vessel. Greater receptivity to what can be received from above and imparted to below not only means in the present, but also applies to what can be drawn from the past and transmitted into

†For greater detail see the author's *School of Kabbalah*.

the future. Thus the group is a crucial vehicle in *Avodah*, the Hebrew word for work and worship. However, before becoming a member of such an assembly various prerequisites have to be met.

8. Prerequisites

Following the sequence of the Tree upwards, the first thing that is required of the Kabbalist is that he or she is relatively prepared to be wherever and whenever they are wanted. This means they must place the Work as a top priority in their lives. Moreover, they should be free of problems that could influence their commitment. These include personal as well as practical pressures that might corrupt as well as retard flexibility. To add to this reliability a high level of external stability and internal integrity is vital, so that the person is not only well rooted in ordinary life, but able to be effective, and indeed, influential if need be. Professional, or even social status, is irrelevant provided the motive is to be of service. A kabbalistic lawyer, businessman, or craftswoman, whose work is respected is more use in the world than a holy hippy, or transcendental tramp. Kabbalah is not the way of those who withdraw from life. This is the contact with *Malkhut*.

Awareness of *Yesod* and its strengths and weaknesses is crucial in the Work. To know one's projections upon oneself, others and situations is to recognise the ego's power to transmit or block what is coming from deep within the psyche. To observe and have command over the processes of action, thinking and feeling that fluctuate within the ego is to be able to use it rather than be used by it. This requires the capacity to rise above the opposing tendencies of wilfulness coming from the right side of the Tree and will-lessness from the left. To be able to lift consciousness, at will, out of the purely yesodic personal into the triad of awakening is to achieve mastery over the four lower halls of the psyche, and come under the will of either the self or *Tiferet*, or the direction of one's teacher, if one cannot maintain the state on one's own. This is another reason why a group is important in the early stages. The support of others as well as one's instructor is a great aid in the initial steps of the Work, before we develop the important prerequisite of willingness, without which nothing can be done.

Underlying all the foregoing is the issue of commitment. Many

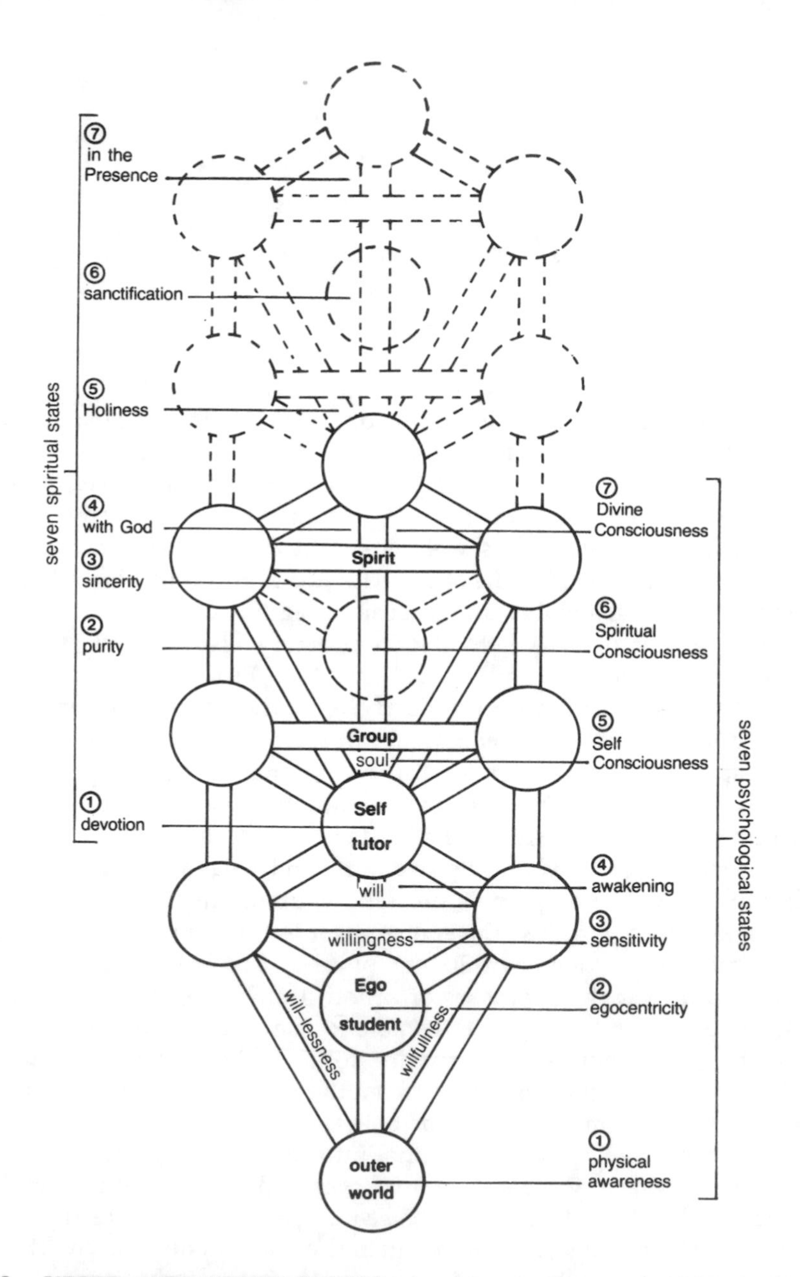

8. UPPER AND LOWER HALLS

The seven psychological stages of development have to be passed through before the seven spiritual steps can be taken. No level can be missed or there would be imbalance, although experience of higher levels is sometimes given by Grace. However for most Kabbalists the merit of diligent work is the way to rise safely and hold what has been given. The path proper begins at the Self.

people come in contact with spiritual work out of curiosity. Fortunately, Kabbalah is a deep and complex subject and soon bores or frightens the curious away. Some are attracted to it out of need. This may be a purely psychological attraction. If so, then a crisis will occur in which the person is confronted with the possible loss of identity as his individuality is diminished in relation to the scale of spiritual work. An encounter with the cosmic level of existence reduces one's self-importance, from either negative or positive inflation to its true place, and this often turns people away from Kabbalah. To give up all one has, including vanity or suffering, and become as a child is not easy. However, if the need is a spiritual one, then the deep yearning is fulfilled by the surrender of one's will to the Work and then the Divine. Ultimately, the latter is the only commitment.

Upon entering the triad of the soul, a series of tests is initiated. Here contact with good and evil is to be expected. Power is given to one to see how it is handled and temptation in many subtle forms is encountered. Values that you think you hold, may be challenged inwardly, or in external situations, in order to make sure you are is reliable in the invisible as well as the practical world. The fact that only you may know that you are being immoral about something small, like stealing paper clips, is an illusion, because by this time one has the unseen supervisor of the soul, which monitors all activities, to see if one is up to the work that may be given at some time. Real responsibility cannot be handed to someone with a split psyche and morality. If it were given to a gifted but corrupt person, then the Teaching could be distorted. Such people spread much delusion amongst those whose souls they have been given to instruct. These tests are applied over many years as the Kabbalist progresses up the Tree. It has to be, so as to be sure that the quality of the Work remains pure. That is why many good individuals in spiritual work seem to have such difficult lives. These trials, however, are not just to seek out weaknesses, but to strengthen the being of the person, so that they may become better and finer vessels in which to receive the Light flowing down from on high.

When a person has reached the place of soul through diligent inner and outer effort, they establish the possibility of a permanent link with the third level of the self. The first two are the Crown of the physical and the *Tiferet* of the psychological organism. Often an initiation ceremony into the *Malkhut* of the Spiritual world marks the entry into the first of the Seven Halls of Heaven. Such a ceremony may be a public acknowledgement or an essentially private moment of recognition. Schools may differ in how they indicate transformation. However, whatever the form is, the most important factor is that from that point on, the person, while still in obedience to the instructions of his senior or directly under the Will of God, is now fully responsible for his actions. This is the coming of age in the Work. Here begins spiritual adulthood, although there are still six further stages to go before reaching the seventh Heaven. Thus while you have access to the higher realms, and will be given powers and knowledge that cannot be learnt, even from others, you still have the choice of free will, and may deviate for many reasons, ranging from a moment of pettiness to allying oneself with Lucifer himself. Indeed, this demonic son of God will now constantly approach the Kabbalist from every angle as he climbs higher in order to test the various stages of Devotion, Purity and Sincerity before reaching the level in the fourth Heaven of being in the presence of God. Even then the middle path up through the Halls of Holiness and Sanctification to the place before the Abyss that lies in front of the Divine Face will not be without its testing, for Satan, in Hebrew, means the Tester.

However, before you reach these exalted regions much has to be done, for the aim of the Work is not just to realise yourself alone. To be more explicit, the second and third journeys of acquiring experience and imparting go on simultaneously. It is not just a question of getting to the top, then coming down again before finally returning home. It is a process of ascent, while simultaneously passing on to the levels immediately below, material that is still fresh in experience. This gives an insight into why there is a spiritual hierarchy. The great spiritual leader is concerned, like a general with the grand strategy of humanity. Such beings have an over-view of things which less developed people cannot hope to grasp, such as the life span of a civilisation. Moses came into this class. Senior commanders, such as great masters like Baal Shem Tov, would be involved with specific epochs and places like the Hassidic movement in Eastern Europe, whilst sages, like Cordovero who founded a particular school, would be concerned with specific lines of transmission. Lesser saints would supervise groups or be responsible for watching over individual people. Those who are being spoken about may be incarnate or discarnate, depending on the needs of the situation.

In some cases, a great personage may be born just to initiate one impulse, like Isaac Luria, whose short life's work altered the direction of Kabbalah, whilst others may return regularly in order to instruct those close to them. Of these, we read little, although they may recall past lives and reveal who they were to their immediate circle.

All these prerequisites are necessary if the Work is to be carried out well. If there is a major defect in the individual, or the group, then it will never function correctly. Indeed, any attempt to harness the influx of the higher worlds under improper conditions will only precipitate a breakdown in the individual and a break-up of the group. Even Lucifer cannot work without some order, and the demonic tendency to chaos merely implements laws that disintegrate and disperse the accumulated energy and form, back to their primary elements. Having examined the development of the individual in relation to the group, let us now look in greater detail at the aim of the kabbalistic Work.

9. Aim

The aim of kabbalistic Work is to act as the conscious agent of transformation between the upper and lower worlds. That is to say the raising of energy, matter and awareness from the ordinary level to a higher state, and the bringing down and transmission of power, substance and consciousness from the realms of soul, spirit and Divinity, so that the natural world may experience Paradise, Heaven and the presence of God on Earth.

While the aim is not uncommon to all religious traditions, its implementation is often beyond the capability of most individuals and institutions. This is either because there is no understanding of what is required, or because the existing methods over time have become corrupt and can no longer act as sacred vehicles for interaction between the worlds. To live a devout life, to study and even to perform religious practices may eventually lead to this capability. As the lives of many good people have demonstrated, this is possible without esoteric instruction and methods, but the process is very long and not guaranteed in one lifetime. Moreover, the rituals of synagogue, church and mosque cannot always be relied on to bring about such transformations, although when the conditions are right, and everyone is in a particularly good state, even the most simple or elaborate service can generate a remarkable atmosphere, but this is rare. Thus, for some, the conventional approach is not enough, because however pious a congregation may be, it is too often cluttered with rigid customs and attitudes to facilitate any flow or unification between the worlds.

When you consider the ordinary ego state of most people during a religious service with its rare moments of higher consciousness, and then set them up against the many hours spent dreaming by day and night each year, then it is clear that there is only a small percentage of real spirituality in people's lives. Such a minute amount of lift can only have a limited effect on raising the general consciousness of the human race. Something more potent has to take on the task, and this is where the esoteric schools within the orthodox (and sometimes not so orthodox) traditions have to accept the responsibility. More than one great teacher has said that if there were only a few more thousand spiritually advanced people in the world, then the course of history would be changed. War and crime would diminish and then vanish, and many economic and social injustices would be corrected if the human race could begin to perceive (unconsciously at first) its familyhood. This state has been touched at the high points of civilisation, when the balance of the Creative forces have been in equilibrium, or there has been enough true spirituality to generate a moral conscience in that society. The Buddhist Emperor Ashoka's India was such a case. Alas, this condition has usually only lasted, at the most, over the one generation that was sensitive enough to provide the spiritual fulcrum. The focussing of this Heavenly pivot in the world is the first general aim of the Work. As one rabbi remarked, "The righteous are the foundation of the World".

It will be appreciated that a great deal of preparation has to be done before such changes can be brought about. Centuries of labour often bearing no obvious fruit must pass before even the groundwork can be laid. Many Kabbalists, Sufis and Christian mystics have and will never see the effects of their labour. Most of the Kabbalists of Medieval Provence and Catalonia probably had no idea of the impact that their new formulation of the esoteric tradition was to have on Judaism, Christianity and occultism, although it might be suspected that the masters foresaw what they were doing, when they sought to solve the conflict between faith and reason that was confronting their time. The task of today is no way different. We work to help what the Chinese mystics called "the removal of the Capital". This is the continual progression of the Holy Council through time, at the head of which is what the Moslems call the *Katub*, or Pole of the Age, who Kabbalists call the Messiah or Anointed One.

Little is known or can be said about such a person, except that whoever occupies this position, at any moment in history, is the most highly evolved human being present on Earth. This makes that person the Crown of humanity, and therefore its most direct connection between incarnate mankind and God. Below this is a hierarchy of spiritual individuals who hold their place in a pyramid of rank according to their development and destiny. The upper part of this celestial company is small, but well integrated as might be expected, whereas the lower levels are more fluid, with the lowest members entering and departing as they attain different states of consciousness ranging from flashes of enlightenment to routine glimpses during meditation or group work. The purpose of the training to be described is how to reach and experience the bottom sections of this pyramid and so bring the lower and upper worlds into fusion both in the individual and in general life.

The methods by which this is accomplished vary from one century to the next, and from one country to another. Some things that were valid at the time of Abraham are no longer relevant to later generations, although the principles and objectives are the same. Hence, it was decreed, after the destruction of the Temple by the Romans that animal sacrifice should cease and the power of the priests be curtailed. Likewise, as the tradition evolved, so various techniques were discarded and new ones brought in. Contrary to orthodox belief, many of the practices they now perform are relatively recent or have been borrowed from other spiritual traditions, because they were more efficacious. For example, the Christian rosary was adapted from the Moslems during the Crusades, and when the devout Jew declares the Thirteen Principles of Faith, he is also concurring in its author's use of the Greek philosophical method.

Most kabbalistic techniques of work are based on principles contained within the metaphysical scheme of the tradition. This system is an amalgam of ancient Jewish teaching, Babylonian and Persian cosmology, and many other influences such as the gnostics and sufis. The strongest outside factor is neo-platonism which had a profound impact on the Jews of Medieval Spain. Many of its concepts were adapted by the Kabbalists of Gerona to bring about the system we use today. All these external adaptations, however, do not detract from the essential teaching of the tradition which goes back to the first and most Holy Name of God.

10. Vehicle

The first principle of practical work in Kabbalah is the manifestation of the Divine saying I AM THAT I AM. This Name must always be present in operations because it contains the essence of everything done *Ba Ha Shem*, that is "In the Name". The reason, as said, is that it sets out the cycle of coming out of nothingness into something through the focus of the word 'THAT' and then its return, after experiencing all that exists in 'THAT' which leads the manifest consciousness back to its Source from whence it came.

In our first figure of diagram 9 we see the process laid out as a descent and ascent with 'THAT' at its pivot. The second figure shows how the midpoint is like the focus of a lens that reduces the light of consciousness from above into a spot of nothingness in the midst of existence, while simultaneously focussing the reflected light from below into the same void that contains everything, before each beam opens out and passes on in the downward and upward flow of light. This focal point is the position of Adam in a state of innocence, whilst the third figure of the integrated star composed of the now unified upper and lower triangles, represents the Adam of experience and completion. Here the individual and the universe merge as the Image of God.

Mankind is at the place of intersection, which is midway between Heaven and Earth. Thus, we are the only creatures capable of experiencing both upper and lower worlds simultaneously. Tradition tells us that the angelic beings cannot walk the Earth, eat, or propagate; neither can the creatures of the elemental and natural worlds consciously enter into the Heavens and participate directly in the celestial activities. Only human beings can do this, for they alone possess the higher vehicles of individual soul and spirit as well as a physical body, which can bridge the worlds. However, to be able to do this requires either a high degree of evolution in the organisation and refinement of the physical, psychological and spiritual bodies, or a system of

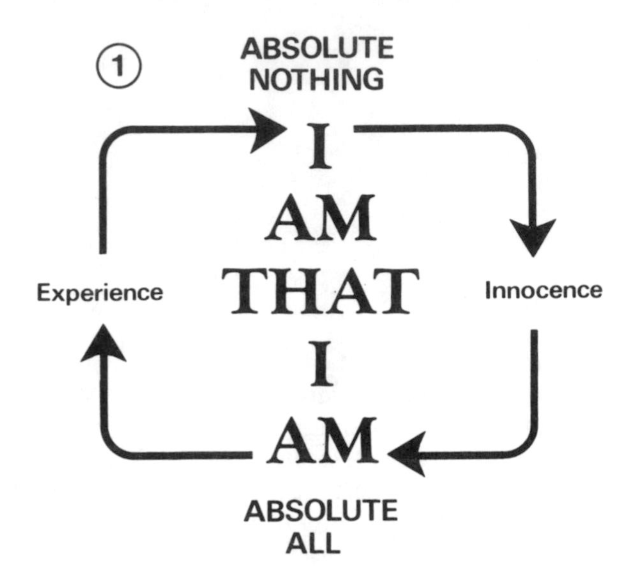

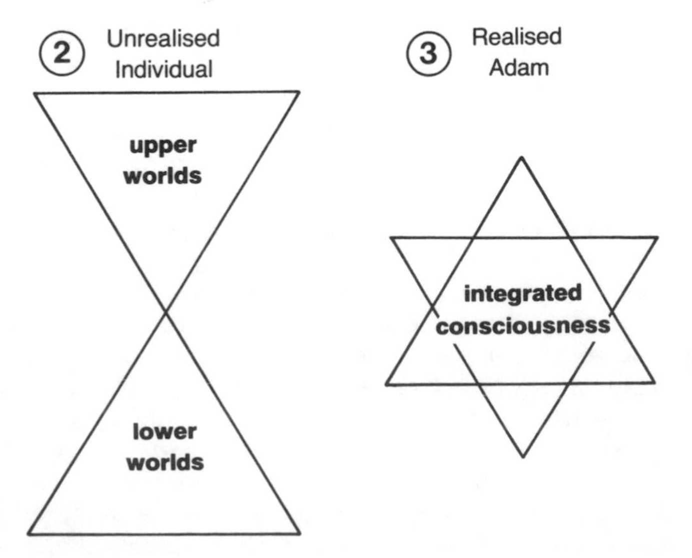

9. **MANIFESTATION**

Here consciousness emerges from ABSOLUTE NOTHING in the first word of the Holy Name. It then goes on to become in the second, be fully manifest in the middle, and then in consciousness return to becoming ABSOLUTE ALL, having passed from innocence to experience of ITSELF. The two lower diagrams symbolise the upper and lower worlds meeting in a focus of human consciousness, and their union in a perfected Adam.

techniques whereby those who have not reached a sufficient level of development to enter at will into the upper worlds, may ride on especially constructed vehicles of ritual, devotion, and contemplation. These vehicles of ascent were called in ancient times the technique of *Merkabah* or chariot riding, which was the old name of Kabbalah.

As might be expected the techniques were usually designed on the basis of the sefirot. This is the second principle. Thus, any exercise is modelled on the dynamics and structure of the Tree, that is, it will contain the major laws of the aim of unity, the interaction of the three pillars and the flow between the upper and lower faces of the Tree. It will also include the principles of the four levels of action, emotion, intellect and will, and the corresponding stages of consciousness in the body—*Malkhut*, ego—*Yesod*, self—*Tiferet*, spiritual knowledge—*Daat*, and contact with the Divine at *Keter*. Some operations may be limited to one or two levels, but the others always have to be present, even if they are not being considered or the exercise will not work.

In this particular exposition we are going to look at a blend of ancient and modern techniques. Traditional methods such as juggling with the Hebrew letters, or praying and contemplating in the orthodox manner have been written about in the *Way of Kabbalah*† and by other authors in detail, so we will not repeat these modes, but speak about the ones that have been developed since medieval times, or have not been described until now. This is now permissible because many esoteric secrets that have been kept discreetly for centuries are now being disclosed in order to meet the needs of our time. With the prospect of a global holocaust, those responsible for the spiritual welfare of mankind have indicated that the Work must be intensified so as to offset the tendency towards conflict and disintegration. This is why one can now buy, in any occult bookshop, material for which many seekers over the ages have made hazardous outer and inner journeys. It is also the reason why books like this are being written. The current generation of Kabbalists needs to be informed and trained more quickly than perhaps any other over the ages.

When it is realised that a kabbalistic operation has to be carried out be it for an individual or for the widest possible purpose, then the technique appropriate must be carefully selected. In some

†*Way of Kabbalah*, published by Gateway Books, Wellow, UK; and Samuel Weiser, York Beach, ME.

cases, there may already be one in existence in the repertoire of the group. This could be a very ancient form that has been handed down, such as certain prayers and rituals, or it might be a ceremony that was constructed in the recent past. If the situation cannot be met by what is already to hand, then something is either modified to suit the occasion, or a totally new technique is designed. Traditional schools, by definition, tend to rely on old methods, but in time the power of these modes fades, as each age has its own peculiar balance of forces. Thus, whilst the sacrifice of the scapegoat was efficacious in Second Temple Jerusalem, it is not appropriate in twentieth century New York (which is not to say that there are not always some people who might consider it as being still valid).

To design and construct a vehicle to meet the moment is a very subtle art which requires more than just a theoretical understanding of kabbalistic principles. It needs a certain experience of the different levels involved and a deep understanding of the nature of the sefirot. Many people believe that by reading and talking about the Tree they know what it is, however time and maturity reveal again and again that what they had thought they knew was not only a fraction of the truth, but often a distorted image of the reality. A common example of this is the statement made by many who have recently mastered the theory of the Tree, that it is quite a rigid system. After some years most students remark that the reverse is in fact true. Indeed, that is why it is called the Tree of Life. Thus, when it comes to designing an exercise, all aspects of the Tree have to be taken into account, because the forces focussed during the operation are very powerful and can easily be miscalculated by the inexperienced. Therefore, one must proceed with prudence.

Following the model of the Tree, every kabbalistic operation must embody the same general principles. It should have a Malkhutian base, so as to earth any energy and ground the participants, and a stable *Yesod* or foundation in which the ordinary ego mind can be held securely by a pattern of actions, thoughts and feelings. It should have a clear Hodian programme of instructions and a good internal and external communication system, as well as a strong Netzahian input of vitality and rhythm, or there will be no power in the flywheel of momentum. The triad of awakening must be activated or the whole operation will just be mechanical. The place of the self should be on maximum alert as the watcher and supervisor, whilst the side triads of the emotional and intellectual complexes are held in balance, so that there is no personal interference or opportunity for demonic intrusion. The soul triad must be as receptive as possible to whatever comes down from the great triad of the Spirit, and last but not least a profound awareness of the Divine Presence, symbolised by *Keter* the Crown, must never be forgotten as one remembers that everything is done *Ba Ha Shem*, in the Holy Name.

Having laid out the general plan of an operation, let us examine some techniques, beginning with *Malkhut* at the base of the Tree.

11. Elements

The training of a Kabbalist uses various techniques for each stage and level. First there are those concerned with self-discovery, both inward and outward, and then the methods by which the student becomes aware of different dimensions of time and space. These are related to one's own life, the scope of the group, and the scale of the tradition. The aspirant will be shown by various means the interior connections he has between different parts of himself, as well as his relationship and function within the group and the tradition. Thus, he comes in contact with the individual, historic and cosmic aspects of the Work in which he will serve.

The process of instruction begins with the individual. The first step is to get to know the body which is the Malkhutian vehicle for the psyche and spirit. If the student remains unaware of the body's structure, dynamics and several levels of intelligence, then not only will much be lost by not seeing the analogue and resonance with the higher worlds, but its powerful influence on the psyche may not be detected, and if necessary controlled. To know the body does not mean that one must be as intimately familiar with its anatomy as a medical student, but to be acquainted with the general principles upon which it is based and how it works. This requires a rudimentary understanding of physiology, so that one can distinguish between different levels of work within the body.

From the kabbalistic view the body can be said to contain four basic levels. The first and densest is that of solids, which would include any structure that supported, carried or operated according to mechanical laws, that is the skeleton, certain organs and muscles. The next would be of fluids which encompass blood, sweat, urine or anything that flows through the organism. The element of air is seen in all the gases present in the blood, organs, and cavities of the body, besides that passing in and out of the lungs. Fire would be the principle behind all the heat and light generated in the tissue which is radiated by the body.

In order to become aware of this elemental division, the student sits or stands in a relaxed position, and focuses the senses on these Malkhutian levels. Beginning with earth, he senses the weight and mineral composition of the body, how it hangs upon the carefully designed structure of bones which are held in position by connective tissue, and the balance and counter-balance of the muscles. The student would then observe how the body moves with great subtlety and precision through every movement in a flow of positions that are held in a momentary equilibrium. This is the mechanical aspect of the body. Next the attention is shifted to the watery element. This is done by a blend of sense and imagination. Thus, the fluid-saturated tissue and organs are perceived as they hold and guide the slowly percolating fluids from their intake at the mouth to their exit in excretion and sweat. It will be noted how the body has quite distinct views about its mass and fluid content, whether it wishes to take on more, or lose some. This gives an insight into the vegetable mind and its effect both on the body and the psyche. By the same principle in reverse, we perceive how the will can influence the state of the metabolism by, for example, excessive drink, or fasting.

The level of air is then examined by controlling the breath and observing the reaction of the body as various quantities are absorbed and penetrate the tissue. It should also be noted that the atmospheric balance in and about the body is crucial to its well-being, and how a shift of consciousness can extract fresh air from a stuffy room. This demonstrates how there are levels within levels, in that a rarer dimension lies within the heavier aspect of the atmosphere that can be tapped and used. The principle of coarse and fine levels of an element is represented by the three intermediate elemental combinations of mud, vapour and flame, which is the earthly counterpart of fire.

The element of fire is examined by becoming conscious not only of the heat but of the radiance that is emitted by the body. This can be detected by very close observation and an attunement to the subtlest level of the physical world. Some people, either by gift or by diligent practice, can glimpse or see the field of light that hovers just above the skin, and others of a more sensitive nature or of greater development, can actually perceive the various lines of the aura as they shimmer around a person. In the early stage of this exercise the aura can be detected by the palm of the hand which registers the different sheafs of bodily radiation as gentle pressure fields set at various distances.

The purpose of this exercise is to acquaint the student with the manifestation of the four worlds in their most physical form. If the experience is developed, then much insight can be gained into the nature of the higher worlds and their relationship to one another. For example, the principle of inter-penetration of body and psyche can be clearly observed in the watery aroma of sweat or breath, which reflects the psyche's condition in the metabolism. In this way the three lower elements can be related to physical, emotional and intellectual states, with fire representing consciousness. Thus solidity is usually concerned with practicality, whilst fluidity associated with moods. As regards gaseousness, people often speak of their minds being foggy or clear, and anyone who has seen a corpse knows that the light of consciousness has departed from it, in that it emits no heat and the eye has no radiance.

This exercise in bodily awareness may be taken even further in that the consciousness of the student can be made to penetrate and observe the work of various areas of the interior anatomy and ascertain their performance, and so learn much about his own psyche by elemental analogy. For example, much insight could be gained about the feeling triad of the psyche if you could perceive the flow of the circulation, and its patterns and characteristics, of which heartache and sluggishness are examples. Likewise, a great deal could be gathered by being acquainted with the working of the autonomic nervous system which corresponds to the *Yesod* of the body, and therefore, relate to the ego and its habitual reflexes. Everyone knows about the beating of the heart and intake of breath in moments of crisis, but how many people are aware of the less spectacular shifts within the central nervous system that relate to the self. If we noted the habitual tightening throat, or the ever cramped shoulder, we might register that we had a malfunctioning psyche long before disease set in in the body.

Perhaps one of the most important lessons to be gained from this Malkhutian study is that the body has a definite mind of its own. It protests if it is pushed, and resists any threat to it by its owner, such as excessive strain, as well as to any outside assault. Over a period of time the will of the body can be trained, but it is not easy as it relies on ancient instinctive processes, such as sleep as well as recently acquired habits. Conscious experience of the body brings one into direct contact with its intelligence. This can be an encounter of confrontation or co-operation, depending on the objective of the student. For example, sometimes habits have to be broken because they misuse or waste valuable energy. Occasionally, the body has to be coerced into a hyper effort in order to accomplish something on a higher level. Fasting or working overtime, or performing much quicker or slower actions than the usual rhythm, or even breaking rhythm, can be means of attaining certain inner states. These, like rapid breathing for a short period must always be used intelligently, because whilst the body has enormous resources it does have limits and its capability, if not its will, may be broken. The yoga freak and damaged junky illustrate such excesses.

The foregoing exercises may be varied in many ways, but their prime purpose is to not only make the Kabbalist aware of the elemental levels at work within the body, but root the Work to the Earth, so that the student can return to *terra firma* any time he or she feels out of depth, after entering the higher realms. This retrieval method is as vital as an astronaut's ability to abort his mission, because an ungrounded mystic can get into serious trouble if he is not in touch with physical reality. Indeed, one should always terminate a kabbalistic operation by becoming conscious of the body. Symbolically stamping the feet is a good way to establish contact with *Malkhut* again after an exercise.

The next chapter takes us up the Tree to teach us how to use *Yesod*, and its power of imagery as a tool.

12. Imagination

Yesod or the Foundation of the Tree in a human being relates to the ego or the ordinary consciousness. This includes not only the awareness of the external world and the body's state in the form of sensual impression, but the capacity to perceive what is not perceptible to the senses by means of imagination. This is because the non-sefirah of *Daat* or Knowledge lies behind *Yesod*, when two worlds, or Trees, are related to each other. Thus, the *Yesod* of the psyche overlays the *Daat* of the body, and the *Daat* of the psyche underlies the *Yesod* of the world of the Spirit. By studying the nature of the relationship between *Daat* and *Yesod* in the lower worlds, it is possible to become acquainted with how the same combination might operate in the higher worlds and levels of being.

Taking the level of ego, the one to which we have most access, we can see how, for example, the *Yesod* of the psyche can know about events going on in the body. Contrary to general belief, we do not perceive the body directly, but through the agency of the central nervous system, that is the *Malkhut* of the psyche, which is the simultaneous *Tiferet* of the body. The lower part of the physical Tree, which is composed of the electronic, chemical, tissue, organic and mechanical levels are out of direct cognisance of the psyche. It is only by the medium of the etheric field, which joins the upper face of the body to the lower face of the psyche, and the sefirot that make up these two faces, that we experience our bodies. The way this occurs is unconsciously via the functions of the side sefirot of psycho-biological processes, and consciously through the sefirot of the central column. The latter are made up of three levels. The bottommost is a general awareness of the body's condition, which only comes into prominence during a crisis, such as a toothache, when the autonomic system passes the problem onto the central nervous system, whilst the topmost of the place of the self comes to the fore when a moment of self-consciousness is present, again perhaps because of a crisis. Between these two conditions is the ordinary awareness of the ego, which is informed about the body's condition in detail by the physical *Daat* in the form of a sense-based image. This capacity to produce readable images is useful to the Kabbalist because it gives the facility to explore the worlds above and beneath normal range of sensual and psychological perception with knowledge and skill, if applied.

The reason for this is that the *Daat—Yesod* combination is a door between worlds through which consciousness can come down or go up. Thus, it is possible to not only look into the most minute recesses of one's own physical organism, but also to penetrate, through imagination, the most remote corners of the psyche, and even cast into symbolic forms material coming through the *Daat* of the psyche from the realm of Spirit. This is why the practice of the art of imagination and guided imagery is part of Kabbalist training. Some people regard this as a relatively new idea, but if they read the books of Enoch, apocalyptic literature, and the methods of the rabbis in the Second Temple period, they will recognise the technique as quite ancient.

To demonstrate and practise the use of applied imagery as a means of viewing different levels and evoking their properties, we will use a simple exercise based on the four elements and levels found in the physical body, so as to show how a Kabbalist can extend the vision of consciousness beyond its usual range. This exercise should be done under the direction of an experienced guide.

First the student lies down on the floor and arranges himself like a human landscape with mountains and valleys composed of his body and limbs. After making himself comfortable he freezes into a deep rigidity and imagines that he is an island surrounded by the sea of the floor. He does not move but observes how after a time tensions set in and his body wants to move. He does not adjust his limbs because he is now made of solid rock and can only shift gradually to ease any discomfort. By doing this he perceives his body on the scale of a real island, and this enlarges his appreciation of time so that he senses the passing of years instead of minutes. As the moments elongate he imagines the coming and going of the seasons and the expansion and contraction of the rocky strata within the body. He notes an unacceptable stiffness in one limb, and suddenly there is an earthquake as the muscles of this human mountain go into spasm. The island shudders several times before the new configuration of the posture emerges. As the student becomes increasingly cold or hot, he observes the mineral intelligence within his body react in its slow motion as bones strain and grind within the pressures of the situation. Perhaps for a moment the student understands what it is like to be a landscape and recognises that it too has movement and life in accordance with its mineral perception of time and space.

The next exercise is to experience water and the vegetable world. In this the student begins by rolling himself into a ball. This is a cell in the primordial ocean. At first you imagine the vast watery depths below and above as the powerful currents carry the cell along in a flow. Whilst holding this in the imagination you note all the watery processes within, observing closely the vegetable principle at work as it grows, feeds and dies throughout our lives. You see hair and skin as leaves and bark, and blood as sap. You note the intelligence of the organs and how they select and reject material from the fluids passing through them. You begin to open out to cell posture as the limbs become roots and branches that wave about in the watery space enclosing us. You flower into an elegant pattern and wait to be fertilized. You conceive and gestate fruit, and give birth to other vegetables that grope with a dim consciousness towards the earth below and the air and light above. Maybe for an instant you enter the cellular world of plants and recognise that many of your motivations come from this kingdom, that the seeking of a home, a mate and children is not an animal or human drive, but derives from the primeval intelligence of that first cell which emerged in the primordial waters to bridge the evolutionary gap between inorganic and organic consciousness.

The third exercise is to imagine we are standing alone or with others upon a great plain. Above, a vast ocean of air moves in a state of mild breeze, whilst we crawl or walk on the ground and feed. Acting out this situation with our arms as wings, we mingle with our own kind ignoring all other creatures except those that we fear might eat us and those we eat. Circling round our flock, we avoid enemies and associate with friends, pecking those who are lower in the order to keep our place. We court and are challenged to a fight by a rival, but before we compete for favours there is a cry of alarm which all take up. Raising our wings-arms, we all fly up and away in panic before following our leader, who is at this moment, the strongest member of our company. We climb up on the wind to gain a safe vantage point from which to view everything below. The danger having gone, we begin to enjoy ourselves, 'following my leader' about the room-sky. Our leader sweeps and turns, swoops and climbs in a complex set of manoeuvres that have taken the flock millions of years to perfect. The air is our calm friend today, although tomorrow it may drive us earthwards in a storm. We descend on its gusts and streams to land once more upon our feeding ground. From this enactment we can perceive the animal in us, and recognise the powerful forces that operate upon society, and our own unconscious depths, to prevent people from becoming individuals. We also glimpse something about the nature of the element air and its higher counterpart, the Spirit.

The last exercise is to experience fire or consciousness. This may be done by becoming a human being, which is not an easy matter. Let the student take up the posture of Rodin's statue "the Thinker" who sits pondering with his chin in his hand. Let him remain outwardly quite still and consider what he has learnt from the three previous exercises. Let the mind contemplate the implication of the evolutionary processes still at work within. Let the heart feel the difference in the levels and the body sense their operation, even at this moment of reflection. Allow the beam of consciousness to extend backwards in time to experience not only what has just been seen, but the historic epochs of mineral, vegetable and animal phases of dominance before man came upon the Earth. Then allow the aim of consciousness to reverse and project into the future and the possibilities that lie before mankind, including the choice of its own destruction. Perhaps some illumination will reveal an insight or prophecy about yourself or the human race. In that moment you may experience what it is to be beyond the realm of nature and in touch with the Light of Eternity. This is a human being's capacity.

13. Preparation

Drawing together the exercises involving the body, that is the *Malkhut* of the psychological Tree, let us synchronise them into a kabbalistic practice. The body of a human being is modelled upon Adam Kadmon, who in turn is an image of the Divine. Therefore, an individual's body is a reflection of the sefirotic pattern of the Tree of Life. As such it can be used as an instrument to receive and impart what comes down into the *Malkhut* of the psyche from the Spirit and beyond. Indeed, the body is the last stage in any kabbalistic process, and if whatever is flowing down does not reach the body, then the operation is incomplete.

Taking the body as a Tree in itself, we can teach it, and ourselves, to become aware of its resonance with Adam Kadmon, consciously relating its matter, energy and consciousness to the structure and dynamics of the Tree. The first part of this exercise is to stand upright in the attention position and become aware of the body as a whole. Having perceived it as a unity in which everything contained within its field is working in unison, we then begin to separate out the various aspects in sequence. We begin by swaying the body gently from side to side in order to observe the two pillars. We note their relationship and how in most of us, the right side is more powerful and active, whilst the left is more gentle and passive. This is seen in cutting a slice of bread in which the left hand steadies whilst the right actively works. Having seen this, we will observe that our consciousness is centred on a line that runs from our crown, through the middle of our brain, throat and heart, to our pubis and feet. If we ignore this axis we are unbalanced in more ways than one. In work or rest the body and psyche always seek equilibrium. This is the central column.

Having established the three pillars you then divide the body horizontally at the level of the solar plexus, thus separating the upper and lower faces from each other. You then observe the four elements or levels: earth and water which correspond to the legs and gut, and air and fire which may be seen as related to the lungs and brain. Using the experience gained in your training exercise, you may begin to sense more keenly the meaning of these levels within our bodies. This is perceived if we allow the attention to rise slowly from the feet to the crown of the head whilst taking in the various levels and pillars to be found in the body. This exercise will not only enhance the idea of your physiology being an image of the Tree, but will prepare it for any kabbalistic operation that you might be about to do. This preliminary action is vital, for the body's will and intelligence, as already noted, can interfere with any deep process if it is not asked to co-operate or at least be quiescent.

Taking body consciousness to a yet more refined level, you may now begin to place the sefirot upon it. Beginning with *Malkhut* you can imagine this to be centred around the feet in contact with the earth. Here you are not using the interpenetrating scheme, but the simple scheme of one Tree. The sefirah of *Yesod* is traditionally placed on the genitals from which the ego derives its power and identity in the way it presents itself. The two sefirot of action, *Hod* and *Netzah*, are usually related to the hips where they function as the active and passive connections with the lower part of the body, whilst *Tiferet*, the centre of the Tree, lies over the solar plexus, the pivot of the body. The two sefirot of *Gevurah* and *Hesed* relate to the heart and are set out on either side of that organ. They are sometimes seen as the two chambers of the lungs where the blood changes from venous to arterial, that is the intermingling of water and air. The non-sefirah, *Daat*, is traditionally placed over the throat but the face with its organs of sense perception and expression may be included, as they illustrate the inflowing and outflowing of knowledge in the eyes, ears, nose and mouth. These organs are themselves expressions of the four elements in that the eyes are related to light, the nose and ears to air, the tongue to water, and the rest of the body to touch, that is earth. *Binah* and *Hochmah*, the sefirot of understanding and wisdom are related to the two hemispheres of the brain, whilst *Keter* is seen as a Crown set upon the head.

While many people know this kabbalistic scheme, there are few who have actually experienced what it means. As one teacher remarked, "Some think that to know the name of anything is to comprehend it". In Kabbalah this is very apparent by the lack of real understanding of, for example, *Hod* and *Netzah*; many expositions dismiss these two vital sefirot with a vague sentence or two. No! One is not a Kabbalist because one can read the texts in the original Hebrew. Indeed, mere learning invariably distorts simple principles by the complication of numerous cross-references. Nothing can make up for direct experience of the sefirot in action or personal entry into even the lowest of the heavenly Halls. No amount of scholarship can match the moment when one passes through the dark glass of *Daat* and into the next world. However, before we get to this stage there has to be much preparation. This involves bringing theory and practice together so as to generate the right conditions for something to happen. So far, we have seen how an individual makes his body ready. Now comes a procedure which many Kabbalists follow in order to bring their body, soul and spirit into closer relationship.

Before beginning whatever has to be done, the Kabbalist stands to, and in attention, with his arms by his side. He then leads his consciousness up from *Malkhut* at the feet, through *Yesod* to the pelvic cavity that lies within the triads composed by *Yesod, Hod, Netzah* and *Tiferet*. As he says the names of the sefirot in sequence, he then climbs up the 'lightning flash' to focus upon *Tiferet* before moving up into the chest cavity that contains *Gevurah* and *Hesed* where he pauses for breath. From here he rises to *Daat* and silently speaks this name before proceeding, as he raises his hands to the sefirot of the brain and the crown so completing the sequence. By this time, the hands should be well to each side and above the head with the palms up, although some Kabbalists like the Sufis, face the left one down so as to impart what is received. The body is now fully alert and co-ordinated, with the psyche and spirit at the ready for the next stage of any operation.

14. Ritual

Having set out our first series of exercises based upon the *Malkhut* of the body and the imaginative faculty of *Yesod*, let us proceed by examining some more related to the three triads centred on the ego. Here we see how the principles of the Tree generate the form and dynamic of an operation. However, whilst the level of the Tree involved remains the same, the way it is explored and developed can be varied, giving rise to many possibilities. These variations of a principle are related to whatever is the aim of the project. The great beauty of Kabbalah is that every generation can design its own method according to the need of the time and the place, although if one examines the texts of different epochs with the Tree in mind, one can discern the same essential principles, despite the vast difference in form, language and culture. Thus we find that the design of the Tabernacle in the Sinai desert is echoed in the Temple in Jerusalem, in the layout of the church and mosque, as well as in the Freemason's Lodge and the occultist's sanctuary.

Taking the great lower triad bounded by *Malkhut, Hod* and *Netzah*, which contain three small triads centred at *Yesod*, we shall describe three methods of sensitising the processes of action, thinking and feeling that are associated with them. The triad of action is made up of *Malkhut*, that is the body, *Yesod*, the ego, and *Netzah* which is the sefirah behind the instinctive and psychological involuntary processes. By this is meant all those rhythms and routines of the psyche and body that form the patterns of everyday life, like dressing automatically, remembering multiplication tables, or anything that does not require any thinking through. Let us suppose that we wish to perform a simple ritual, which is the working mode of this triad. Its aim, in this case, is to alert the triad and make the student aware of its qualities.

The first thing is to formulate the objective. This we have done. We now set out the process into a sequence, so as to build up and focus the attention and so charge the situation. Thus, there has to be a preparation stage, an initiation of the operation, a development of the impulse, a climax and a resolution before coming back to earth, with, we hope, an advanced degree of comprehension and experience. Here is a rising up through the four levels and a return to equilibrium.

Having decided what is to be done, all the physical factors are then gathered together and arranged in an order that has a kabbalistic significance in relation to what we wish to do. This may mean arranging a room or a corner in such a way that it not only becomes a special space, but by its particular setup will become a structure that will aid the Kabbalist to hold and direct the principles invoked. Thus, there has to be a space that has been specially created for the operation and one or more objects in it that will serve as the limiting factors and axis of the operation to contain and direct the energy of the ritual. An example of this may be a room that faces East which has a table-altar upon which stand two candlesticks. The significance of the East is self-evident to Jews, Christians and sun worshippers alike, as the solar point of arising is an archetypal direction. The altar is likewise symbolic as the field of attention with its two candlesticks representing the two pillars. The space between represents the third unseen presence of consciousness and will.

The student now begins to prepare himself. At first he ablutes, that is, he washes his hands and face and makes his body clean and comfortable. Some people might carry this to its extreme when a major ritual is about to be performed. In this case a bath is often required. With a minor exercise the symbolic ritual of washing the hands and face may suffice. Again, fresh clothes or ritual vestments are usually put on in a major enterprise. This is done to inform the body and lower psyche that something special is about to be performed. It also helps to evoke the body's awareness and obedience to the will that must not be distracted. If you are a Jew, then a *tallit* or prayer shawl and *yarmulke* cap is sufficient for a ritual garment. If not, then anything, from a hat only used on such occasions to an elaborate and specially designed robe may be put on to indicate that a kabbalistic operation is to be performed. Such vestments should not be worn on any other occasion or they will lose whatever sacred power they may acquire during such rituals and so become debased in substance. When such objects are used out of context they can be used by the perverse for quite a different purpose, although at high spiritual cost.

The act of putting the garment on should be a ritual in itself. It must be done with full consciousness of what it represents. In the Bible the priestly vestments relate to the three levels of the psyche, spirit, and Divinity.† One composite robe with the appropriate symbols can suffice. When this is done and the student is aware that he is about to leave the state of ordinary consciousness, then he proceeds to the place of ritual, where with others, or alone, the operation is begun. This may be with a period of silence in which the awareness is extended, as set out in the chapter on Elements, throughout the body, as consciousness of the mineral, vegetable and animal levels draw the being into a heightened sense of physical unity. This is held until the ego is in equilibrium and the body consents to become quiescent as the field of consciousness is opened.

As the hands of the Kabbalist are raised to receive whatever might be given, so an invocation is uttered. This might consist of a single prayer of praise or petition, or a complex progression of words that take the person up the Tree from *Malkhut* to *Keter*. The effect of this is usually quite striking, because by setting up a physical and psychological vessel, there begins the collection of what is called 'the Dew of Heaven' that is continually falling from the higher worlds. This is the spiritual mannah that nourishes the human race, although only a small proportion are sensitive enough to be conscious of it without special techniques. The accumulation of this celestial substance usually raises the Kabbalist further by its conversion into psychic energy. This, however, can only occur in those who have developed enough of their inner capability to be able to convert the celestial influx passing down. To do this requires much practice and experience—but one must begin somewhere.

Having reached a point of contact, through the *Tiferet* of the self, the ritual may then proceed on to its particular objective. In this case it is not to receive and transmit higher influences, but to request, if it be Divine Will, that you may learn more about the nature of ritual. At such a moment a match might be struck high overhead and its flame brought down to light the candles. It must be said "might" for this is only one way of representing a principle. During this act of ignition you may realise how out of Nothingness came Light, the symbol of Divine Will and the highest World Emanation. As the flame is lowered the words, "Thy will be done"

†See Chap. 33--*Kabbalah and Exodus* (Wellow, UK: Gateway and York Beach, ME: Samuel Weiser).

should be said, in this case, to remind the Kabbalist that nothing may be carried out without the Holy One's permission, or the operation is no more than an act of magic or human manipulation of subtle powers. This is crucial, because later the inexperienced may find, that like the sorcerer's apprentice, they cannot handle the forces released, and panic. This can have dire consequences on the unbalanced and should not be attempted without a tutor.

On lighting each candle, bearing in mind which represents what pillar, the ritual may then be taken further in exercises to develop the art of conscious action with a sacred purpose. Orthodox and ancient forms of this mode are to be found in synagogue and church ritual. However, special rituals may be made up by the Kabbalist, so as to meet an individual need or a specific objective, such as healing. This, however, requires much knowledge, and we are not yet at this point. Therefore, let us confine ourselves just to studying the principles of ritual. Having completed the exercise in preparation, the process is then reversed. After a period of silence in which consciousness is stretched to its limit to mark the summit of the operation, the Kabbalist then gives thanks for whatever has been received. After the hands have been lowered and the verbal descent of the Tree is complete, the candles may then be blown out with the words, "Holy! Holy! Holy! Art Thou Lord of Hosts, Thy Glory fills all the Worlds".

After a pause you then stamp the feet to earth and disrobe, so bringing the body and psyche back into the mundane condition, while still retaining an awareness of the higher worlds for as long as possible. Over the years the effects of such operations will cease to fade, as everything the Kabbalist does in life will become a sacred ritual. As one student noted, "I learnt much about Kabbalah from my teacher by just watching him practice his profession". This is the method of ritual in daily life which is the practical way of the Work.

15. Contemplation

The technique of contemplation applies to the triad formed by *Malkhut, Yesod* and *Hod*. This combination is found on the passive side of the Tree, and so one would expect it to be reflective rather than active. This is reinforced by the fact that the sefirot of the body and ego are matched by *Hod,* which is concerned with the collection and communication of information within the body and the psyche. To learn about the nature of this functional triad the following exercise can be used.

After making the preliminary preparations to indicate to the body and psyche that a kabbalistic exercise is about to take place, the student sits down in silence before a table prepared with paper, pens, compass, ruler and inks. The student then makes a prayer asking to be shown insights into the question being posed. Let us assume that the question is "What is the nature of the four ego types?" That is those sub-triads that surround the ego and connect with *Malkhut* and *Tiferet*. Having made the petition the process of contemplation begins.

The first part of the exercise is to set up a frame of reference, like the ritual, but this time in the abstract. Thus, you carefully lay out the sheet of paper and square its base line to the table with its long axis aligned to the solar plexus, that is *Tiferet*. Then you proceed to draw with the ruler the line of the central column of the Tree. Taking the compass and inserting it into the middle of the line, a circle is then drawn. This process is repeated above and below with the pivot of each circle placed where the middle circle's circumference bisects the axis line. This will give the three interpenetrating circles that mark out of the positions of the sefirot. Thus, the Crown comes where the upper circle bisects the axis line at the top, whilst *Daat* is located at its pivot. *Tiferet* is the central circle's pivot point, with *Yesod* at the place where the lower curve of the inner circle bisects the axis. This is the pivot of the lower circle. *Malkhut* comes where the lower curve of this circle touches the bottommost point on the central line. The side sefirot are marked

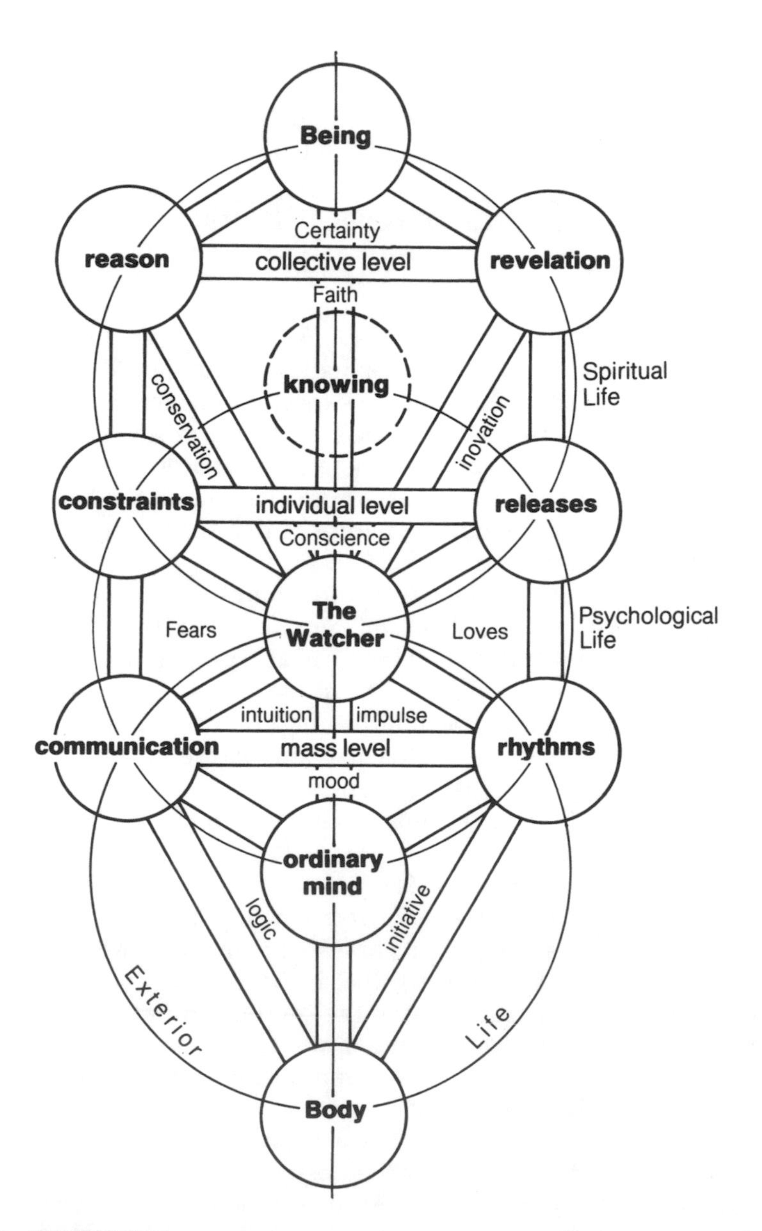

10. **GEOMETRY**

In this Tree the geometry is used to divide and differentiate the various aspects of the psyche in detail. Keywords are associated with certain areas so as to illuminate experience and transform theory into reality. To contemplate the Tree is to see it in terms of one's own life and so begin to enter into its form and dynamic. By this method one can correct any imbalance in its geometry.

out by the three points of intersection made up by the circles on either side. To complete the geometry of the Tree, lines are ruled between the relative sefirot and the pillars. Out of this all the triads should emerge. The sefirot are then indicated by small circles and the paths made thicker by doubling the guidelines.

To draw the Tree and the sefirot is a contemplative act. It connects one with the geometry of its structure, so that one begins to perceive during its construction the form and dynamic that compose it. To use another person's Tree or study it from a book is not enough. One has personally to enter into contact with the Tree and participate in its extraordinary beautiful symmetry. Here, we experience the meaning of Truth being Beauty, and Beauty being Truth, as we, by our contemplative action resonate with the Divine principles contained within it. In some kabbalistic groups to draw one's own Tree and then one's own Jacob's Ladder of the four worlds, is considered an initiation in itself because it is done as a formal ritual to indicate a commitment to the Work. To have one's own Tree in sight at home or work is to be ever aware of the Way of Kabbalah, in the same manner as a cross or a calligraph of the Name of Allah on the wall is a reminder to a Christian or to a Moslem.

Having drawn up the Tree, coloured inks are now applied to separate out the various levels. Following the guidelines in the Book of Exodus, we leave the triad *Keter, Hochmah* and *Binah* white, as the colour of pure light, but paint the great triad of *Binah, Hochmah* and *Tiferet* blue to represent the Spirit. The side triads from *Hochmah* and *Binah* down to *Hod* and *Netzah,* including *Gevurah* and *Hesed,* centred on *Tiferet,* are coloured purple, with a lighter shade to indicate the triad of the soul. The triads of the lower face of the Tree can be coloured in red of various hues with a purple-red in the triad of awakening. Here, we have the colour of flesh and blood separated from the blue of the heavens by purple, the blend of the two. This exercise should generate much thought about the different triads.

Having completed our frame of reference, you now turn to our question and begin to contemplate the nature of the four ego triads by using the Tree. In this, our triad of thinking is led, by conscious will, to dwell upon the diagram. Now the thinking triad works not only automatically, but with extraordinary skill. It will draw upon facts and observations made over many years and apply them to the problem. In the Watcher of the self, you can observe the analysis at work. For example, the triad will deduce from the layout of the four ego triads that the lower two, connected with *Malkhut* will be concerned with the outside world and the body, while the two upper triads will relate, through their connection to *Tiferet* with more introspective matters (in contrast to the thinking mind being used) because they are partially segregated by the line of ordinary consciousness stretched between *Hod* and *Netzah*. This reveals that these two inner triads are often only perceived as thoughts and feelings that rise occasionally to the surface of consciousness like fish. It will also be noted that by their association with the side pillars, the left hand triads must be passive whilst their complements are active. This leads the thinking triad to conclude that it itself must be an outward reflecting process that takes the facts it can perceive and systematically processes them, while the upper left hand components of *Hod, Tiferet* and *Yesod* must work by intuition, that is, its logic is not so discernible or reliable, because it is overlaid by the feelings and the normally dormant awakening triad.

Now the same process of analysis can be applied upon the other side to conclude that the lower right triad, like its double of physical action is inclined to take the initiative psychologically, whilst its upper counterpart can unconsciously manipulate a situation from beyond the threshold of the liminal line between *Hod* and *Netzah*. An example of this is when someone creates tension by silently building up a pressure of anxiety or anger. Likewise, the mechanics of how the four triads must gain and lose ascendancy from mood to mood may be discerned, as well as the fact that a triad of a given moment must have its counterbalance. Thus a powerful intuition, in the top left, will precipitate a strong reflex in the lower right so that practical action will want to check out a hunch or intuition. Many discoveries and conclusions can come by the technique of contemplation. For instance, speculation on the effects of these triads on health or inner growth can be explored by analogy, and projections of the same processes at work in the deep psyche can throw light on the same four triads of the Spiritual Tree. In this way a theoretical understanding of the way various parts of the Tree operate is enhanced.

It will be clear that all this is but a part of a total working method. However like ritual, contemplation on its own is limited. Action and thinking must be balanced, and if you look at our diagram, you will see that they are complemented by the third triad of feeling, which in its central and inner position reconciles the lower outer two. This gives us a clue to its nature and function, which we shall explore in the next chapter. Meanwhile, let us conclude our exercise of the thinking triad by considering what contemplation is. If you examine the Tree, you will see that above the thinking triad are the sefirot of *Hod, Gevurah* and *Binah* with their adjacent triads of intuition, emotion and concepts. Being on the passive pillar they are supportive by nature, so that you can see how the cleverness of *Hod*, the discernment of *Gevurah* and the reasoning of *Binah* might act as an unconscious background to the process of contemplation and help formulate its conclusions. In this way, what is being contemplated is considered at many levels. Superficial and lateral thought occurs when only the thinking triad is being used. This is because the triad on its own is no more than a brilliant instrument. It is seen at its worst in the clever fool who believes that logic is all. However, the operation is to train one to become aware of the higher and deeper levels of experience and so we move on to examine the technics of devotion which belong to the triad of feeling, which completes the ego-centred great triangle of the lower face of the Tree.

16. Devotion

The feeling triad is situated between *Netzah, Hod* and *Yesod,* so it has no direct connection with *Malkhut* and the body. However, there is a process of resonance between it and the corresponding triad of the body which relates to the organs. In this way, the feelings are often associated with the heart, the stomach and the intestines, in the same way the triad of action is manifested in the corresponding triad of the muscles, and the thinking function in the triad of nerves. All these correspondences are not direct communications, but what are called referred connections. This is particularly true of the feelings and is the reason we feel stomach cramp or heartache in difficult situations.

The capacity for such a response is due to the fact that the feeling triad is in contact with both pillars and therefore can become active or passive. Moreover, its connections with the ego makes it particularly susceptible to the loading of events that stimulate this or that response. Under ordinary conditions, the usual pattern is that the feelings are influenced either by what is being projected in from the outside world through the ego, or what unconscious influences are at play from within the psyche. In kabbalistic training the process is reversed, in that the sensitivity of this triad is used to conscious advantage, so that it can receive and transmit, by way of the feeling triad, whatever is thought to be useful in a given situation. For example, by conscious projection through this triad a tense confrontation can be eased and a way through to a resolution be made. "Blessed are the Peacemakers", said one great Kabbalist. This requires, however, a high degree of consciousness being combined with training that can apply the principles we are examining.

As we have seen, there are various levels of will. There is the body's considerable volition and the wilfulness and will-lessness of the side pillars. These can be controlled either by a conscious intention coming from the self of a person, the direction of an instructor, or by the application of discipline based on the rules of the tradition such as "Thou shalt not bear false witness". The state of willingness, associated with the feeling triad, has to be cultivated by practice in accordance with the theory that the self comes to the aid of an individual open to its direction. In this way there is a constant watch over the inclinations of the yesodic ego to command according to its limited comprehension. This we will come to later. If the situation of willingness can be maintained, then many things become possible.

The first thing to occur is that the struggle between the three triads of thinking, action and feeling stops for as long as willingness is sustained. This means that no energy is wasted and that, on the contrary, it is conserved. As a result, there is an accumulation of power that is not usually experienced or available in the *Katnut* or lesser state of consciousness. Moreover, the body becomes less tense and increasingly alert to external events, whilst inwardly a greater sensitivity to what is happening in the psyche is acquired. In order to reach this state, various exercises to develop the feeling triad can be devised.

A simple example is to sit in a chair and remain there in silence for half an hour. After a while the body will begin to be bored. It will want to move, cough or get something to eat or smoke. It will create aches and pains and will even invent strange sensations in order to get some action going. If one simply allows all this to go on, but is obedient to the idea of becoming willing, then the conflict is minimised. After a period of time, the body will stage a crisis, like wanting to go to the toilet, but if this is met with quiet acceptance, then the demands will subside. Such a moment must, of course, be subject to commonsense. Do not force the body beyond its proper limit. Such an exercise should be carried out over several weeks, so that in time the body will accept considerable periods of physical stillness without complaint.

Another example of getting to know and command the feeling triad is to observe its patterns. It will be noticed in daily experience that the feelings have a general cycle. In the morning one often feels this way, at midday after lunch usually that, and in the evening, yet another set of feelings. If these habits are not enacted (and this includes the bad feelings too) then the day will seem to be different. Here we discover that contrary to popular belief, most of our feelings run like clockwork, and are not so prone to change after all. An example of this is that we always feel the same pleasure or apprehension when we come into a particular place and meet certain people. Indeed, some individuals we know always arouse deep dislike without fail, even though nothing has been said or done by them to us. The kabbalistic student is trained to observe thoughts, actions and feelings all the time, so as to realise how he or she is at the mercy of their habitual dominance. The great lower triad that contains these three sub triads, centred on the ego, is for most people just like a psychological computer with a set of triggers that are continually repeating a complex of patterns acquired over many years. Unless one knows this and can recognise them, they cannot be changed or put to good purpose, because in spite of their mechanicalness some are very useful, if only to act as tools in particular situations.

In order to have a command over these psychological habits one has to have a stable will. Now many people believe this is possible to acquire without help. Indeed, many believe they possess will already. This is an illusion. Free will belongs to those who know themselves to at least the degree of being able to separate ego from self, and few even know there is a difference. Most people are dominated by physical and social considerations. They cannot and will not change their situation because their security is based on material possessions or on the good opinion of others. It takes a crisis or a great impulse of will to prize an individual out of the grasp of *Malkhut* or *Yesod*. Further, whilst a crisis may precipitate such a transformation, it often cannot be sustained without assistance from outside, which is why many people fall back into their old ways, or worse, get lost by not looking for help.

In Kabbalah the help comes from a senior or tutor, who acts as the temporary self to the individual. For example, an exercise might be given at the end of a meeting and such a project will be carried out during the week. This could be to remember the face of each member of the group at ten o'clock in the morning, noon, and three o'clock in the afternoon. The order is carried out obediently, not because the student wants the good favour of the instructor, but because it will help to encourage self-development. By recalling the exercise at those times, no matter what is being done, you are not only learning how to command consciousness, but increasing the capacity of the feeling triad's sensitivity. This will open the door to the triad of awakening above, and so gain access to the higher levels of the Tree. Moreover, from such a practice, the beginning of Love begins for one's companions in the Work. Further receptivity will be enhanced and with it the ability to perceive one's own inner state which is the prerequisite of all operations. What is perhaps the most relevant element in this particular exercise is that a covenant with oneself rather than one's instructor is met by real commitment, and this is the essence of obedience which arises out of real willingness.

Traditionally the feeling triad is the one of devotion. Here, however, we have to understand that devotion is not just the obvious acts of prayer or meditation. In Kabbalah one is taught that devotion also means reliability in whatever one is given to carry out. This quality of character is crucial, because it is usually the feeling triad that rebels when under pressure, and therefore, it is vital that it be obedient to the will. Obedience comes after long practise and many backslidings, but perseverance develops stamina and power. When the feelings come under inner authority, then prayer and meditation deepen to a degree undreamed of in the normal state of being.

In classical Kabbalah, there is a practice called *Devekut,* that is 'cleavage unto God'. In this exercise, there is a constant recollection of WHO is always with us, WHO knows us better than we know ourselves, and from WHOM we may learn what real devotion is. To be in the *Gadlut* of greater state of consciousness is to strive to be alert in all of the three sub triads. Alas, this is not easy, because at their centre is the complex and subtle mind of ego which will precipitate action without consultation, divert the thinking processes on a whim, and distort a feeling because of a prejudice. This yesodic mind is the focus of a continuous flow of images and conversations. In order to master the phenomenon, we must comprehend the ego's nature. This requires another set of training exercises, for without knowing the ego's capacity to block even the Light gained from *Devekut,* we can do no serious work.

17. Ego

In traditional Kabbalah, the sefirah of *Yesod*, or the Foundation, has several symbols. One is the unilluminated mirror which reflects only that which is projected upon it, unlike *Tiferet*, the illuminated mirror, which also shines as well as reflects. The lesser mirror of ego tells us that it has no active power, but merely images whatever comes into its field. However, like an ordinary mirror, its image is remarkably convincing, if you do not realise that it is just a reflection. Moreover, it should be noted, that like most looking-glasses, it has flaws that can present an imperfect picture. In some cases, the image can be so distorted that the reality it is mirroring is totally unrecognisable. This often occurs when a person is under duress and panics. If the condition becomes chronic, then it may be seen as neurosis, and if permanent, as a state of madness. This is why the understanding and command of *Yesod* in any spiritual work is vital, for any major imbalance of the ego will be magnified and corrupt whatever is being reflected, no matter how spiritual.

Another traditional symbol for the yesodic ego is the Moon, with the Sun at the *Tiferet* of the self. This echoes the idea behind the two kinds of mirror. If we examine the symbolism of the moon, we will learn much by analogue about the nature of the ego mind. Here, we have the application of 'as above, so below' principle, so beloved by all esoteric traditions, for the same laws apply to the macrocosm of the universe as they do to the microcosm of a human being.

Like the moon, the ego has a face that is always seen and a face that is not. This tells us that there is a certain fixity present that always turns towards or away from consciousness. Thus, there is an unseen side to the ego about which most of us know little. The face that we are familiar with, like the moon, has a definite geography, or rather lunography. In us, this is what is called the personality, or the mask we wear to the world. It is composed of mountains and valleys, craters and seas of habits and attitudes long frozen into a configuration, like the face of the moon. In most people this is acquired in early life and remains unaltered until death. While many of the skills and ploys of the personality may be useful in negotiating ordinary life and striving in the professional and social scene, they are often useless and even dangerous to any in spiritual work, because they can prevent, or even destroy possibilities of inner growth. For example, so called good manners can stop the truth being spoken. In Kabbalah this could mean a lack of honesty between the student and tutor, or between *Yesod* and *Tiferet*. Many people are too polite to themselves when considering unpalatable truths as bad taste or unacceptable.

In order to obviate such an occurrence, exercises are given out by an instructor to observe the nature and working of the yesodic ego, so as to identify its patterns and weaknesses. Such a project might be to take the symbol of the moon and relate its phases to fluctuations in the ego. Thus, the new Moon might be seen as the stage when one begins to awaken in the morning. Here, a thin crescent of consciousness slowly emerges from the unseen side of the moon where the inward looking dream face has been illuminated during the night. The first quarter could be regarded as a period of half awareness when the concentration is not fully engaged, whilst the full Moon could be seen as the state when the personality is totally projected outwards and everything is on the surface. The last quarter, and the degrees in between, might be considered as a phase of retreat or the beginning of introspection, when the interest in outer things is waning. The dark moon describes, in its lack of light, that the ego is either asleep, or turned totally inwards in reflection or reverie. Observing all these phases in oneself, and others, will reveal much about the scope of the ego and its ability to alter its state in contrast to the constancy of the Sun, which always shines whatever condition clouds its face.

Taking the lunar symbol further, in order to show how the technique of analogue is useful for exploration, one might be asked to consider the phenomenon of the eclipse. The lunar eclipse, when the Earth's shadow passes over the moon, could be seen as the body overshadowing the ego, either in illness or some physical activity that occludes its reflection; whilst the solar eclipse, when the moon stands between the sun and the Earth, is quite identifiable as the ego preventing the light of the self from reaching *Malkhut* and the World. To ponder one's findings, when applying this approach, will deepen the comprehension of *Yesod* and allow a more objective penetration when it comes to look at the operation of one's own ego.

From what has been said, it will be seen that the ego has a distinct and complex character. It undergoes constant change, its degree of consciousness alters and focuses in a full circle of directions, and it has an unseen side. Now, whilst the observable face might be very familiar, at least to others, the hidden side is not. Most of us recognise that we have thoughts and feelings and do actions that we do not show to the outer world, but few realise the significance or power of these unrevealed aspects of our ego. Many of these hidden activities relate to our fears and hopes, and sometimes to our fantasies. These in most people are largely unconscious and cause much trouble as they interfere with any possibility of perceiving reality, be it inner or outer. The Kabbalist cannot afford to allow such an intrusion into the flow of light from above or that which is coming in from below. It would thwart the pursuit of self-knowledge and the opportunity to be useful to the Work.

This is why many of the exercises in the early stages of Kabbalistic discipline are concerned with studying and separating out habits and attitudes that are detrimental to progress. You are first of all taught, for example, to leave any egotistic elements, like status, whether of inflation or deflation, outside the door of the study house. Later this rule applies to general life, in that you perform your worldly tasks in a state of continual detachment because the ego will latch itself onto almost anything and claim it for its own. It will at times, moreover, not only try to interfere with ordinary situations, but seek to control spiritual ones. It will, as control of it becomes serious, and therefore a threat to its long-established autonomy, begin to resist any reduction of its ego-esteem. Indeed at the critical point, it will start to fight. At first it manifests as simple resistance, but later as a conflict develops, the ego turns from simple obstinacy to subtle cunning, as it seeks to retain its authority by subterfuge or by feigning token assent. This process is continuous throughout life, for an undisciplined ego will seek to take advantage of any lapse in the Kabbalist's watchfulness.

The exercises concerned with mastering the ego are many. For instance, some are designed to use the body as a control factor. Heavy physical work, for example, can bring to the surface a violent protest from the ego which has an image of itself as being very spiritual, and 'above' such toil. Another exercise might be to make ego act out of 'character' in a real life but contrived situation. Yet another project could be to expose the ego to others involved in the Work by speaking honestly about one's life and aspirations. Here the audience must not only be discerning but also merciful and interested in the truth. (This is the soul triad.) After a while, you soon know whether it is the ego or the self speaking. Moreover, you also discover that even the ego has spiritual ambitions and fantasies.

Generally, the instructor acts as the self in these exercises. Such a person must also be working on his or her ego, because there is the dangerous phenomenon of projection when the student sees the tutor as an idealised *Tiferet* to his or her own *Yesod*. This situation can be a great temptation for both parties. A good tutor will watch out for the symptoms of projection and correct the imbalance. Obedience is not submission to your teacher, but to the Teaching, which represents a manifestation of the Truth. The cultivation of one's own *Tiferet* is the best way of putting *Yesod* in its proper place, but this takes some time. Meanwhile, the different techniques discussed and practised based on the triads surrounding *Yesod* will begin to set its components into their correct acting, feeling and thinking parts. These methods will, over a period, make the particular nature of one's ego emerge as a distinct sub-personality. However, while much attention is devoted to the curtailing of *Yesod*'s useless habits, one must also develop its considerable range of skills. We have already touched on the ego's capacity to deal with images, so let us now explore and develop this talent so that *Yesod* might be encouraged, like the body, to participate with willingness in the Work. In this way ego becomes co-operative and not disruptive. This is vital, for without *Yesod*'s help very little can be accomplished; one is a blind artist whose visions can never be painted. Therefore, in the next chapter, we shall look at *Yesod* as the screen of consciousness.

18. Imagery

Judging by its position on the Tree of the psyche, *Yesod* is a complex sefirah. This complexity, as noted, is increased by the fact that the *Daat* of the body underlies it and connects it with the physical world. As such, the ego is the place where the impressions gathered by the senses and material generated by the psyche are cast into an intelligible image. This means that not only are the electrical impulses from the eyes, ears, nose, tongue and skin interpreted into recognisable signals, upon which action may be based, but so are feelings, thoughts, and inner actions. The latter material is cast in a variety of forms from flashes to complex moods, single ideas to intricate metaphysical themes, simple reactions to detailed manoeuvres. All these, plus the occasional mystical experience with its strange symbols, are projected upon the screen of *Yesod* that day and night produces a continuous show of illuminations, delusions, dreams and realities.

The first exercise to be given is devoted to distinguishing what the body contributes. Here you are told to observe how we have a body image which is held by *Yesod* over our whole life. Anything that does not concur with it is registered, be it a scratch on the finger or the loss of a limb. *Yesod* knows for example, by ache or bump, bruise or strange taste, that something is amiss in the same way as a good driver suspects all is not well by an unfamiliar vibration or noise in his vehicle. The interior image of the body is a good place to begin differentiating the various levels. For example, one can tell the difference between physical cardiac pain and emotional heartache, although they are often closely associated. After a series of exercises in identifying the differing qualities of the worlds, like remembering a place and then seeing it in reality, or reading a recipe and then following it, one should be able to move on to examine the anatomy of the psyche by means of *Yesod*'s mirror.

Normally, the ego only reflects events in the lower psyche. That is whatever you are doing, thinking or feeling about at that moment. These preoccupations are not difficult to spot and isolate. However, what is not so easy is to perceive the forces that underlie *Yesod*'s activity. These factors may come in response to external stimulus, like a stolen kiss, where the reaction of frigidity might reveal physical repulsion, checked emotion or the power of concepts about love, timing or infidelity. There is also the possibility that the ego is being influenced by your personal devil or angel. This is an old fashioned way of saying that a constraint is coming from the level of the soul concerning your inner morality. Great skill and much experience is required to identify the reality of what is really happening. Many people are told again and again by their souls what to do or not to do in oblique and sometimes direct communications, but they still do not recognise what level is speaking because they do not listen. The Kabbalist must take note of anything unusual, be it an external or internal signal, for it may be a directive from the self to be on the alert for some crucial moment that is about to occur. What today are called synchronistic happenings that echo interior events were called omens in former times. To recognise such phenomena requires constant observation of the yesodic processes of daily life.

After a period of watching, a picture begins to emerge of one's inner activity. Now the psyche, like the body has many routine patterns, but they are not so well defined, because they belong to a subtler world than the body. However, because we know that the processes are based upon the Tree, we can at last perceive their general principles. One of the first things to be recognised is the fact that it is not easy to penetrate up the path between *Yesod* and *Tiferet*. This is because it emerges out of the hidden side of the ego—the back of the moon, which is largely unknown. By the constant collection of fragments of information the Kabbalist learns, by inference, what is this hidden aspect of the ego. Help can be given by your tutor or other students about this blind area, but much trust has to be established between people before you take their view into serious account. The picture that is built up of your hidden or shadow-side has to be checked and rechecked before the pathway of integrity, between the ego and self, is fully opened.

The traditional method of gaining access to the shadow and beyond is to interpret dreams that are memorable. Generally speaking most dreams reflect the digestive processing of material being absorbed by the psyche, but occasionally a dream will be so clear or potent, as to still remain in the memory by morning. These are the ones to be examined. To analyse every dream is like having an x-ray of the intestines after every meal. Commonsense will tell one what is remarkable, because most dreams fade as they should, once their essential substance has been extracted by the psyche. Those which remain are meant to be noted by the conscious aspect of the psyche and pondered, for their content requires special attention.

Dreams, according to Kabbalah, may be classified as normal psychological processing, or as those concerned with individual development, or prophetic vision. The first is related to the ego and the functional triads of the Tree, the second to the soul and the third to the triad of the Spirit. There is a fourth but that belongs to contact with the Divine, and is therefore beyond the present discussion. Those dreams relating to the individual are usually highly dramatic and often disturbing. They will be an emotive mixture of symbolism and elements of the person's life. Very often, but not always, they will come at a crucial point in that person's development, and indicate some decision or initiation. You should record and reflect upon these alone, or with others who are skilled or objective about such things. Dreams of prophecy are rare but they also have a distinct quality. They likewise are strikingly lucid, but unlike the other dreams are impersonal, although they instill awe in their dreamer. These also should be noted for reflection and interpretation.

Traditionally, Joseph is related to the sefirah of *Yesod*. This is because he was a dreamer and an interpreter of dreams. Indeed, his coat of many colours represents the ego, and his raising to be the grand vizier to Pharaoh symbolises the talented and disciplined yesodic servant of the ruler of the self. To be able to interpret dreams requires both a gift and much knowledge. In Kabbalah an understanding of the Tree is a great aid, for one can examine a dream in the light of the sefirot and gather much more information from it. First the main elements of the dream are divided into their sefirotic qualities. Then the characters or symbols involved are related to archetypes associated with each sefirah. Thus, the severe or gentle factors may be seen as *Gevurah* and *Hesed*, while the dark and powerful mother figure could be related to *Binah*. The trickster, in most dreams, belongs to *Hod*, and the sensuous figure sometimes encountered, to *Netzah*. As the configuration of archetypes begins to reveal its loading and emphasis, so the levels and their relationships start to emerge. Blended with a well-informed background of the individual and a good understanding of their nature and problems, a useful kabbalistic interpretation can be given. However, such consultations should be used with discretion, or a morbid preoccupation with one's psychological process can begin to unbalance the person, like a hypochondriac's obsession with the body. One must always work within the equilibrium of the Tree.

Normally, *Yesod* acts as the unconscious screen for both the body and psyche, but as we have already seen, it may also be consciously directed by imagination. This capacity is unique to a human being because of the gift of free will. Now the capacity to create images means that one can plan the future as well as remember the past. It also means that you can formulate images to be projected, as any artist, writer or musician knows. This ability may be applied, as we have seen, to kabbalistic work in creating a simple or elaborate ritual. It can also be used to penetrate beyond the veil of ego unconsciousness, that is the line stretched between *Hod* and *Netzah*, and so glimpse the workings of the inner psyche or the upper worlds. This, however, also requires much skill, because the operation can be very disturbing to the uninformed person who has no real grasp of, or training to deal with, the forces involved. Here we enter the frontier zone of personal darkness beyond which few people go, except in dreams or in moments of heightened consciousness.

In Kabbalah, such an excursion can be undertaken in controlled conditions. These are in the company of a trusted and experienced tutor, or group of good companions under strict spiritual discipline. The reason for this prudence is that this is the area where some people, on experiencing increasing sensitivity, become aware either of their own psychological defects, or the presence of those who inhabit this twilight border between the two lower worlds. This is the realm of Hecate and the Witch of Endor, sorcery and the creatures who cannot for the moment touch the Earth nor enter into paradise. However, there is a way straight through this psychic forest that we tread each night in safety, and this is the path between *Yesod* and *Tiferet*, whose name and practice gives good safeguard. The traditional title of this path is *Zadek* or righteous integrity.

What follows is an exercise designed to walk the *Zadek* path using the mirror of *Yesod* both to create and reflect, in guided imagery, an insight into the higher worlds and the state of our souls. In this way we can see how it is done and what can be gained on the basis that the objective is self-knowledge. Here begins the art of using *Yesod*'s imagery consciously.

19. Excursion

To have experience of the higher worlds is not unusual. It can happen in sleep or ordinary consciousness. But here it is spontaneous, a gift of Heaven. Under these conditions there is no personal control or capability, except to look and learn. What is shown is under Providential guidance, so that no exploration beyond what is presented is possible. Some people have these experiences when gravely ill, like the woman who weary of life, yearned for death. She was taken up through the various levels of existence during a deep depression and shown the Throne of Heaven from which a Voice issued, commanding her to return to Earth and complete what she had been born for. The details of the event with its cosmic landscapes and beings was remarkably similar to the accounts set out in the early apocalyptic writings like the Book of Enoch, except here the place was not the Judean Desert, but a suburb of London. The implication is that the upper worlds are an objective reality that people can recognise at any point in history, for they exist in a different order of time.

Another case of a glimpse into the higher worlds was the man about to take a sip of whisky in a London pub. As he put the glass to his mouth, his surroundings faded and he saw before him a vast glittering wheel turning slowly in a black void of space. The wheel was composed of myriads of golden strands which he knew to be the lives and destinies of all the human race. Having had his obsessive question about rebirth answered, the sights and sounds of the pub returned, and he stood for a long time without drinking, wondering whether he was going mad. Both the instances quoted were the result of inner crisis and the response of Grace to a profound puzzlement. In the first case, the woman decided to return to life, remarried. The man, alas, could not cope with the situation confronting him and later killed himself. This illustrates the power of such experiences, and why a gradual and disciplined approach is absolutely vital so as to be able to handle them. It is also the reason why drugs, which allow rapid access to the higher regions, are discouraged. One may see the wondrous sights of Heaven and Hell, but few drug takers can hold such an experience and make sense of it. Many never want to intrude into the other worlds again, and like Jack of the Beanstalk's encounter with the giant, who can blame them for cutting down the plant that had given them access to cosmic experience too early.

To go on a conscious excursion into the next world requires a seasoned guide and map. The map is provided by Jacob's Ladder, which shows the various levels and frontiers to be crossed. The guide should be someone, preferably your tutor, who has been there before and knows the way both there and back, and more important, what to do in an emergency, as sometimes happens. This is why the study and practice of Kabbalah is limited to the mature and stable. In this exercise we are to go on a short flight to the ceiling of the physical world, and just beyond. It will be a training run and a reconnaissance following a set flight plan.

First, the student and his guide must be in a place where they will not be disturbed. Then they must make themselves at ease, so that the body will not distract the attention. In ancient times fasting and a short period of celibacy, followed by both physical and psychological ablution made up the preparation for such an excursion. This meant a bath and entering into a state of devotion, purity and sincerity. In this case, we only wish to make a limited journey, and so we ablute accordingly with a washing of the hands and face. Having prepared, the student under the direction of his guide, comes into a state of attention and awaits instruction.

After the invocation of the Tree and permission from the Holy One that the operation be approved or aborted, according to Divine Will, the guide then takes the student through the first stages of becoming conscious of different levels. First the elemental levels are contacted within the body, then the vegetable and animal souls, which are calmed and told to wait. Then the ego is attended to and instructed, so that it obeys the direction of the guide, who gives out the following instructions, with a pause in between each sentence to allow the images and the experiences to unite. The excursion follows roughly in this form. The guide says:

"You sense the chair you are seated upon—Feel the weight of your body—Become aware of the room--Close your eyes—Perceive your thoughts and feelings—Awaken—Differentiate between the ego mind and that which watches within—Hold that position—Now begin to ascend—First imagine yourself hovering above the house—Become a bird—Now climb higher, so as to see the neighbourhood—Go higher—Look out over the whole area—Observe the houses and streets—Watch the people go about their lives—Shift the scale—Perceive the town as a single organism—Catch the sense of its life—Is it at work or play?—Is it expanding or declining?—Climb higher and take note of what kind of bird you are—Look out over the country—See all the lines of communication between the towns—Become aware of the electronic signals in the air about you—Fly yet higher and note the state of your bird—Observe the coasts and frontiers of the land—Ascend further—View the whole continent—Recognise the geography and see the peoples who live there—Reflect on their different characters and histories—Climb higher and take in our hemisphere of the world—Observe the advance of day and night—Note the seasons above and below the Equator—Fly higher and perceive your own state—Look at the globe of the Earth and feel its life—Move out past the moon—Go beyond the planets, one by one—Watch yourself—See the sun's size diminish as you leave the solar system—Hover amongst the constellations—Draw back from our galaxy—Hold your position in the silence of deep space and listen—Listen—Listen."

After a long pause the guide speaks again. "Now return—Come back into the Milky Way—Move through the constellations—Enter the solar system—Approach the Earth—Move by the moon—Penetrate the atmosphere—Look down on the oceans—Descend through the clouds—Fly towards our country—Float over our town—Swoop down to this house—Hover for a moment and observe your bird, before you become human and find yourself sitting in this room—Open your eyes and feel your body on the chair."

After a pause in which to recover, reflect for a while on the experience before any analysis. When the student and his guide are ready, the student should then debrief, like a pilot after a mission. He should give first a general account of the voyage, and then the detailed examination can begin. During this, the guide should not suggest anything, but just comment or ask questions. The debriefing should be divided between what was seen and heard in the universe, and how the bird was experienced. The observation of what was picked up in this case is less important than the information gathered about the soul through the symbol of the bird. Its size, form and state would be very informative both to the tutor and the student. A scruffy bird with a damaged wing or an over-weighted flyer indicate much, as would a creature with cunning claws or weak eyes. These discrepancies seen as aspects of the psyche can be interpreted and worked on so as to attain improvement.

From the foregoing, it can be seen how much could be gathered about your state and what it is like to leave the Earth, if only for a few moments. In longer and deeper excursions, more could be learned, but these should not be attempted until there is a certain familiarity with working in this manner. The practice should not be done too frequently. Moreover the journey should be varied over different ranges, so as to develop the power of projection. It is important not to overreach your capability, but always to retain contact with the Earth. If a student loses it, the guide should order him back and even tap or shake (only if necessary) the student, should he not respond to verbal instruction. You should always begin and end with consciousness of the body and each journey should be completed by a descent of the Tree and a stamping of the feet, after giving thanks for what has been received. This both earths those present and reminds them that the objective is not the pursuit of occult phenomena, but preparation and training for the service of God. This brings us to the counterbalance that must always be present in such work. Ascent towards Heaven must always be balanced by a deep contact with the Earth. Here is where tradition plays its part to bring about balance, and so we will next examine the Tradition in relation to manifestation in the world.

20. Tradition

To retain contact with the world below is essential for several kabbalistic reasons. The first is that it keeps a solid balance that checks any inclination to drown in the psychological world or fly away into the realm of the Spirit. The second reason for maintaining a terrestrial contact is that it allows what has been received from above to be imparted to the Earth, which is part of the process of conscious unification between the worlds.

The need to be well grounded is emphasised in kabbalistic work because when the focus of attention moves out of normal ego consciousness into the unknown, the individual can extend consciousness up Jacob's Ladder without danger of splitting the body and psyche. This sometimes happens with drug users, who force a separation, or in psychic experiments by the unprepared that isolate aspects of the being from external reality. Exploring the higher worlds is like visiting an unfamiliar city. After finding a place to live you first get to know your own house, and then the surrounding streets. Having established what is home, the exploration then extends out to the adjoining districts. Later the more distant areas of the city are explored until the general geography is known. After each excursion a return to home is vital, in order to rest and digest what has been seen. Over a period, you gain an insight into the life of the city: its high and low sections, its administrative zone, centres of art and science, work and play. Slowly all becomes familiar. Even the dangerous and criminal areas begin to fit into the layers of a complex infrastructure that goes to make up the character of the city. So it is when exploring the upper worlds, and like the situation in the city, you always return to home base with its anchor of security.

In most spiritual traditions this place of familiarity and safety is found in the customs and practices of formal religion. A tradition may be elaborate in form, a modified compromise or a simple set of beliefs. It can be orthodox or even heretical, depending on your point of view of what is important. What does matter is that the mode holds a spiritual significance for the practitioners of that rite. The truly spiritual do not quarrel over which sect is correct. It is a sign of spiritual ignorance when the form is considered more important than the content of the Teaching. What should be taken into account, however, is whether the form of the tradition helps or hinders the devotee. Does it aid in the contact with the higher worlds or not?

Dark elements always hover near any spiritual work, like moths to a candle, because they wish to draw on its power. Therefore, the integrity of a tradition is crucial, for sacred ceremonies open a door from below into an inner holy space and structure that has been created, often over a long period, by the tradition. This invisible temple, which exists in the world of Formation, provides an approach to the Gate of the Spirit. It is called both in Christian and Jewish Kabbalah the *Malkhut ha Shamaim*, or the Kingdom of Heaven; through its rites one may reach, by traversing the seven great palaces of Heaven, the Presence of the Divine.

Now the outer material form of the inner temple may be seen in terms of a great cathedral, a stone circle, or an old synagogue. It may even manifest in a room set aside for such religious practice. The key to such a place is to be found in the form and dynamic of an orthodox liturgy or in a simple prayer repeated with deep sincerity. It does not matter what the mode is; what counts is the intention. A day's prayer in Jerusalem without real intent is worthless, while a moment's full consciousness, as one says the Holy Name on a London bus, may bring knowledge of God. This, for the Kabbalist, Sufi or Christian mystic is the aim. Buildings, books, liturgy and rites are secondary. This, however, does not invalidate traditional modes of worship; they have their purpose for the people who need a form for a guide. Without such religious customs and practices society would be barbaric and devoid of a social-religious focus and standards.

Throughout the ages there has always been this apparent split between the mystics and the orthodoxy of any religion, with the mystics usually accused of being antinomianist, that is, opposed to traditional law. This is quite untrue in most cases, as many Kabbalists for example have adapted Kabbalah to religious custom; some indeed added a deeper dimension to the existing liturgy, and although at the time there was a conservative resistance, today many of these additions are considered quite traditional. What is always forgotten is that every religion begins as a mystical revelation. It is usually when the Teaching has become priestcraft or spiritually dim that mystics have trouble, especially when they try to revive some atrophied practice that binds, instead of releasing, the soul of the congregation.

Taking an objective look at a tradition one can see that it is divided into several recognisable levels. First comes the mineral in the church, synagogue or mosque building. This is the *Malkhut*. Then there is the congregation at *Yesod*. Into this the generations are born and die with marriage and funeral ceremonies celebrating the vegetable cycle of life. The animal element is present in the social activities and the sense of community with its elders giving the seal of tribal approval. The soul dimension is manifest in commitment of circumcision and baptism, and the vows made at barmitzvah and confirmation. Beliefs spoken of on the Sabbath relate to the spiritual, each sect having its own view on the meaning of life. The universal aspects of the faith are seen in the annual cycle of festivals which celebrate the history of the tradition and the cosmic pattern of the year. Few Jews and Christians recognise their festivals as overlaying ancient spring or harvest rites. The deepest mysteries of religion are often only touched upon or hinted at during high Holy Days or moments in the Sabbath service. Those who wish to penetrate this veil must often seek elsewhere to find the door into the esoteric depths of their faith. However, this does not mean that they cannot participate, or use the traditional mode of their religion to attain entry into the Promised Land.

With intelligent application a student may use the form most familiar to his or her culture to a greater or lesser degree. Some Kabbalists are ultra orthodox and fulfil as many of the six hundred and thirteen commandments as possible. Others are less strict and adhere to a modicum of precepts, whilst others keep the bare minimum, but with complete integrity. As one rabbi observed, the greatest law was "To love others as oneself". If we realised WHO the Self was then this saying would take on its ultimate meaning of I AM THAT I AM. In this way we see again how intention is always the measure of a sacred action. Using this criterion one may participate in an existing service, design one's own rite or blend ancient and modern methods in order to rise up and relate to God. The middle way is followed in this book.

The traditional approach of maintaining a connection between one's place in time and space and the Divine is well worked out in a cycle of daily and annual rituals, devotions and contemplations. This working method is the most common, because it has been in existence for millennia and is well tried. Whilst tradition has the advantage of a vast backup of collective power and experience, it also has the disadvantage that it can drown the individual, as it imposes a social conformity which is often mistaken for spirituality. We see this in the manners and dress of extreme sects. The strange irony is that real spirituality always has the quality of true individuality despite concurrence of view, so that apparently widely divergent Buddhists and Kabbalists can discuss questions without essential disagreement, because they are both in contact with the same cosmic world. This is rare for those encased in too much outer form and little inner comprehension of their tradition. The Spanish Inquisition demonstrated this well.

For the Kabbalist the use of tradition is influenced by temperament and background. Unless one has a strong reaction at this point, the wisest thing is to use those elements of one's upbringing that evoke the *Gadlut* or greater state. These may be rituals, prayers and symbols or ideas that draw upon the deep memory of one's roots as well as personal experience. Use these forms to remember the Holy One in the morning, remind one of God during the day and bring the Divine into consciousness in the evening. Try to recall, in between these times, who one is and why one is here on Earth. Maintain this awareness of being incarnate day and night whilst constantly remembering that one is in the presence of God. Change the form of the recollection when it loses its freshness and gradually go deeper into those moments set aside for meditation. To repeat a Holy Name whenever one recalls God is slowly to realise what it means as one recalls the Source. In this way Adam reflects the Divine gaze as that moment unites with Eternity. This is the aim of every tradition with an esoteric heart.

21. Day

Having looked at the general cultural background of a tradition, let us examine how it might be used by a Kabbalist in his everyday life. Firstly an individual must recognise where he stands in relation to the world in which he lives. Most people are classified by physique, intelligence, social class and nation. To the world an individual is an amalgam of these labels, whether he accepts it or not. This means that a certain mode of conduct is expected. The prudent Kabbalist does not resist these expectations because he operates from a different level and can work within a social framework without being untrue. As one well-known Kabbalist said "Be in the world, but not of it". This requires not only spiritual maturity but great skill in mundane matters. For example, an individual may seem to be doing business when he is in fact testing an initiate for reliability. Only the perceptive would know the difference. Thus, one may perform the same outer actions as the conventional professional, but have quite an opposite objective. Two people in the same office or workshop can serve very different Gods.

Taking a day as a model, the first moments after waking can be used to advantage. That peculiarly lucid state of consciousness between dreaming and waking reveals the presence of the Watcher of the self as it observes the dreams fade and the body come into view. At such a moment prayers may be said or deep questions asked. Perhaps a problem posed the night before has received an answer, or the day ahead needs deeper planning. Reflection on how to approach this or that situation is considered from the point of view of the Work, and not personal gain. Action to be taken is seen in terms of interior consequence rather than an exterior solution, for the Kabbalist recognises that everything done on Earth influences the balance of the universe, so that nothing is without its effect, no matter how small.

After carrying out whatever ablutions have been decided upon, the Kabbalist then sets aside a period for a morning ritual, devotion or contemplation. Some combine all three approaches. A ritual might consist of laying *Tefillin* in the orthodox Jewish way. In this, two boxes containing certain scriptures and inscribed with the initials of the Name of God are strapped onto the head and arm whilst praying. At the other extreme a Kabbalist may do no more than place a hat on his or her head to mark the moment, whilst another might sit facing a certain direction for half an hour in silent meditation. One person might, in their devotion, repeat the Name of God over and over in an endless chant, whilst another could be slowly saying each word of a prayer and weighing its meaning. Yet another might just contemplate the Sefirotic Tree, or light a candle and consider why light is the symbol of Divinity. There are many possibilities and variations of the same intention.

After contact between above and below has been established, the Kabbalist then goes out into the world. Whether at home or away, in the market-place or factory, office or field, the intention to be conscious of God is ever present. For much of the time '*Devekut*', or cleavage to the Divine, will be lost, but it must be striven for nevertheless. In time a pattern will be set up in body and psyche that will help to retain the state, and indeed, providential reminders will be forthcoming after a while, both from this world and above, as the selected times of the day are approached. The suggested hours of ten a.m., noon, and four p.m. could be used to recall your aim. Another set of reminders could be at particular junctions in your daily routine. A coffee break or a point in a journey could be utilised; so could an interval in a work process, or recurring high mark of the day. Any time or place may be applied as a beacon. So can certain people, like the man who always passes you on the way to the station or the woman who brings in the mail. One 18th-century Kabbalist said, "One should learn from the thief. He is ever watchful and takes every opportunity for gain. It is the same in the matters of the Spirit."

The midday break should be used for inner as well as outer nourishment. Besides the exercises in conscious action and his emotional state in relating to others, the Kabbalist could contemplate the World at the daily zenith of the sun. In the morning the body is in one state and in the evening another. At midday it responds to the life about it in a particular way, which you can observe in order to pick up the full range of the body's capacity when the sun is high. At the noon Nature is opened right out in response to the cosmic influx, before beginning to fade towards night. At such a time you can experience things about the World as at no other. It is the climax of outward expansion when the sun is at its maximum point of radiation. At this moment the zenith of light stands in opposition to the darkness of midnight. Holding the consciousness through the moment of noon can reveal much about the nature of good and evil, cosmic cycles and the Divine reflected in the sun.

The afternoon brings about the waning of the body and the waxing of the psyche. If the morning is concerned, as traditional Kabbalah suggests, with the active pillar, then the afternoon reveals the more reflective column that begins to look back on what has been done. The same techniques used in the morning are applied again, but with different times and places to remind one of what the Work is about. When the daily round of a monastery is examined, it will be seen that the same criteria are applied. The various offices repeated every day perform a similar function, but in a secluded and orthodox situation. Kabbalah, however, is not a withdrawn order; it operates right in the midst of life. This makes it more difficult as regards distractions, but it also offers a unique variety of opportunities in which to act directly upon a situation. Thus, while you are reminded by routine of the cycle of creation, you can also be involved in the unusual events, no matter how small, that make up the drama of existence.

An evening routine may include a formal meditation. If there is not a group meeting, the time can be spent at private work or play. The latter, however, to the committed Kabbalist, is still an opportunity to study and practise. A game of badminton or chess can reveal some hidden animal traits in your character, and a swimming session can be used to learn something about negotiating the watery world of the psyche. Social occasions are excellent times to observe the personality at work, and in the little battles between the ego and self, which seems to have the upper hand. Differences of opinion over small or grave matters can indicate wilfulness in oneself, as well as others, and the test of spiritual pride is always present when with people not involved with spiritual work. To remain inwardly awake at a party is not easy, and many a serious student has made a fool of himself, although no one else except those on the Path would have noticed it.

At the end of the day comes the time for reflection. This may be done with others, or alone. Many individuals may analyse what happened that day with partners or friends who judge everything according to ego, but few relate it to a set of principles. Most people consider gain or loss in terms of cash or position, but the person under spiritual discipline sees everything from the viewpoint of inner success or failure. These assessments might be in the form of an intimate conversation with spiritual companions who do not judge, but gently reflect what lessons might be learned. Originally, this was the point of confession, here used not just for penance, but for constructive reflection. For example, an incident on that day might be a warning light or the indication of deep change. Good companions are more than helpful on the Way. They are vital as there are many pitfalls and diversions that you cannot see for yourself.

The final act of the day is the last session of ritual, prayer or contemplation. This again is a matter of personal choice. The minimum that is required is that it be based on the Tree, in that you rise up from *Malkhut* to *Keter* to acknowledge God, and are grateful for what you have received that day. After this formality, the last moments before sleep can be used to distil the essence of what has been experienced. In this process details of the day are paired away into a simple summary that is pondered upon with its arising questions, until sleep overtakes the consciousness. These questions will be taken deep into the psyche and considered during the night, so that there may be an answer in the morning on awakening. This daily cycle should be repeated with periodic modifications. Over the years the accumulation and refinement of the experience gathered will bear profound fruit, for it produces what is called the Wine of Merit. Merit is the result of Work, and this, in time, is matched by Grace.

22. Festivals

To complete this consideration of the mundane aspect of Kabbalah, let us look at the annual festivals. Now in all religions there is a yearly cycle of celebrations. These are usually based upon the ancient recognition that there are rhythms in the cosmos which rule our lives. The solstices and equinoxes are obvious examples of crucial turning points of the year and many Jewish and Christian high Holy Days are to be found to coincide with them. These mark not only the waxing and waning of natural processes, but the tides of spiritual forces. Ceremonies performed at such moments indicate a respect for these nodal points and seek to catch the cosmic rhythm manifesting at that time, as the celestial balance shifts from ebb to flow and back again.

The harvest festivals are clear instances of ancient rites adapted to Judaism and Christianity, and so are the winter celebrations of Christmas and Channukah. The former celebrates the coming into the world of a great Light, signified by the Star of Bethlehem, and the marking of the beginning of the New Testament; the latter, the rededication of the desecrated Temple after a period of desolation and spiritual darkness, with lights that increase in number over eight days. Both in fact come at the time of year when nature is at its nadir and the life principle is at its weakest, that is just at the point when the sun is about to turn up again in its progression round the zodiac. This winter solstice is the period when the soul is least fettered by the flesh and can easily rise into the realm of the Spirit. On the daily model, it is like the state of inner freedom often experienced at midnight when the body is at its least active. Here we begin to see how the Kabbalist might begin to view and use these annual celebrations as a mode of study and work.

If you consider each festival from its esoteric standpoint, its outer aspect is in the story and its associated rituals, and its inner in symbolism and content. Thus, the celebrations of Easter and Passover that come at the same time of the year can take on a deeper significance than is generally realised. Both these festivals relate to Spring, to a renewal of life after Winter. Historically they coincide because the Last Supper was in fact the Pascal feast. To participate in either is to experience rebirth; one tradition seeing it as the resurrection of an individual, and the other of a nation being reborn. Both in essence are saying the same thing as they speak of the promise of spiritual freedom after a period of physical bondage, as represented by Egypt, and the taking of Jesus by the authorities. Viewed this way, one begins to perceive how those who designed these festivals tried to incorporate several levels into them.

A little reflection will reveal the same content and intention in either of the two stories. Both speak about preparation, trial, despair, doubt and the breakthrough experienced by anyone on the spiritual path. Both describe in detail the resistance of the world to anything new and the confrontation with the authorities of their time. Each celebration speaks of sacrifice and departure. Both Jew and Christian sense an anticipation of a new epoch, although few recognise what it really means. To the Kabbalist both festivals speak quite clearly about initiation, and so to participate in an Easter or Passover service becomes, with perception, a deeply profound experience, because it is more than just a celebration of what happened many centuries ago. It is what is occurring inwardly, in that very moment, that becomes significant.

The Kabbalist can relate to the whole annual round of Holy Days in this way as he or she moves through the rituals and prayers with a consciousness of their present reality. By this method the student can not only reflect upon his or her own spiritual situation, but draw upon the vast collective experience held by the form of the festival. In this manner, it is possible to perceive the cosmic implication of the festival's function. You might for example, glimpse the juxtaposition of terrestrial and celestial forces and sense the state of mankind. You could, with sufficient perception catch sight of the communal soul of that tradition and be shown its level of maturity. It is quite possible, for instance, to key into the life of the existing generation and see if it is waxing or waning, or have an insight into the spiritual depth of individuals participating in the festival. This is the cosmic dimension.

As we can appreciate, there are many possibilities available whilst taking part in such activities. However, while you may draw from these great accumulators of spiritual power, you must also give back in return. Thus, the Kabbalist, in his public worship, tries to make an inner connection between Heaven and Earth. In this way, a channel is opened through which it is possible to bring down into the congregation present some of the spiritual substance accumulated over the centuries by the ceremony. If one is operating from *Tiferet*, then the flow will occur, and whilst no one else may notice it, the quality of the service will be raised, although some people might detect a slight change of atmosphere, or a degree of purity present. They might even sense a certain severity if it is needed, or a touch of loving-kindness, should the service be too much on the Judgement side of the Tree. Whatever is required, will, if the Kabbalist is in the correct state, be imparted from above.

The implication of this is that one may practise Kabbalah, which means 'to receive', in a public place. This is not only indeed so, but is one of the main objectives of the Work. However, it has to be done with tremendous discrimination and should not be attempted until the first stages of training are complete. However, it will be observed, that descent of the spirit can occur quite spontaneously at baptisms, barmitzvahs, weddings and funerals when a Kabbalist has become aware of an inner light beaming down upon those participating in the ceremony. If one is the fortunate agent of such Grace at that moment, then thanks should be given. Such events are not rare, but they can only occur if the person is open, knows what is happening and can allow the transmission.

Returning again to the theme of festivals, it can be seen that much may be learnt from their essential content, provided one does not become lost in the detail. Every festival has its particular message, and if studied and practised in the right way it will reveal many secrets embedded in it by its creators. Take for example the festival of All Saints, in the autumn, which celebrates the existence of those who have reached some degree of spirituality. This is quite different to All Souls, who have not reached this level. Its purpose is the acknowledgement of an illustrious group of beings who may be seen as the Body of Christ or the House of Israel, the Blessed Ones or the Inner Council of Mankind according to the terms of your tradition. If one could be in the right state during a service dedicated to these great souls, then it might be possible to experience who and what they are. You might even be allowed to glimpse the world they live in and even become dimly aware of their task in the universe. During such a ceremony, contact might be made with your own particular inner teacher, or at least with those in charge of your section. Thus, the festival is not just remembrance of their existence, but a meeting place, in time, between us below and those above who are involved with the Work.

So the annual cycle of festivals is more than a round of traditional customs. They are the mark points of cosmic fluctuations within which rituals, devotion and contemplation are designed. For the Kabbalist they can also be a doorway into mystical experience as he uses the great physical, psychological and spiritual vehicles of these festivals to gain access to the higher worlds. Consider the millions of people round the world celebrating a New Year. Such a festival is a quite tangible construction whose approach and departure in time, can be sensed like a great ship coming and then going. Festivals are massive temples in the World of Formation that are entered, at certain points or the year, by a mass of people, although they can be contemplated by a solitary mystic who may choose to go there at a less busy time. This leads us on to the notion that you may wander about and explore the inner worlds at will, for perhaps by now you being to perceive the reality of these subtler realms that permeate our fondly imagined solid world. However, before proceeding further we must never forget to retain our contact with the mundane level of existence; for this reason it is good to adopt, as an anchor in life, some of the customs of our upbringing which keep us in touch with the Earth. For this reason, we will examine the seventh day or the Sabbath, which marks the *Malkhut* of Creation when God rested and reflected on what had been done.

23. Sabbath

Resuming our progression up the Tree, let us blend the exoteric with the esoteric to perceive the bridge between the outer and inner aspects of a traditional celebration. The fourth commandment is that the Sabbath should be sanctified. This Injunction comes between the commandments related to God and those related to human beings. It is indeed the point of interaction between the Divine and lower worlds, because it belongs to the first of what are called the seven lower sefirot of construction. In this arrangement it relates to *Hesed,* or Loving-kindness and Mercy.

The Sabbath is a day of rest and reflection. On it, the committed Jew and Christian worship God in the three approaches of ritual, devotion and contemplation. The Kabbalist uses these same modes to enter the fourth condition, of mystical experience. In this way the orthodox form is used as a method by which one may enter the higher realms. In public worship, this is done by the various services held in the synagogue and church. However, very often the real level of these gatherings is usually not much higher than a social meeting, with the spiritual element giving it an occasional touch of other-worldliness. For most people, this is sufficient. To read from the scrolls of the Law, or to take communion, is often as much of a spiritual experience as most people want. To try to live by the precepts of tradition is also too much for many, for it is an enormous commitment that few can keep. The Kabbalist knows this from personal experience, but strives, nevertheless, to meet the criteria of the Spirit, although he may not be seen by the conventional as a good Jew or Christian.

Because of the difficult conditions found in church and synagogue many mystics down the ages have held private Sabbath celebrations that run parallel to public worship. They may take place before or after the regular services in secluded rooms without the distractions of the usual places of gathering. Occasionally one reads of or hears about such a meeting of perhaps two or three people, although some Kabbalists prefer to celebrate the Sabbath in solitude. This does not mean that they are alone by any means, because if they attain the inner levels of soul and spirit, they are connected inevitably with the beings operating on those planes. Here begins kabbalistic communication.

Let us imagine how such an individual might go about his Sabbath. Taking the bare essentials we will follow a service through, from its inception to its conclusion. Assuming that the normal ablutions have been carried out, and the person is wearing fresh clothes, we would find him in a place especially dedicated to the purpose. This as noted, could be a corner of a room where an altar has been erected, which may consist of a pair of candlesticks or whatever symbol has significance to the worshipper. After a period of silence in which to bring the elemental body into equilibrium and the vegetable and animal soul under the will, the service is initiated by an invocation. This can be by the ascent of the Tree and the evocation of the Holy Names, or by whatever formula awakens the person's being to the higher worlds. This could be followed by a deep and long silence.

The purpose of the silence is to bring into harmony all the disparate aspects of the psyche. Certain problems, for example, may be plaguing one. To set these aside takes a little time. Perhaps one is feeling in a particularly inappropriate mood, or anticipating what is going to happen tomorrow. When these inner distractions have been reduced to the minimum, for they can never be totally eliminated, the yesodic ego is given something to occupy its attention and draw it into the operation. This can be the repetition of a Divine Name, a prayer to move the heart or a kabbalistic idea to contemplate.

The sounding of a Holy Name such as 'the Living Almighty' is like a mantra. It should be spoken with great reverence with its reverberation penetrating throughout the body and psyche. It may be said aloud, but only with the full awareness of Whom one is naming, respecting the commandment not to take the Lord's Name in vain, or without consciousness. Indeed we are told it gives great pleasure to the Divine to see the Name come into full manifestation, as it is the final part of the process of bringing Divinity into the physical world. It is the conscious realisation of I AM THAT I AM that enables Adam to help God to behold God.

The same can be said of any prayer touching the heart, like, "Lord have mercy upon us". Here the love that is extended from above is returned from below by the devotee, and thus there is a deeply emotional dialogue between creature and Creator. This analogy of lovers is common to many traditions, for it speaks of the profound interchange that can occur during devotion. To express love to God and know one is loved in return is to experience the greatest intimacy possible, for when people draw that close to the Divine, then they are nearer to God than they are to themselves.

The act of contemplation can also stimulate a mystical experience. While pondering the verses on the death of Moses who was not allowed to enter the Promised Land, one might perceive how it is possible just to fall short of the mark. This could lead on to what might be impeding progress in one's own spiritual life, thence to a reflection upon a particular problem out of which arises a solution. Such an insight could remove the difficulty and allow a movement forward into a new space. This piercing of a veil can make us aware that Divinity is always present to aid us. Such an experience might last an instant but be recalled each time we read the passage which we had been contemplating that Sabbath.

The normal use of the Bible is traditional, the cycle of the scriptures being read in a weekly sequence. However, in Kabbalah, it may be applied in an unusual way, the portion to be examined depending on the Will of the Holy Spirit. After the invocation and a petition for guidance, the Kabbalist places himself in a deep state of receptivity, listening with great intent to what might be received from above. The Bible is then taken and opened at apparent random and the chapter presented read with infinite care. Often the content is directly relevant to the moment. Frequently, questions being posed at that time, such as "Should I take such an action on a certain issue?" are answered and clarified by the text, either by the precise instruction of a verse or in the form of a parable that clearly relates to our situation. The lesson is then pondered so that further information may emerge out of what has been presented. Obviously, this mode of working requires enormous honesty to check any fantasy that may intrude to distort what has been given. If the reading is obscure at the time, then it should be held in the mind for the rest of the week until some event reveals its significance.

The final part of the Sabbath service is to return to silence after saying various prayers of praise or petition. These may be traditional or especially designed for that occasion. When they have been uttered, the Kabbalist then withdraws as deeply as possible into the self and waits in a fully alert *Tiferet* before the door of *Daat*, the place of Knowledge. If nothing occurs this must be accepted. Should something happen the person may not know it has until the action is over, when he realises that he has been somewhere else other than where he is now. In this experience, there is a moment of union, of knowing and of being known. It may be no more than a split second, but it is quite distinctive and memorable, although nothing precise can be remembered of the moment. However, what is clear is that he was in touch with a higher world.

Having completed the order of the service the Kabbalist then begins to return to the lower world of Action. This is accomplished by the acts of thanksgiving and descent of the Tree so as to bring consciousness down into the ego and body, and so to the earth. While such a Sabbath can be made more simple or elaborate, what must be remembered is that it will only be effective if the *Kavanah* or intention is correct. No amount of ritual, prayer or contemplation will bring down the Holy Spirit if the person is not truly receptive; and this, it will be recalled, is the root meaning of the word *Kabbalah*. Having outlined some of the routine and cyclic exercises of the tradition, let us now examine a technique that can be used occasionally for gathering information from beyond the threshold of ordinary consciousness.

24. Journey

So far we have seen how an individual can use various methods to move from Malkhutian body consciousness up to the *Tiferet* of the self. We have been shown how this is done by private work and the use of public occasions. Most of what has been discussed has been preparation, but now we may begin to perceive how everything is moving towards generating an inner vessel. This interior vehicle is strengthened by constant practice and study of Kabbalah. After a while, things that were previously not possible, like insights into the upper world, begin to be received from above, because there is now an instrument within the psyche by which one can exercise and examine what has up to now remained hidden.

The following method shows how this growing faculty may be developed and used in determining one's state or anything else that may be relevant that is within range of the study. The technique can be done within a group or practised in private. As before, it requires an experienced guide to lead the student to a place where he will not be disturbed. Let us assume that these conditions have been obtained, that the Tree has been evoked and permission from on High has been granted. After a pause to accustom the body and psyche to the situation, the guide then proceeds roughly in the following manner.

First the student is asked if he is in a state of readiness. This the student checks, observing, from the position of the inner watcher of *Tiferet*, the routine processes of body and mind. On declaring readiness, the guide then asks the student to imagine himself standing up and going out of the room. This the student does by projecting, in imagination, what will be observed on leaving the room and a position is taken up outside the house. The scene is then visualised in great detail as the prevailing conditions are examined and perceived by the extended senses. The voyager then moves on out of sensual range into pure imagination. Here memory of the locality is brought fully into action as consciousness shifts out of direct contact with the *Malkhutian* body and into strictly *Yesodic* imagery. The guide then instructs the student to leave the immediate area and travel out into the countryside. This is done, the student still observing a recognisable landscape, as he moves by memory along a familiar highway.

The student is then asked to turn off into a side lane and go to a wood that is quite unknown. Having entered it, he goes right into its depths where there is no sight or sound of the modern world. After a long pause to adjust and appreciate the place, he is then asked to proceed to the very centre of the wood. Here there is a clearing where the traveller is to rest because it is late and growing dark. After a short sleep he is told to wake up. If he is sufficiently absorbed in the situation and responds to direction without being distracted, then consciousness has crossed the first threshold into his inner world, and the next stage can proceed.

On awakening in the clearing, the traveller is told to find that it is quite dark. The stars can be seen above and the moon is just rising. Nearby, there is a horse eating grass. The traveller observes that he is wearing different clothes. These might be of any style or period. It does not matter at this point. As dawn breaks, he mounts the horse and rides out of the wood and into the nearest town. Here, he discovers a city that is like no other ever seen. It is both strange and familiar. All the people in the streets look at the traveller with recognition. The traveller knows some of them well, but most are only vaguely familiar or total strangers. As he rides along the streets and passes the various private and public buildings their condition is noted and a series of questions is asked to ascertain the state of the town, such as, "Is it happy? If not, why not?" Moving on, the traveller leaves the town, although some of the inhabitants accompany him to the town's limit. The dress and manner of these followers should be noted.

After an eventful day's ride across grass, desert and marsh, the sea is reached. There on the beach the traveller is told to rest and sleep a deep sleep in which a strange dream occurs. This, like all unusual events, should be noted for analysis later. In the morning a boat is found riding at anchor just off shore. It is waiting for the traveller. He leaves the horse to grass and goes out to the boat, but not before having a good look at it to see what kind of vessel it is, what condition it is in and to record its name. Once on board the crew appear. Mark each of them. Your life may depend on their skill. Walk round the decks and examine the boat from above and below. What does it carry for cargo? The guide should be by now no more than a voice.

Find the captain's cabin. Is he/she there? If so, what is she/he like? Note that the boat has now set sail. Go up on deck and watch the land slip away. Observe the state of the sea and how the boat is handled. At first all is calm, but soon a squall comes up and then a full-blown gale. How do you react? How does the captain respond and the crew perform as all around the sea boils and lightning and heavy rain split and blur the sky? Observe everything. Note areas of stress and strength. Time passes. The storm begins to abate. The sky clears and the sea becomes calm. As the boat and crew recover equilibrium, record any damage. Land is seen. The captain directs the helmsman as the boat moves towards a port. The boat approaches the harbour but does not tie up. Instead, it lies just off shore, whilst you look through a telescope the captain has given you. Gather what you can about this far country. It is another world. Note how the buildings are not like any others on earth, nor are the people. Just as you begin to react to the nature of this strange land, the captain orders the boat to weigh anchor and return home.

The student, still deep in this guided fantasy, is then brought back across the sea, taking note all the time of what is happening, until the home shore is reached. There the boat is left and the horse-ride back across the country to the town is re-experienced, noting if there are any differences in the landscape, or the traveller. On reaching the town he observes any changes there, especially in the attitude of the townspeople. When the traveller returns to the wood, dusk is falling. As sun sets he dismounts and lies down to rest. After a night's sleep, he awakens and realises that his original clothes have been restored. He then sets out for home, leaving the wood for the familiar countryside before returning to the house and room that the operation is taking place in. Here he is brought back into physical consciousness by coming down the Tree and stamping the feet. After a suitable pause, the debriefing can begin.

As should have been gathered, the journey relates to various levels, with each stage and symbol containing much information about one's inner condition. The first shift occurs in the wood, where one is lifted out of the physical realm by entering an unfamiliar clearing. The wood is the vegetable principle and the horse the animal soul. The sleep, night sky and moon induce and evoke the experience of entering into the realm of *Yesod* and the unconscious. The journey out of the wood and into the town take one deeper into the psyche where the town and its inhabitants tell one much about the state of the psychological organism and the various sub-personalities that govern our inner life. The few townspeople, that is, interested aspects, who follow one out are aids or hindrances to our development, whilst the cross-country ride is the inner terrain we have to traverse in order to reach the threshold of the deep emotional level, represented by the sea. Here the style of boat and its condition give us some idea of our capacity to move in that world, and the crew the emotional complexes that make or mar its performance. The captain, if there is one, can be seen as the inner guide whose way of dealing with the storm indicates what to expect when confronted with a crisis of the first order. The distant shore is the deepest part of the psyche that is rarely experienced, except in illumination. Here the dream that might have revealed some insight while one was asleep on the sea-shore may be related to what was consciously seen of the strange port from the boat. All the information gathered about the people and buildings at this entrance to the unconscious should be considered as a glimpse into the higher levels of the psyche, which act as the frontier and veil to the hinterland of the world of the Spirit.

Much prudence must be exercised in the analysis of the data revealed in the imagery. At first one should simply note what occurred without comment. Later, in discussion, one may begin to perceive the various levels and differentiate between mundane imagining and real vision. This takes time and practice. One should consider each element of the account and relate it to what one actually knows about oneself, or if one is the guide, about the student, although there must be no interference with his conviction, if he judges it to be the one thing and you another. People must teach themselves, with the minimum of projection from the instructor. Further detail can be added by returning to certain points in the journey and re-creating the situation, so as to get a higher resolution of image to interpret from. After the debriefing has made some sort of sense, the student should then write out a report whilst it is still fresh and file it for further reference and reflection. The operation could be repeated from time to time and later, under strict self-discipline, may be done on his own.

The foregoing technique is an ancient one, illustrating how to exploit *Yesod's* capacity to act as the non-luminous mirror of the psyche. In this case the range has been extended a little beyond the extent of our first exercise. In skilled and intelligent hands it is a fine instrument and can be developed so as to be able to penetrate to all but the highest level of the psyche. However, it must be used sparingly, otherwise conscious imagination turns into uncontrolled fantasy, which is far from the objective of Kabbalah. The line between the mystic visionary and the mad is not, as generally believed, very small. There is a wide gap defined by great discipline and a definite aim, ordered knowledge and self-command. The lunatic may see impressive images of truth, but these are usually tainted or distorted by ego-oriented fantasies and dreams. The Kabbalist does not seek the grandiose, but the essence of what is embodied in these visions. Therefore the student relates all that has been seen to the Tree and its laws. If one knows it well, then each element of the journey will identify itself quickly and many puzzling things will fall into place. To illustrate this point, let us explore one of the most important factors in our journey, so as to interpret it in greater detail. In the next chapter, we will look at the captain as the symbol of the first stage of selfhood that brings one into contact with the Inner Teacher.

25. Captain

The notion of an inner teacher is not strange to Kabbalah. Many Kabbalists down the centuries have spoken of their *maggid* or celestial instructor. Sometimes the teacher has just been a voice, like the mentor of the great Safed Kabbalist, Joseph Karo, and sometimes they have been figures visible to the eye, like the *maggid* of the Gaon of Vilna, who was once seen by two students through a window, but not to be found with the rabbi when they entered his study. More often than not it is an inner instructor who directs the Kabbalist—when it is needed—and advises on matters that the Kabbalist cannot read about or have access to on Earth. Legends say that the greatest Kabbalists were taught by Elijah himself who is responsible for the spiritual direction of the Tradition. Other stories tell us that Elijah not only turns up in many disguises to aid those on the inner path, but manifests as the *Khidr* or 'the Green One', in the Sufi tradition, where he performs the same role. According to folklore Elijah had neither father nor mother, like Malkizedek, who initiated Abraham at the beginning of the tradition. All this suggest that other strange characters like Hermes Trismegestus and Thoth were none other than Enoch, the Initiated, the first fully realised human being, but in different forms.

For ordinary people the likelihood of being taught by the highest teacher is remote, although many just beginning spiritual work often want nothing less. This is due either to innocence or ambition. If it were to happen, then all the power and responsibility that goes with it would crush or explode the student. The spiritual cyclist, however skilful, is not ready to pilot the supersonic jets of Heaven, although many dream they can. This is a *Yesodic* illusion, as are many fantasies about instruction coming from the upper worlds. That is why such communications must be tested and approached with prudence, by dealing with the phenomenon of inner signals in stages so that the student becomes familiar with what is happening and can deal with it.

The first stage is to learn how to discriminate between different levels. For example the voice of the body, which has a distinct character, must be distinguished from the voice of the ego, which can adopt many disguises in order to get its way. Then one has to develop an ear for intruding intelligences that sometimes whisper or call from the sidelines. These can be either very crude or extremely subtle. They are to be recognised, and then ignored. Also to be recognised are the various negative aspects of one's own psyche, like certain memories that warn or encourage, or particular ideas that thrust and weedle their biased views into the consciousness. These may be from the distant past or a current opinion that can taint a real experience. The psyche has many such voices; some are obvious and others hardly noticeable and yet more powerful than can be imagined. The archetypal principles, for instance, that embody the sefirot are extremely potent. These, when out of balance, can often distort a truth. The Trickster of *Hod* is a prime example. This clever function can easily cloud the most lucid inner instruction by a brilliant quotation of something it has read but never understood. Many insights have been drowned in this way.

The most interesting archetype from the point of view of this chapter is the Inner Teacher who resides at the centre of the Tree at *Tiferet*. Called the Seat of Solomon, this sefirah is the focal point of many paths and triads. As the place of the self, it occupies the position of being the most directly informed focus in the psyche, for it perceives the worlds below and has access to those above. It connects with nearly all the sefirot of the Tree and has direct contact with the individual and collective unconscious, as well as the soul and the spirit. It is therefore the most qualified sefirah in terms of all round experience. As such it operates as the Inner Teacher.

In the guided inner journey of the last chapter the boat on the sea may be regarded as the vessel by which consciousness negotiates the volatile waters of the psyche. As we saw, the captain can be understood as the one who knows the ways of the sea and how to handle the boat in difficult times. If we reflect on how the boat was managed during the storm, as well as all the finer points of seamanship throughout the voyage, we may catch a glimpse of the nature of our own Inner Teacher.

To develop this further, it is possible to go back, after invoking the Tree and asking permission, to look at the captain and his/her cabin in greater detail. One might, for example, scrutinise more carefully the captain's face for clues as to his/her order of intelligence. It may be a mask or wise old man or woman, or a countenance that does not belong to this world at all. The captain could turn out to be an experienced but drunken sailor, which would suggest that perhaps there is more Grace than Judgement watching over us. In some cases, there is no captain, which might indicate that no direct relation with the self is apparent. Observation of the captain's uniform and its condition could be highly informative. A slapdash skipper would reveal much, as would an impeccable naval officer. One might find one has a clever pirate, which suggests some liaison with the Lucifer principle. Such contacts are quite capable of influencing the captain of some people's ships at certain crisis points in their development. The story of Faust tells this tale.

As one can see, much can be learned by this exercise about the situation and state of the self. Here it must be understood that the self is made up of three components. The lowest is the Keter or Crown of the body. This level is very susceptible to self-glory, if there is great physical vitality. The second level is the psychological, whose subtle versatility is tested and tempted by powerful forces within and without the psyche until it can maintain a stability even in the gravest crisis. This is the aspect we are examining at the moment. The highest facet of the self is the lowest part or *Malkhut* of the Spirit. Here is the true supervisor of the lower levels, who slowly emerges into our experience, as our mentor and friend.

The image of our captain tells us much about self stage. It also gives us the opportunity to redress any imbalance we observe on board the ship. For example, suppose discipline amongst the crew is slipshod, it is possible, by an act of conscious imagination, to alter the situation. This action will correct the discrepancy at the psychological level, and it should follow, if the intention is genuine, that one's inner performance will improve. Here we are applying the tool of symbol in reverse. That is, instead of being receptive to what is being said the process is turned round in a conscious act which can affect the as yet unconscious part of our psyche. This, of course, must only be done in self-evident cases of neglect or rebelliousness.

In the early stages of spiritual work very little is known about the workings of the psyche, and indeed, many avoid this area because it is too fraught with trouble, pain and conflict to be dealt with directly. Now while an excessive preoccupation with one's psychological anatomy is as unhealthy as hypochondria, a certain amount of work has to be done. This is because there are in all of us certain imbalances due to genetics, environment, fate and karma. These problems cannot and should not be avoided because they contain vital lessons for our development. Conscious reflection on the ways of the psyche under skilled instruction is necessary, and here the foregoing exercise is most useful. As time goes on, the unconscious becomes illuminated and converted into consciousness. This is done by relating one's life to both external and internal work. The workings of the psyche can be seen by introspective analysis or external conditions. Both reflect our problems and their solutions in our relationship to life and the Work. However, before you apply the technique described, you must know what you are about, or more harm than good will be done. In order not to interfere with normal psychological processes, you should consult either your outer instructor for advice or contact the Inner Teacher, deep in the unconscious.

In order to be able to do this much practice must be carried out in the active imagination. Many sessions have to be experienced before beginning to form a clear idea about the various levels and aspects of the body and the psyche. As a precaution, while you should note everything that happens, you should not act on everything that is suggested, unless its message makes sense or the truth of it is obvious. It is a mistake to be lured beyond one's capacity or attempt an impossible suggestion. Some people become over enthusiastic with their first inner instructions and imagine that they are in contact with the highest beings. It must be remembered that we are still working at a relatively low level and demonic elements like to interfere, especially when the person does not know friend from foe. Therefore, in the next exercise we will set out a ritual so as to avoid unwelcome intrusion, and so go directly to our Inner Teacher. Even our captain could be a disguised member of the opposition, in the same way that some gurus are wolves in sheep's clothing.

26. Inner Teacher

In this exercise we intend to penetrate deeper. Therefore our preparations must be increasingly thorough. This does not imply that they should be elaborate, but that the intention has more to it than just to explore the inner regions of our psyche or the upper worlds. We have to have a specific reason. This means that our aim is to be more limited, with greater focus of power. Here we begin to understand the dynamics of our consciousness, for if we take the traditional symbol of light we can see how a narrower beam produces greater intensity and deeper penetration. Such a beam of consciousness can be obtained by giving the structure and dynamics of the exercise a tighter form.

The mode of generating such an inner laser beam is first of all to set out the aim of the operation. Up till now we have simply observed the inner realms and noted what we have seen. In this case we formulate a definite objective. Here it can be a question that has not been answered by the usual means. It might be about some metaphysical problem or something related to our lives. It could be about correct personal conduct, or the solution to a current issue. It certainly has to be a question of some gravity. No trivial matter should be considered, for not only will this bar access to the Inner Teacher, but it will devalue the exercise for future use; and one of the objectives of the exercise is to build up a contact that can be used periodically, for the rest of our lives.

Having formulated a question we then proceed to prepare for the inner ascent. This is carried out in the suggested way of ablution and evocation of the Tree. Initially it is best done with a tutor or trusted companion under instruction. This is advisable because an inexperienced student could be panicked, if led off course or faulted in procedure. The operation should take place in a dedicated space, so that no unwelcome visitors of any world are likely to interfere. By this time you should have some ceremonial symbol to wear during such sessions. As we have suggested, this could be anything from a complete traditional outfit to a simple object hung round the neck. This is a reminder to the body and lower psyche that you are about to enter another dimension. To add weight to the occasion, you can, by an act of imagination, don a ceremonial robe of your own design. This might be a cloak or some all-enveloping garment which evokes the three traditional sacred prerequisites of devotion, purity and sincerity. The colours could be purple and blue, according to the Book of Exodus, with red and white representing the lowest and highest worlds.

The function of these interior robes, based on the priestly raiment, is to enclose and protect their wearer, as well as act as the symbol of the higher bodies we all possess, but of which we do not as yet have conscious knowledge. In most people these inner bodies are very under developed, so that only a vague sense of their presence is perceived. Here the garments are used to enhance the Kabbalist's awareness of these levels, so making for greater sensitivity. Like a physical equivalent, much thought and work must go into the design of such vestments. The more refined they are, the subtler the receptivity of the person who wears them, because the creation and formation of these symbols affect the higher vehicles they represent.

Having dressed for the occasion you now make yourselves ready for the action. First you ask permission from the Most High; if this is given by the inner voice or a sign, the mission proceeds. You begin the ascent in total silence for a few moments. When the sense of a door being opened is experienced, you then approach the threshold of normal awareness. This position is held for a moment before stepping into the realm of conscious imagination. From here you start to ascend, going first to a place above where you are physically. After looking down on the landscape as if it were at the bottom of the sea, you gaze upward so as to perceive reality in a different way. In this state you convert the winds into watery currents swirling about, and rising and falling above and below. Ignoring anything that might appear to be nosing about in these depths, you rise up towards the light filtering down from the distant surface high above. Ascending by degrees you float up through the various levels of lessening density, looking neither to left or right, although you might see out of the corner of the mind's eye all sorts of intriguing sights. Just below the surface you stop and float for a moment with it just above the head. You do not look back down into the depths, but keep the gaze only on the veiled light beyond the waves. From here it can be seen more clearly than ever experienced in the world below.

On breaking the surface of the sea of *Yetzirah* you take a deep breath of Beriatic air and see a landscape of quite another world. It is cosmic in appearance. As you swim ashore vast mountains can be seen with one particularly tall peak in their midst, upon which a jewel of a city can be made out. Clambering up onto the shore you rest a while to dry out your garments, which takes no time in the fresh and clear atmosphere of the place. Before setting off inland, look back at the sea and see how moody it is. On the surface it looks calm, but there is much turbulence deep down. You move on, away from the shore and begin to climb up the foothills of the great range. After picking a way over several ridges and along some valleys, you become aware of beings that watch your progress, although you may or may not see them. You do not bother to find out what they are because your attention is caught by the sight of a beautiful building on the crest of a high hill. It is clearly the home of some holy person because it emanates light and peace. You climb up to it by a path that has obviously been used by others, and approach the place. You open the gate and enter, taking note of all that is to be seen in the garden as you come up to the door and knock.

After a moment's pause in which to make ready to meet your Inner Teacher, the door opens and there stands a being with deeply penetrating, yet kindly eyes. You are greeted and invited in. Let nothing be missed, be on the maximum alert as you are led into an upper room. Before sitting down opposite your interior mentor, look around and take note of everything in the room. If asked a question, reply with courtesy, but no fear. When the moment is right ask the main question you have been holding. Listen for the answer. It will be given. If other questions arise, keep asking again and again, until it is indicated that the conversation is over. Having received all that you can, ask what you can do in return. Take note of what is said and carry out whatever you have been instructed to do there, or elsewhere, when the time comes. At a certain moment the meeting will be clearly over. After paying respect to your spiritual superior, retire graciously, after asking permission to visit again. This might or might not be granted. Take your leave at the door of the house, and after seeing it shut, start down the hill to the seashore.

On gaining the shore, reflect for a moment on what has happened, and look towards the distant city on the mountain top. One day you may go there. Then turn your back on the scene, and with gaze fixed on the sky above, walk into the sea and allow the waves to break over your head. Begin to swim. Diving down and away from the surface, sink into the depths until you come to just above the bottom. Float there for a moment and sense the weight, pressure and flow of this ocean of the psyche. Again ignore whatever creatures might approach you, and convert the water back into air and the image of yourself hovering above the local landscape. Observe the sights and sounds of the neighbourhood, descend to the house, and into the room where you are seated. Thank the Holy One for what was given and come down the Tree to *Malkhut*. Let the inner robes remain. They will dissolve of their own accord, until they become a permanent feature of your interior world. Stamp your feet and enter life at the ordinary level. Relax and reflect.

During the debriefing note down all the questions asked and the answers given, in a book especially devoted to the purpose. This must be done first. Then reflect on what was observed about the Teacher and the upper room. Do a drawing of the place adding, even if later, details missed while debriefing. Recall the books and symbols about the place, the robes worn, and any other unusual features of the room or person. Some of these might be recognised or need to be researched, so as to identify their meaning or connection with another time and place. These can be useful clues into one's own history, which leads us onto the next exercise of distant memory. But first we must tie up our present exercise by saying that if you are invited to return by the Teacher, then do not neglect to renew the contact, because it is easily lost. After a series of such sessions, stretching over several years, you will eventually be able to go there almost directly and speak with your mentor.

27. Memories

In Kabbalah, the concept of transmigration or reincarnation is accepted. Known in Hebrew as the process of *Gilgulim*, or Wheels, it means the repeated turnings of rebirth. It is referred to in the Zohar, the great Kabbalistic classic of the Middle Ages, and frequently mentioned by Kabbalists in 16th century Palestine. The idea of recurring lives was dropped in later times as Kabbalah became regarded, by Western educated Jews, as irrational and fell into disrepute. Nevertheless, whilst cultural patterns may change, the laws of the universe do not. Therefore we take into account the notion of a chain of lives in order to understand our present fate and what our spiritual work might be. This past can be explored by the imaginative technique under Kabbalist supervision, and so give insights into our personal destiny.

All of us have memories. Indeed one exercise is to recall our earliest moments of consciousness, so as to recapture the flavour of our *Tiferet* view of the world before the ego of *Yesod* was clouded over by education. These moments are a clue to our nature and the things to which we can relate. Some individuals for example, connect with places and others with people, whilst others are aware of small things and others the large. A collection of these memories can give a very clear picture of our fate and its development. It is the same when carrying out a similar exercise in terms of previous lives.

One often hears about people who feel that they lived in ancient Egypt or were certain great personages in history. This may be so, but it is more likely that it is an identification or association based on a need to be different, especially in an area where nothing can be proved and it carries a certain romantic charisma. If it were true, then more often than not the person will never speak of the matter, because it is too precious a realisation to be worn as an ornament by the ego. As to the notion of memories of several former lives this might be considered, if one accepts that a soul can remember remarkable moments in the same way that one recalls certain days.

Life for many individuals is a routine of seeking security, food and relationships against a background of general circumstances that, for most people, does not become notable unless there is intense suffering, deep love or a glimpse of higher things which leave a trace in the psyche. These moments are the memories that people dimly recall when they visit certain old places, or see historical objects. An individual who, for example, actually remembers the plan of a vanished town quite clearly, is recalling a deeply etched memory that has not been erased by the postmortem process of death. A long or dramatic life in that place has left its mark on the soul.

If we accept the teaching that the soul has passed through more than one body, we can see how those who were incarnated many millennia ago might have matured over many lives to become old souls, as against young ones who have only been on Earth a few times. These older souls, moreover, like the elders of any generation would become more pronounced in character and will, according to their inclination and development. Thus the wise and good may influence the inner lives of their contemporaries, while the clever but evil old souls dominate external history. Younger souls in contrast are innocent and less marked in character and fate, as they grope their way through life. This tells us much about the composition and state of the world population. In earlier times the number of mature souls would be small, although we are told, on account of the primitive conditions on Earth, these were of especially high calibre, such as the prophets who chose to remain below rather than ascend to spiritual regions of existence. This might explain the remarkable level of esoteric knowledge to be found amid the wide ignorance and extensive violence of the ancient world, for there was as yet no middle management of the spiritually orientated.

In order to find out how we might fit into this scheme, let us begin by reflecting on the memories behind our consciousness. This deep stratum is generally only accessible in moments of heightened consciousness, or by seeing and being in a situation that seems strangely familiar. This can occur in certain fatal meetings. It is almost as if one was being reminded of some incident involving them, but long ago. Sometimes very powerful emotions of fear or love are evoked in such encounters. These incidents should be noted and collected. When enough have been gathered together, then a common quality will often emerge. Take for example, people with whom we fall in love or have as constant friends. They will nearly all share the same characteristics. While this may be seen as the attraction to certain types, there is often a sense of mutual recognition that forms a deep connection in which some unfinished business is worked out over months or a lifetime. Here is the law of karma reminding one of previous relationships in another time and place.

As regards places, a book about some remote country can spark off a strange yearning or instant interest to find out more about the area and its history. Take the example of people who feel at home in particular cities and find they know their way round even though they have never been to them in that lifetime. While most people regard this phenomenon as just odd, the Kabbalist sees it as a window into a past life. However if it is treated as no more than flicking through an album out of curiosity, then it is of no real use. By this it is meant that the significance of these ancient memories is lost and an important aid to inner development wasted, because if one knew why one remembered them, then some vital clue about one's present life could be gained. Let us make an imaginary investigation into such an example so as to learn what we can about it.

Suppose a man had the experience of being profoundly moved as a boy by seeing a picture of Toledo, the old capital of Castille in an encyclopedia. He does not know why, except that he knows that he must go there one day. Later as a student he visits the city and finds it strangely familiar. This perplexes him. He recalls the picture but this does not explain the sense of coming home. Some years afterwards he enters a Kabbalah group and is put through the following exercise aimed at opening up a door into his deep memory.

Led by his instructor he is asked, after the ritual of evoking the Tree, to go deep in memory and imagine a room. This he does, exploring with the mind's eye the floor, walls and furniture. He then goes on to describe what he can see, with remarkable clarity, outside the window. Fine details of what the streets are like emerge, so that gradually a picture is built up of a town that is obviously Toledo. Now while this could be ordinary memory, the period seen is not today, but the 13th century, for the people in the streets are wearing medieval dress. Later in the visualisation he sees a group of Jews in deep meditation and study in a house in the Juderia. They are obviously Kabbalists. Subsequent research and another visit to the town reveals that it was indeed a Kabbalistic centre at that time, and that he, unknown until then, had Spanish Jewish ancestory. As he wanders about the narrow lanes of the ancient Jewish quarter he finds that he is conscious of specific Kabbalists who lived there. One name in particular recurs and this man's work relates to his own view. This gives the student an extraordinary sense of being among companions.†

Such an insight not only relates the individual to his past but grants access to knowledge that no learned thesis on Spanish Kabbalah could provide. Thus a link with the chain of the tradition is established between the student and the group of souls he has been working with over the centuries. The implication of this is enormous because it reveals the scale and depth of the Work which transcends physical time and space.

Naturally everything seen in the visualisation must be checked as far as it can be, to see that it is not romanticising. Often confirmation of the material received comes unexpectedly, like a sketch made during a session, of an unvisited city matching a photograph obtained later. Sometimes places are so well described that someone who knows the site will recognise it and confirm some pertinent detail.

Arising out of such sessions can come the identity of one's spiritual supervisor. This may be someone with whom one has worked in the past. Hints on his identity are sometimes indicated, in that a name persistently crops up in conversation, books, dreams and even a magazine. One must of course check that fantasy has not taken over before accepting anything as valid. If an identity does present itself, then only facts, as yet unknown, can verify the credibility of the phenomenon. If these emerge within a short time, like finding out the place of birth of such a person by a series of coincidences, then it can be taken seriously. Even then, one must regard such identities with discrimination for there are beings in the invisible realms who like to mislead. Always consider any information given with great caution and act upon it only if it makes sense, and fits into the larger scheme.

All the foregoing of course lends itself to delusion. This is why it has rarely been written about. Many people today are using the same technique of guided imagination in psychological work, but without the grand design it can lead to much confusion. Therefore,

†This incident was in fact the author's experience.

we speak here from the Kabbalist viewpoint, so as to make a clear distinction between different disciplines that use the same process. What is laid out in this chapter is a blend of the psychic and spiritual, held and checked by the practical, that is a combination of the three lower worlds. This is made possible by evoking the Tree and asking permission of the Holy One. If the moment or the motivation is not right, then the operation is not permitted to proceed. The practice of this principle is essential in all kabbalistic work which takes one out of contact with the physical world. No one with neurotic or psychotic tendencies should be allowed to take part in these operations, as it will enhance their malady. That is why Kabbalah was restricted to the mature. We apply this balance by returning to look at daily life, so as to remain well grounded, whilst still progressing up the Tree.

28. Daily Life

One of the most important kabbalistic exercises is to be aware all the time. This means to be constantly watchful, that is to be operating not from the ordinary consciousness of the yesodic ego, but from the self of *Tiferet*. This is no easy matter, as distractions from within and without constantly draw the attention away from being in the Seat of Solomon. However, you must persist, so that gradually such a degree of consciousness is maintained that nothing significant is missed in either the upper or lower worlds. This practice is vital in that it enables you to perceive the reality of any situation, and perhaps be of use in the transmission of higher influences to the Earth. However, before this can be done with any real effect you must be able to enter the state of *Gadlut* at will.

As we discussed earlier there are two basic states common to most of us. The *Katnut* or yesodic consciousness and the *Gadlut* or greater condition. The latter is attained by Grace or deliberate effort to hold this position. It is done by incessant practice which alerts the *Hod-Tiferet-Netzah* triad of awakening. Here, the individual experiences a keenness of the senses and a lucidity of psychological awareness that can detect not only what is going on inside oneself, but often in others. Such a condition should eventually become the norm in everyday life for the Kabbalist. This is essential because it allows a link between Heaven and Earth to be established within the individual, which can be of use in the outer world.

The application of the awakened state is that one watches life without interfering in the normal yesodic process, unless necessary. From this point of view, many things can be seen that are normally unnoticed. For example, one's own and other's unconscious motivations become apparent and so do trends, such as community tension, that are often only recognised as dangerous when it is too late and there is a riot. Besides the utilitarian function of a higher degree of consciousness than the ego, much can be learnt about one's own unconscious character. If you take each day as a microcosm of your life, many things emerge to surprise, please and displease. For example, you will observe certain parental attitudes that you acquired during early upbringing and how they colour and often distort your view of others. You may also note that there are particular ideas that dominate you without your knowledge, like not trusting, which may come from some long forgotten personal experience or some notion imbibed from your culture which inhibits social or racial intercourse. These are the more obvious things to detect. A little deeper observation carried out over some time will reveal many other unconscious attitudes that govern our lives. Indeed, we learn that there is a massive set of emotive and conceptual complexes that rules us without our knowledge.

The identification and modification of such unseen, deeply hidden attitudes, emotional responses and reflex actions is part of the process of self-perfection. Indeed, becoming acquainted with these unconscious aspects of one's nature is just as important as learning about the remote past or what the higher realms are like. In fact much of the Work will be to deal with this level as you operate within the pressures of the collective unconsciousness. Therefore the cleaning and polishing of the two mirrors of the ego and self is essential, so that they may reflect, without blemish or distortion, a true picture of the world and the light that shines down from above.

The daily exercise of direct contact with ordinary life is absolutely necessary because it completes the octave of the Tree that stretches from *Keter* the Crown to *Malkhut* the Kingdom. Without this link with the mundane, nothing real can happen, for the flow is incomplete and any good impulse remains only in *Yesodic* imagination. Thus, one must be fully present at work and play, during serious and amusing moments, social occasions and whilst alone, or even making love. There is no time when you should not be present, observing and reflecting at what is going on within and without. In this way you begin to realise that you are always being watched, if not by your mentor, then that other deeper self which is always present, although you may forget it.

To live one's daily life like this is not easy. It doubles the burden of living. However, there are benefits far beyond the effort put in. Not only do you start to appreciate life more, but you perceive the rhythms of existence. This gives you the knowledge of when to act, because you will recognise the right moment, and not make effort when the tide is flowing the wrong way. It allows you to see the pattern of your life and know what is advantageous and what is detrimental. This is what the Chinese call "Moving with the Tao". In kabbalistic terms it means shifting with the balance of the Tree of Creation as it alternates its emphasis within the three pillars. At one point, for example, the stress of a situation might be on Severity and therefore great restraint may be required. At another stage, the pillar of Mercy might be active, and so all effort is devoted to exploiting the process of expansion, whilst at another time the middle pillar of Clemency might be operational, and so the individual waits to see which side is to become prominent before moving.

The foregoing principles can be applied to a personal or a general situation. There may be a time, for instance, when certain important decisions have to be made about leaving a job. If the conditions are seen from the *Gadlut* state, then the possibilities open or closed will become self evident and one will respond accordingly. If the trend is *Gevuric* or curtailing, then it should be acknowledged and accepted, unless a confrontation is right and will achieve its objective. Here is real Judgment. On the other hand, it may be a period when *Hesed* brings abundance and one should make hay while the sun shines, before the opposite pillar reverses the tide. The Kabbalist may also observe current affairs in this way, identifying certain tendencies long before the media or economic and political commentators notice it. For example, often the most sensitive or intelligent members of a community recognise quite early on the dangers of a situation in a country. This happened in Germany when certain Jews left long before the Second World War. It is interesting to note that many Kabbalists left Spain some time before the great expulsion of 1492. They could not only see what was to happen, but took precautions so as to preserve the tradition, which we now inherit.

Self-observation in everyday life not only earths you, but serves as the working method in the market place of the world. While private study and secluded group practice are important, much effort has to be made under the conditions of mundane reality. Here, there are no special concessions, no tutor to keep an eye on one, no sympathetic companions or carefully tailored conditions. It is as it is, and this is how life, for most of us, has to be dealt with. If you cannot manage the ordinary problems of living, then Kabbalah is not for you. There has to be a good level of competence and a familiarity with things of this world, or what is brought down from the higher realms will never come into manifestation. If you have not one real skill then you cannot transmit the teaching, or communicate the essence of what Kabbalah is about. You must be effective in life, even if it is only some small ability that allows the expression of what you are working towards. You need not be the master of a profession because you can be an excellent servant. To know how to sweep the floor with consciousness, as one rabbi did while he contemplated the universe, is as valid as the captain of industry who had a small room in his tower block to which he retired for a period each day to meditate.

According to tradition, every Kabbalist should have a trade; that is, not only have a means of livelihood by which he earns his bread, but a profession that is relevant to his nature and its development. Thus, being a gangster is not conducive to a spiritual life although, as noted, even a thief can teach a Kabbalist how to be observant. Right livelihood, as the Buddhists call it, is part of a Kabbalist's way of living. Preferably, it should be as close to the perfect as possible, so that the gifts given by the Almighty are used to the full. These are often not recognised for many years until the professional or social conditioning imposed on us has lost its force and we seek what we really want to do with our lives. This, however, can only come about after the early stages of self-development and the dominance of the ego and its ambitions or fears have been dealt with. That again is the reaon why Kabbalah should only be seriously taken up in maturity, when the true calibre of our being begins to emerge. This takes us up to the long term exercise of examining ourselves in relation to others and the world. Here, we begin to see how we may fit into and take part in the Work of Unification.

29. Fate

As consciousness increases so does the awareness of great and small, depth and height. This means that the Kabbalist not only observes the minutiae of every day, but begins to discern the patterns in his or her life as a whole. This detection of the interconnectedness of everything must happen because all things are indeed linked at every level. It is seen in space, as the relationship between things in a given moment and in time, in the unfolding of events, because every entity in existence moves in a rhythm that has been ebbing and flowing since the universe began. Clearly only those with a high degree of spiritual consciousness can perceive the cosmic pattern, but it is possible for those, even quite early into kabbalistic work, to pick out the design of their own fate. This is done by an ordered reflection.

The first part of the process is to consider the present. Here, we look at our own state as impartially as possible, either alone or with the help of a trustworthy companion. This may be your own instructor, a good friend, or a skilled professional who might be the practitioner of one of the many arts devoted to self study from the ancient discipline of astrology to modern psychological analysis. In all cases the supervisor should possess a comprehension of the cosmic view which goes much deeper than just the personal. To probe only the psyche is to become immersed in an essentially fluid and ever-changing world, and without reference to a higher order many people have been lost to reality, drowned by their dreams. Therefore, it is vital that all assistance has the transpersonal dimension. Indeed, it is better to have a down-to-earth adviser than a brilliant theorist who is full of comment but has no experiential wisdom in their being.

The reflection of the present may be set out in diagrammatic form. First you contemplate your relationship with God. This is usually done during the daily meditation. Then you consider your relationship with yourself by focusing upon the state of the Spirit, the condition of the psyche and the health of the body. This will indicate the general situation as regards your interior being. After this comes the examination of your outer world.

The first thing taken into account is your relationship to your most intimate companion. Here will be seen the world's immediate reactions to what one is at the moment. A long and deep view of your partner's response will indicate either advance or retreat, growth or stagnation in the art of relationship. Many things unperceived about oneself will be reflected by your partner. Of course, you must take into account his/her psychological projections, but even so, your choice of partner indicates your own nature and inclinations. Thus we get a precise mirror of our fate, that all inclusive pattern that reveals our mode of being. In the creative tensions of a close relationship many aspects of our character are exposed, and for this we must be grateful, even though it might be painful. To avoid such encounters and what is brought out in them is to miss one of life's most important working areas. Friendship, love affairs and marriage are designed by providence to aid and increase development and many who retreat into safe solitude remain out of touch with their destiny. There are times to be alone, but in excess and without contact with life one becomes ego-centred and prone to delusion.

The next level to examine is your family. This may or may not be blood relationship. As many have discovered, their circle of friends is often closer and more supportive than their own kith and kin. This group will reveal, by its various components, connections with the various aspects of oneself. The presence of an outwardly moody person amongst your intimates indicates an inner moodiness of everyone attached to them. A look at each character of your circle will tell much about who you are and where you are. The proverb about being judged by your friends is put to good use by the Kabbalist. Your position in the circle as the leader or follower, the joker or charmer, the fool or wise one is extremely informative. There is much to be learnt about your strengths or weaknesses, role and function from these reflections. Friends and even enemies acknowledge your talents and ask for their application or restriction, like jealousy of a good talker. These gifts are an indication of one's potential use to the Work, as well as our fatal path.

Our path through life is largely determined by our gifts and our capacity to use them in the environment we live. Reality is not concerned with illusion and you will be where you are because of what you have or have not done with them. Egotism, optimism or cynicism may blind you and maybe others, about your capability, but Providence knows better and sends opportunities for you to find out and explore what you might be. If you recognise your hour and meet it, you may come into your own. Many a person with delusions about what should be done if they were given a chance has failed to match the inevitable moment, because their ideas were not based on anything but yesodic dreams. A sense of reality is vital to the Kabbalist, otherwise nothing can be accomplished. Therefore, the criterion of what is feasible and what is not, is related to every occasion that fate presents. Impeccable honesty about each opportunity and its possibilities is practised. In this way a less gifted person can be more effective than many more talented people who waste the limited number of opportunities given to accomplish certain things.

To establish a general picture of your life situation, there should be a session of reflection preferably each week, or at least once a month. In this way the past and its relationship to the future may be considered. To miss a session is to break the continuity and lose the gradual accumulation and cohesion of the picture of, say, recurring incidents which become seen as strands that are clearly trends in your fate. People who do not pause to reflect wonder why certain things always happen to them. They never look up in time to avert an avoidable disaster or take advantage of an obvious opportunity. To be immersed in nothing but Yesodic concerns is to be out of touch with the self, and therefore, with the real potential of one's life. Sometimes, the self of *Tiferet* will indicate, by some unusual interior or exterior action, an oncoming event, but very often we miss this signal and are caught by surprise. This is why periodic reflection is vital. It is learning how to watch over our fate and not allow ourselves just to be carried by circumstance. In this way we rise above being a victim, even though we may not be able to change the external pattern.

If we review our past from the standpoint of *Tiferet*, that is as honestly as we can, we should, at the age of around thirty, have some sense of who we are. We may not yet know what our particular work is, but some indication of what kind of training we need should be apparent by then. By training is meant not the formal study at university or in the workshop, but what the soul has to pass through in order to mature. Initially, this may have been a tough childhood, an easy youth or a difficult coming of age.

Seen with the inner view, such periods may appear the opposite to the conventional view of life which is success-orientated. The sons and daughters of the privileged often have little experience of, or aptitude for, self-reliance, whilst the socially deprived may know more about God than an archbishop. It is not unusual, for example, to find the rich to be mean and imprisoned by their possessions and the poor to be free and generous, in spite of their limited conditions. However, we speak here of people who are involved with some kind of spiritual work where mastery of intense difficulties bring about a deep strength and integrity. Many worldly-wise people are outwardly strong, but quite amoral which later precipitates an inner collapse in the face of changed external conditions. The Kabbalist should be able to handle the most difficult crisis fate provides.

To begin to piece together the pattern in your life is to start to see the laws of fate. For example, you begin to discern that certain events were inevitable, that the meeting or parting with this person was ordained, and that a particular set of circumstances were simply unavoidable. After a time, there emerges the sense of some kind of plan, and you suspect that the whole of your life is indeed supervised, so that the maximum can be gained from every situation, good or bad. This it would seem is equally true for everyone, although most people are not conscious of the fact, because they only see the surface of events. To realise the possibilities in each moment is one of life's great secrets, and when you begin to flow with the tides of descending creation and ascending evolution, much unnecessary suffering is removed. For example, when you look back at events that no longer affect the immediate present, it can often be seen that much of the pain generated was caused by wilful resistance to the inevitable. Most of this comes from the ego which cannot see beyond its habits and convenience, and this usually means those fantasies we have about ourselves. When we recognise our useful patterns, we can allow more useful tendencies to develop. These will help us for a time until they too become redundant. Thus, we utilise the forms we have been given to help mould our fate consciously. This means we may be able to influence the future.

However more important than the future is how one performs in the present, both in the personal area and in relation to Kabbalah. Only what is done in the present can change the future, although not always in the way we imagine. To live out your fate consciously is to begin to know what your destiny might be. This means how your gifts may contribute to the operation of unifying the Worlds in mankind. Here we start to perceive the spiritual strand of our lives carried over perhaps centuries, even millennia. In order to have an insight into this cosmic stratum of being you must paradoxically maintain an alert watchfulness on the ever moving moment "now", for it is the key to time. In this way, we may be shown how the pattern of our fate has led up to each moment to reveal that it is the only place we can be, even if it is in the midst of a major crisis. To the Kabbalist there are two order of crises; those caused by faulty conduct which act as correctives, and those that test integrity. Each fate contains at least one of these major trials. People engaged in the Work usually get more. Here is a part of the training for which most people are not prepared. Therefore the next chapter is devoted to the theme of trial.

30. Trials

All of us experience crisis. It is a part of life. We see this law in our personal lives and in the world about us. It applies to private and public events, to individuals and communities. It can also relate to mankind as a whole, and by speculative observation, probably to the individual planets and the whole solar system. What then is a crisis? In Kabbalah it is when the flow of existence, at whatever level we are looking, reaches a stage when resistance matches progress. At such a time the pressure increases to a critical point where the flow is turned back, or breaks through a barrier. Seen at extremes it may be regarded as a moment of passing inconvenience or a major disturbance to the status quo. Either way it makes life difficult, if not impossible. To the Kabbalist, there is always more than what appears on the surface. Crises are seen as effects, not causes, and these when examined in depth often totally change the view of the occurrence.

The mechanism of a crisis is that when the Tree of a situation is out of balance, or is momentarily one of equilibrium, then the loading of that situation is about to be changed. Thus, for example, if a person is too severe, then either more severity is applied to create a reaction, or Mercy is introduced to correct the imbalance. This usually precipitates a crisis, like a bad judgement which induces conscience that brings the person back towards the central column of Clemency. In an individual's life it can be excessive indulgence against a strict upbringing, or in a larger sphere a revolution opposing oppression, both leading, in time, to greater personal and political maturity. On the vertical scale crisis can occur when one level is in conflict with another. The most frequent in the individual is when the ego is about to relinquish its power to the self. This is a major crisis that can result in either level holding ascendency for a period, until the matter is settled in favour of evolution, because in the long run the cosmic process will always win, even if it takes many lives. Lesser crises can occur within each sefirah or triad, so that we may witness or experience, for example, a Hodian crisis when the person realises that facts are not enough; or a passive emotional crisis when old fears seek to hold back an impulse to love without reservation, as they struggle with dynamic complexes in the triad of active emotion. The solution lies in equilibrium, but this is often not seen until the episode is past.

There are minor and major crises. The minor are to be observed every day, and whilst these may be managed with relative ease, they should not be regarded as unimportant. If one reflects, it will be noted that major crises are often precipitated by a minor one. For example, on a large scale, it only took one man to shoot another and his wife to start the First World War. Likewise, a casual remark can cause a quarrel or trigger a turning point in someone's life. The reason for this is that many small factors can build up to a major event. The persistent criticism that undermines a marriage is an example, so is an increasing unease which can make a person suddenly leave an outwardly pleasant but stale situation without anyone in it knowing why. We should take note of each crisis that presents itself and search for its root and where its conflict is directing us.

A major crisis is easy to identify. It is usually spectacular and will often be remembered as one of the most productive periods of our lives, although at the time we thought it hell. However, to some, a crisis is a way of life. This can be a pathological way of gaining attention, or a constant warning that they are not on target. For most of us big crises come at turning points in our lives. They usually have a long build up and often their foreshadow touches us, in indicative events, some time before they actually occur, like a rattle in a car engine before it breaks down. This is the use of reflection, so that we are not caught entirely unawares. Sometimes, because of such fore-knowledge, we can avoid a catastrophe, although this is not always possible, but at least we can prepare the sea captain who battens the hatches for a storm. However, for the Kabbalist, the objective is not just to survive, but to learn as much as possible from the experience, because very often these periods of disruption are when the most direct knowledge is gained about oneself and existence.

Seen from the cosmic point of view, the dimension alters and one begins to see such critical events as spiritual tests. Now according to Tradition, Satan is the tester. Indeed, his name means just this. As one of the Benai Elohim, the Sons of God, it is his task to pressure the righteous and test their genuineness. We see this described in great detail in the Book of Job, when God allows Satan to try this remarkably fortunate man by taking everything from him and afflicting his soul. Throughout the book, Job complains to God that his punishment is unjust, as he has done nothing wrong. His friends who do not understand what is happening, naturally assume he must have broken some law to come into such trouble. This issue, however, is not about karma or the law of retribution, but about whether Job will crack under the strain and lose his integrity. The wager between God and the devil may seem on the surface odd and unfair, but the contest between evil and good is vital to Creation because it makes Adam bear witness to the fact that mankind has free will, can rise above physical and psychological circumstances and still hold the Divine Light on the Earth. Satan failed with Job, and all was restored to the man with yet more increase. However, the battle still goes on in each generation, as the Job in every evolving individual is tested almost to breaking point. If there is a break, then that is the person's own decision, for Satan is not permitted to destroy the soul.

This is one of the reasons why people on the Way are often tried so severely. When they have been proved they can be given much and bear the heavy load of spiritual Work. When one considers how few follow the Path beyond the honeymoon stage, then the weight of responsibility involved has to be carried by those capable of holding it. If a person in charge of training souls, should fail then many will fall, and that must not happen. Indeed, when such individuals have cracked, then whole schools have become corrupt, and many seekers lost for that lifetime. The vessel must be thoroughly tested before it is allowed to be filled with heavenly dew.

If a crisis is to be regarded as a test, then even the most unfortunate circumstances can be put to good use. This transforms the situation into a Kabbalistic exercise and changes its whole aspect. Thus, the break-up of a relationship can be seen as the working out of karma, whilst the coming together and confrontation of another couple may be regarded as a chance to develop Gevuric courage or Hesedic compassion in one or both of them. An on-going crisis in the family may become the workshop of several souls, as might a strike at work be the spur to an individual's realisation about the mass mind and how he or she is facing in the opposite direction. Every situation of tension has its creative element. Conflict and its resolution are normal in the process of evolution. Most plays and books are about the confrontation between good and evil. Great literature develops the issue in depth, like Tolstoy's *Resurrection,* where a man struggles with his conscience. In the mass media the theme is the same; the baddies have their moment, but in the end they must lose, or evil will rule and cause anarchy in society and the universe. Here the archetypal confrontation between order and chaos in the cosmic drama is acted out in individual and the collective consciousness.

The key to a safe passage through the great and small dramas of Creation is correct conduct. By this I do not mean conventional customs, which are often outmoded patterns of behaviour, but acting from true integrity. In the Bible it is spoken of as righteousness. A person who lives in this way is called a *Zadek* in Kabbalah. To be such an individual means that one moves according to conscience, that is the way of the soul. This triad composed of *Gevurah, Hesed* and *Tiferet* gives the qualities of discernment, courage and love of the Good, Truth and Beauty. To think or dream about behaving according to these criteria is not enough. As one sage said, "Anyone can be an angel if their feathers are not ruffled." Therefore life, or fate, to be more precise, creates situations in which one's integrity is both tested and deepened as a result. Such examinations are not always at our convenience because usually there are others also involved. These may be people who are consciously being put to the test, or bystanders in the process of being woken up by the shock, because it is a fact that even the most dozy soul can become conscious when shaken by dramatic events. This is another function of crisis. Thus it is, that all levels have an opportunity to be shaken out of exterior patterns that bind the interior habits which imprison the soul. If history had no drama there would be no civilisation, nor would we have the Great Ones who teach us how to meet the problems of being born, living and dying.

This discussion of crisis and trial leads on to the larger scale of Providence which is the concern of the spiritual levels as it watches over the world and supervises events below. Without a general plan in the universe, and an occasional adjustment to meet special situations, there would be disorder, which is just what the devil thrives upon. Therefore, let us take a look at Providence so as to know a little more about the cosmic theatre in which we act out our parts.

31. Providence

According to kabbalistic tradition, existence unfolds in the form of a grand design. First manifestation emerges from nothingness into a void, which is then filled by the Will of God in the appearance of the sefirot, which in turn organise themselves into the Tree of Life that contains all the principles of manifest existence. Out of this primal instrument of Divine government emerge the three lower worlds of Creation, Formation and Action. These descend in an ordered impulse of consciousness, energy and matter to create, form and make the great Ladder of Jacob stretching between the first *Keter* of total unity to the fullness of multiplicity at the bottommost '*Malkhut*'. This graduated process has distinct levels of laws that increase the further they are from the highest Crown, with each superior level ruling its inferior levels in the same way that man can direct and control the conditions of a garden in order to produce the finest plants. The level of celestial government is general, in that it deals with stars and planets, nature and species. However, in the case of mankind Providence can be concerned with the particular, but only when an individual raises him or herself above the law of the masses.

When the descending impulse of Creation reaches its limit at the elemental level of the most solid of metals, there is an upward turn that becomes a process of cosmic reflection, known to us as evolution. This movement begins the return journey to its source. At the present stage our Earth has completed the making and developing of the mineral, vegetable and animal kingdoms. The human race has only recently arrived on the planet. Here we see the meeting of the natural world of organised matter, energy and intelligence with the levels of soul and spirit. Thus each individual, as a cell of Adam Kadmon enwrapped in a physical body, has access to the higher worlds and contact with their Divine origins. This makes a human being the only creature in existence that can consciously span all the worlds, as he or she grows in the experience of both visible and invisible realms. Such a uniqueness gives us access to Providence and *vice versa*, in that we may individually evolve with help from Providence, which provides the best conditions for us, although we do not always appreciate it at the time. The supervision of Providence is a vast, subtle and complex operation. For most of us its workings are a mystery that gives us just what we need, rather than what we want, at the right time. Its main aim, in accordance with the Will of Heaven, is to help mankind transform the world of Action and the Elements into a paradise on Earth in which the Presence of the Holy One is known by every incarnated being.

Such a project cannot be completed quickly. It is a vast effort extending over many millennia carried on by each generation of aspirants which is composed of people who have committed themselves to this Work of Unification. Paradoxically to help in the process of unification often initially separates those on the Path from the rest of mankind, because few understand what is involved. Moreover many seekers of the Way do not know what its aim is to begin with, despite the fact that Providence tells them each day by its interaction with their lives. For most, such a realisation can only come about over many lives, as accumulated experience brings about insight by degrees and then real knowledge about the purpose of existence. Not everyone is sensitive or intelligent and many in pursuit of widsom or happiness are still children in matters of the soul and spirit. Therefore, Providence designs special situations in which the person seeking truth can find it, so that growth can occur and the next stage be prepared for. This phenomenon takes some time to recognise, but once it is, then the aspirant flows with the movement of Heaven. Here we have a person who lives out fate consciously and uses it for self-development.

Fate is the pattern of one's life. It is the result of all that has gone before in other lives. It is designed by the laws of retribution which deal with both reward and punishment, and the needs of the time in which the person has incarnated. Because of past actions certain relationships with others continue, until the work together is complete. This means that each person has a set of fatal meetings arranged by Providence which cannot be avoided, although they may be discarded once the connection is made. This, however, does not mean that the business is finished. The meeting will recur, if not again in that lifetime, then in another until the issue is resolved. The Kabbalist, therefore, considers each relationship in this light. It might be that one encounter will suffice to complete something from a previous existence, or it could take many years to work through a complex karma with another individual or group. The Kabbalist takes this factor into account in all relationships whether intimate or distant, for they are part of his or her training to become aware of the inter-relatedness of the inner and outer worlds, because nothing is separate in the universe. Here is the underlay of Providence.

In the early days of life a child takes everything for granted. Parents supply food and comfort, and later education and training is given by the community. It is the same on the spiritual path. At the beginning one is handed out all sorts of help. Books come one's way as if by accident. Coincidence brings certain people into contact who can direct one and answer some pertinent question. Situations occur as if by design, rather than the random laws in ordinary life. One meets someone, as if by accident in a remote place, or picks up a spiritual contact in the middle of the market place. It is as if one were being guided and given just what one needs at that moment. This is the hallmark of Providence.

The name Providence is just what it says. It provides with precision and capability because the cosmic level from which it operates can see the overall picture. Thus, two people can be directed towards each other from different sides of the world, and at the right moment be made to meet in Times Square, New York City, or on a mountain between India and Persia where few people go. The Kabbalist is always on the lookout for such incidents, because they not only form a part of the chain of connections, but reveal how the Spirit works in the world. Contrary to a common view, esoteric operations are not always carried out behind locked doors. They are often performed in the market place of the public domain where no one notices them or sees them for what they really are. Usually it is only years later that some people begin to suspect that more happened than was seen or reported. The life of Joshua ben Miriam of Nazareth is a prime example of this. To most of the people in Judea he was an itinerant rabbi, one of many individuals who might have been their deliverer. The authorities saw him as a trouble maker and the possible focus of an uprising. Only a handful of people realised he was more than just a great teacher. It was only much later that it became apparent he was the Anointed One of his time. When Ibn Arabi, many centuries after, met the Katub of his Age, as the Sufis call the Messiah of the period, only he recognised the Katub. He was forbidden to tell the others with him who was present.

To meet the Messiah of one's time is not likely, but one never knows. Perhaps more important is simply to be watchful and see what Providence puts your way. While you may grow to allow Providence to look after you, what is sometimes given, after the ease and encouragement of the early days, is not always what is expected. Indeed it sometimes comes as a great shock to learn that even on the Path you have to earn your keep. This is not a metaphor of business, but a cosmic law of paying a spiritual debt and of increasing your potential and profit, like the good servant in many parables. Thus, you are sometimes posted a problem 'out of the blue', which means out of the sky or Heaven. It might come in the form of someone looking for an entry into the Tradition. Here is where the Kabbalist pays off his account to his early helpers by adding a link in the chain of generations.

Sometimes the task allocated is not so easy or obvious. It might be a difficult relationship in which one partner watches over the other and helps him or her through a spiritual crisis that might last for years. When a certain Hassidic rabbi was asked why had Heaven given him such a shrew of a wife, he replied, "So who else could cope with her?" Being good does not always bring a harmonious life. Many very conscientious people are pushed to their limit by the irresponsible, who seek them out to balance off their own difficulties. This has the effect of testing out the depth of commitment to integrity and improving, by example, the state of the afflicted. One often finds spiritually orientated people engaged in difficult, dangerous and even mad situations because that is where the light is most needed, although the choice to leave is there. Providence arranges these opportunities according to your capability. Here it is worth noting that the easy options are rarely the most profitable. However it takes hindsight to appreciate this when the job is done.

After the Kabbalist has been involved in this type of activity for some years there emerges a set of skills that attracts certain situations. These are heaven-given gifts and indicate the nature of your life's work. Thus talents that are needed and well used, like those of a healer or artist, reveal what is your destiny. Destiny is the long chain of fates that makes up the aim of your reason for existence. Its distinct quality passes from life to life and may be detected, by the observant, in the unique quality that underlies an individual. Thus, the Kabbalist observes his or her performance in whatever task Providence puts their way, because in it is the clue to what they were called forth, created, formed and made for. If you come to see what you are and work within your gifts, then you know your place in the grand design and can happily serve the Holy One from any level. If this state is obtained, then acceptance of whatever work is ordained grants a profound sense of purpose to the Kabbalist's life. This often means that many petty problems and ambitions are curtailed leaving more energy available for the task in hand. However, before this is reached many stages have to be passed through, so that you arrive at such a conviction with the knowledge of experience and not just the theories and fantasies of innocence. In order to do this, we examine the next phase of development and the hazards to be mastered, especially as the psychic faculties awaken, which they do after a sustained period of kabbalistic work.

32. Psychic Faculties

Over a period of time there begins to develop within the Kabbalist certain higher faculties. By these is meant that as the Yetziratic or psychological body develops with diligent work, so do the subtle organs and their sensibilities. Some people are born with these faculties which are regarded as psychic gifts. In the case of the Kabbalist they are the result of conscious work. In the discipline of magic such faculties are deliberately developed, so as to perceive and manipulate the laws of the *Yetziratic* world. In the case of low magic this power to command is all that is sought, but it is at a high price, for more often than not, such powers generate temptation, abuse and eventually psychological confusion, with the more serious loss of access to the worlds beyond, of the Spirit and Divine. High magic, like Kabbalah, seeks to be of service to God, but practitioners of this superior occult art are very rare, for integrity at just the psychological level is difficult to maintain. There has to be the spiritual dimension. This, however, does not mean that the Kabbalist is not put to the temptation of occult powers.

As the psychic senses begin to awaken, so the person becomes increasingly aware of the subtler levels of events nearby, and sometimes from afar. You may, for example, become conscious of someone's innermost intention, or pick up what is really going on behind an apparently ordinary conversation. There can be times when you become conscious of some person not related directly to your own life and not know why, until you hear that an event took place involving that individual in some spiritual situation. Some people find that they are informed about events far across the ocean, or know beforehand that some important event is about to occur, whilst others have the ability to cast their consciousness into the past and find out what actually happened.

At first these faculties arise quite naturally out of the Work. Mostly they grow gradually but occasionally they blossom quite suddenly. To the unprepared this can be somewhat disturbing in that to become aware of the workings of other people's inner processes means that you have the capacity to influence, as well as be influenced, because the flow operates both ways. Many sensitive people, for example, can pick up tension within a household of conflict and come away from it agitated, although they themselves are not personally involved. This same gift of reception can be consciously reversed to transmit good feeling or understanding. But first you must take into account whether it is right to interfere. Here is the test of manipulation.

Let us take a hypothetical situation and draw some lessons from it. A Kabbalist goes out to dinner. During the meal he perceives that his host, the husband, is having an affair with one of the guests. He arrives at this conclusion by a series of insights that are presented to his *Yesod* in flashes. He may have picked up the interior communications between the two people or he might have glimpsed the subtle threads that stretch between them. These can be perceived by the psychic eye as links between the head, heart and pelvic regions. A closer look would determine whether the relationship was a passing encounter or something more serious. This is done by seeing which of the strands is the thickest and at which place their ends are situated. Thus, a head to head predominance would clearly be quite a different relationship from a strong pelvis to pelvis connection. As you can imagine, the possession of such information bears a certain responsibility, and some temptation to those who wish to do good, or ill.

Another example of this problem is when you see, with very precise vision, the solution to another's dilemma. You not only observe the game as an outsider, but have an inner view of what brought the person to this point. It would be easy to speak and advise, but this is not permitted without a clear indication that it is correct, for to interfere with another's karma may cause yet more trouble for him, and a little for yourself. Thus, discretion is tested again and again, so as to prove that you can possess psychic faculties, but must not misuse them. Occasionally the test is reversed and you have a responsibility to speak on the basis of inner knowledge. This exercise must be done with enormous tact, taking into account all the effects that might follow. Consider the Kabbalist at our dinner party. If he spoke to the hostess, who was a close friend, it could be a disaster. If he let the husband know he knew, he might be held responsible for the result, and if he informed the third party – who knows what would happen? And yet, the Kabbalist was shown the situation for some reason. So it may be necessary to speak to the husband or prepare the wife to ride the shock, or just wait. It is a very difficult decision. Such psychic gifts carry their burden.

Whilst these phenomena may occur spontaneously by being stimulated in a dramatic situation, they can also be induced deliberately. For instance, the following technique can be applied after some practice, but it requires first the fact that the psychic centres are operational, and secondly that one can interpret accurately what is shown, because all the information that is received is not reliable. It has to be soundly edited and converted into an intelligible form.

Supposing that you want to see what is your own inner state. After the recommended preparation of ritual and prayer imagine that you are riding a horse on a long journey. You may find yourself crossing a particular landscape in certain weather conditions. From this image much can be deduced. First look at your clothes and the condition of the horse. Observe how you appear, and examine the terrain. It will not always correspond to an outer situation. In tough times, for example, the ride could be up a steep mountain pass on an exhausted horse with sleet in your tired face and a cold wind biting into your worn out coat. At another time, you might find, when you flip this image up to take a reading, that you are riding a yearling through a beautiful summer meadow in fashionable cotton gear, whilst on the horizon dark clouds are to be seen forewarning some trouble ahead of this present good period. This technique is particularly useful when the ordinary mind cannot see clearly what is happening below its habitual thoughts and feelings.

A further application of this method is to project an image, after considering a general question about a situation. What may be presented is, for example, a picture of a battle, with the people involved, playing out their roles as generals or soldiers on either side. A close examination of the image might reveal that someone is not what he appears. The obtrusive watcher in the outer situation might reveal himself as the real field marshall behind the nominal commander. In another case you might wish to know how an absent friend is, and so, after reflecting on his or her face, you visualise them as a ship. Its situation will, if the vision is not fantasy, tell much about their circumstance. Here you must double check with known and hard facts.

The use of such methods is fraught with dangers. You can just be deceiving yourself or others; another responsibility. Therefore, whilst much information may be useful, it must not be acted upon until confirmation is received by external means, or the image is repeated often enough not to be ignored. Even so, to act on insubstantial advice requires great discernment and prudence. This is not the work for the neurotic or psychotic. Such people often have visions, which though at the heart are correct, are usually distorted images to suit their own world picture. They have this faculty because their unbalanced mentality sometimes triggers this psychic function, which feeds deranged images into their already ego-centred *Yesods,* leading to inflated personal view. Everyone has these dark elements in them to a greater or lesser degree, and therefore, even if you are convinced that you are right, you must check assiduously to see if any personal motivation has corrupted the essential modesty required for service.

The temptation to use these psychic skills improperly is a great test. You may justify their use by various reasons ranging from self-knowledge to helping others. While these objectives are valid, it is always the intention that must be watched. Spiritual vanity may allow the abuse of such gifts for what is believed to be the common good, and whilst a person might not think he is performing psychic manipulation, others may perceive magic being worked on themselves or others without their consent, and this is not permitted, however good the reason might be. Many an individual in the early stages of spiritual work has tried to change a situation from the subtle level for the best of reasons, and finished up forgetting what was the original aim. This is because it is very easy to drown in the watery world of *Yetzirah*. One needs good connections both in Heaven and on Earth so as not to be washed away in the powerful currents of the psychic realm and out to sea.

Direct access to the World of Formation brings not only new sensibilities and powers, but contact with those beings who live in that zone. During formal meditation and sleep we pass quite safely through these areas, but as one raises the conscious centre of gravity, so one encounters the inhabitants of the next world. Thus, the ability to discern and handle whatever entitities might emerge out of one's own psyche or the lower levels of *Yetzirah,* must be cultivated so that we may safely approach and enter into the upper worlds.

33. Entities

As you begin to penetrate beyond the line that stretches between *Hod* and *Netzah*, you come into the lower unconscious, which is unconsciousness until you are aware of it. Then like the stars that are not seen in the day, but are nevertheless present, there emerges, as consciousness rises, the middle levels of the psyche with its various constellations of intellectual and emotional complexes. These psychological configurations hold and relate all the memories and ideas imbibed by personal experience or passed on through the collective unconscious of our background. They may be clusters of fears or loves, or groups of positive or negative ideas that take on, at this level, a kind of life of their own sometimes to become distinct and powerful entities within the psyche, like mini-archetypes.

Examples of such entities are the virgin and the whore in women, and the tyrant and the victim in men. These sub-personalities, as they are sometimes called, are legion and are represented, in traditional Kabbalah, as angels and demons. We all know the imp in us that likes to be mischievous and the saint who seeks to be good. We also are acquainted with the Jekyll and Hyde as well as the fool who blunders occasionally into our lives. These are all parts of ourselves created by our own experience and that which is present, like the ancestral parts of the brain, as the ancient archetypal intelligence of the human race. Thus, in addition to containing all biological evolution in our bodies, with its mineral, plant and animal levels, we also have very primitive aspects of the psyche underlying the more sophisticated levels of the unconscious. Thus, a highly educated, urbane man, in time of war or great fear, can become as violent as any savage, because it is there to be aroused, if it is not controlled. The reverse is equally true, in that the collective sage and saint is equally present to be awakened.

The arising of these unconscious aspects normally does not occur except in especially cultivated or dramatic situations, but nevertheless, they are there and sometimes influence our ego consciousness without our knowledge. This is apparent in an unbalanced state like neurosis, where a person fears constant attack, or believes themselves to be all-knowing. As we work towards heightened awareness, these entities emerge to help or hinder our progress towards healing and further evolution. This is why, in spiritual work, a very personal crisis sometimes occurs as split off psychological aspects are exposed to the light of increased consciousness. In the case of those without a discipline or tutor, it occasionally results in a breakdown, whilst among those working under supervision it can be no more than what has been called the 'Down' without the 'Break', because they are carried through this dark night of the soul by experienced support and inner knowledge.

Another set of internal psychological entities to be met are the archetypes. These are focused round the various sefirot. The old planetary gods associated with each sefirah gives a clue to their nature. Thus, the Moon and Artemis are associated with *Yesod*, Mercury with *Hod*, Venus with *Netzah*, Apollo with *Tiferet*, Mars with *Gevurah*, Jupiter with *Hesed*, Pluto with *Daat*, Saturn with *Binah*, Uranus with *Hochmah* and Neptune with *Keter*. Around these principles accrue both individual and collective material which manifests in dreams and drives that both illuminate and motivate the psyche. In cases of madness an archetype sometimes breaks free of the checks and balances of the other sefirot and takes possession of the person. We see this in the compulsive hero, and the nymphomaniac who are dominated respectively by a split off *Gevurah* and *Netzah*. When you enter the domain of these great beings, you must acknowledge their territory and power and tread most carefully. In ancient kabbalistic literature, they were seen as angels and demons with whom one negotiated a middle pillar passage to the higher gates of Heaven.

Besides these internal entities there are those who do not inhabit our psychological body, but draw near to it when they see a possibility of access or communication. These entities may be good, bad and indifferent. Some, for example, can be no more than curious, like dogs or cats that wish to see who has risen up from the physical world and into their time and space. These creatures range from stupid to highly intelligent. They have their place in existence and can be regarded as the flora and fauna of the lower yetziratic world. One treats them as one would animals and plants when out in the wild. Some are harmless and some otherwise. Fortunately, the psyche has an inbuilt sensitivity to danger if something sinister is provoked, but this usually only occurs if one's intention is tainted, as like is drawn to like. Here is the reason why sorcery or dealings with the lower spirits is forbidden in the Bible as is uninvited communication with the dead.

The logic behind such an injunction is that most people are frightened by the unknown, and this is a healthy reaction. One does not go into the jungle without a guide, or a great deal of preparation. To encounter the dead of this level is to contact people who have not yet become used to the idea that they no longer have a body, and this suggests that they have very little inner development. As such they will grasp at any opportunity to attach themselves to the living, which is a very unpleasant experience for the incarnated, as they feel the intrusion of someone else's will into their mind. Many people have been deeply disturbed by such a phenomenon, when playing with calling up the deceased. There is a kabbalistic procedure to contact those great spirits who no longer live on the Earth, but these operations are directed to a level well above the lower yetziratic stratum. Generally speaking the dead are best left alone. They will come of their own accord in a dream or a voice if there is something important to communicate.

If such an unpleasant encounter does occur, and it can, if all the precautions are not taken, such as ablution, setting up the Tree and asking permission, then centre in *Tiferet* at the solar plexus and go directly in consciousness up to *Keter* above the head, and pray for protection, or straight down to *Malkhut* and stamp the feet so as to earth as quickly as possible. Do the same thing if it occurs to someone else, and take them out to walk in the fresh air, preferably into a garden, or where there is an abundance of nature.

Along with all the creatures who inhabit this level of existence are those intelligences that wander about looking for trouble, and those who patrol the zone to police it for that very reason. Sometimes, during a kabbalistic practice, some of the villains will seek to disrupt the operation. It may be out of sheer devilment or a serious attempt to destroy the Work and discourage the participants. This usually occurs when a new group or inexperienced individual is setting up a channel to hold the flow of energies between the upper and lower worlds. Subtle diversions such as strange inner noises are used to interfere with the process of making a vessel. These distractions should be ignored and the opposing force blessed so that its energy is converted and incorporated within the operation, for evil dissolves when met by love. Actual voices are a more difficult matter, because they are not always obviously the Opposition. Sometimes, they will sound very like helpers who come to aid the Work, but after a time, something odd will be detected in their advice and directions. Experience will reveal how there is always a flaw in their recommendations or a perversity in their objectives. The remedy is to treat them with respect and ask them to withdraw in the Name of the Divine. If they do not, then terminate the operation and start again after a suitable time has elapsed, like another day.

This is how many students first contact evil directly. In most human beings there is a mixture of good and bad, with good predominating in the majority. In the non-physical worlds, the difference between the two is more marked, because the composition of a creature has a finer and less complex being. By this is meant that the essence of things becomes more apparent. We see this law very clearly in spiritual work, in that people become more transparently what they are, if one has eyes to see. The immoral man or woman who has developed the psyche, but gone to the devil, is decidedly evil. As Shakespeare said "Lilies that fester smell far worse than weeds". From here on we must be yet more watchful because the opposition, as well as the Companions of the Light, have a keen interest in our development. To gain the allegiance of a developed soul is a great prize to either side. Therefore, there begins, as the soul awakens to self-consciousness, a battle around the person's life which accounts for the many unusual events that take place on an individual's spiritual path.

To become self-conscious is to raise the focus of awareness into the triad of the soul. This means that one becomes directly involved with the great struggle between order and chaos that has gone on since Creation began. At this level, which is the ante-room to the first Heaven, an inexperienced person can be easily blocked or cast down, as the angels and demons within and without struggle to influence us. Ultimately, we have the final word, because here is the place where we exercise the gift of free will that was given to all human beings. To operate consciously in the field of the soul means one has much psychological power, and this can be used, as we alone choose. Thus no one else can be held responsible for our actions, although there will be those who seek to use our power for their own ends. This is where the issue of ethics arises, for unlike man-made laws that can change with newly elected governments, spiritual ethics remain constant because they are based upon Eternal laws. Their purpose is to protect and guide the individual on the Path at every level.

34. Integrity

The soul triad on the Tree is composed of *Tiferet*—Beauty and the self, *Gevurah*—Judgement, and *Hesed*—Mercy. It is the triad of deep emotion and the bridge between the upper and lower faces of the psychological Tree. This means it has access to the worlds of Action and the Spirit, that is the physical level of the particular and the cosmic dimension of Creation. It is a focus and vessel for receiving and imparting material from above to below and *vice versa*. As such it is a crucial triad and one that carries great responsibility. Normally, the soul operates as an unconscious organ of the psyche, but as the Kabbalist begins to work, so it becomes at first alert, and then awakened into consciousness. This brings a number of gifts, but also many problems.

Most people experience the soul as a tinge of conscience, a moment of deep insight or as a dim presence behind their daily thoughts, feelings and actions. Occasionally, direct access to the soul will be experienced when in love or during a crisis, perhaps while observing an emotionally moving scene or in a decisive point in some drama. Besides its qualities of truth, discernment and loving-kindness, it is also the seat of free will. By this is meant that while the ego cannot but react according to habit and the spirit be too remote to be controlled by the will, the soul can and is affected by the way we choose to live our lives as individuals. This is the area of free will which can follow the good or incline towards evil, because we can as wilfully abuse the Laws of Creation as accept and flow with them. The privilege of choice makes for much tension within a human being.

To illustrate by analogue; when an adolescent realises that he is no longer a child and can physically match his parents and teachers, he begins to disobey their rules, in order to prove his individuality. This, of course, is an illusion, because all people of this age go through a rebellious phase before recognising, after a number of disasters, that power means responsibility. It is the same on the path of inner growth when an individual becomes aware that he can use the gifts of the soul for selfish or selfless purposes. Strange as it may seem, you are not prevented from making use of your new powers, although a teacher or Providence will point out the unpleasant consequences that result from any actions contrary to the laws of existence. Like adolescents, some people ignore such advice and quite ruthlessly explore their capacity to exploit situations that often make others suffer. For a time nothing seems to happen, and they begin to believe that they are immune from cosmic reaction, often ignoring a warning, comment or incident that hints at what could happen if they do not stop. What they fail to understand is that they are being given time to reconsider what they are doing and realise they may jeopardize what they have acquired. God is merciful.

Usually there are three stages of warning given out by retribution before things become critical. The first is often a gentle tap to draw the attention that something is off the mark. If there is a positive response you can correct your course with little or no payment beyond remorse. The second stage is frequently in the form of a small accident or significant incident that jolts the conscience. This is sometimes enough to indicate that something must be done to retrieve the situation. If this is ignored, then a major event, like an illness or series of disasters brings your evil momentum to an abrupt halt. The scale of such events will range according to the degree of self-will and the influence the person has. These might be anything from losing a job or partner, to madness, and even death. The more evolved the person, the greater the responsibility and the response of providential justice, whose task it is to limit evil before it does too much damage to the souls of others and the Work. Not a few people who have perverted knowledge and powers acquired on the Path have lost all they had. As a once great occultist who sought fame and found disgrace remarked at the end of his lost life, "I wonder what it was all about?" He had forgotten the aim of his tradition and served the god of his own ego.

To avoid such tragic calamities there have always been systems of ethics given out by spiritual traditions. The Jew has the Ten Commandments, the Christian the Lord's Prayer and the Buddhist the Eightfold Path. In essence they are always the same. At first sight they appear to relate to ordinary life situations, but if we look closer, we will see that they apply to the higher worlds also. Thus, for example, you do not murder another's soul, which is quite possible for someone with occult power. Nor do you steal or commit adultery at this level, meaning that you do not take for yourself that which belongs to God, or improperly mix those elements that should not be related, like black magic. Neither do you bear false witness, because this cuts one off from the truth, or covet another's spiritual properties. These ethics are designed not only to give guidelines through the highly volatile world of the psyche, but to safeguard against the intrusion of evil.

In the line "Deliver us from evil" from the prayer of Joshua ben Miriam of Nazareth is the implication that you will be faced by such an encounter. Now this prayer was given to people already on the Way, that means who were already operating at the soul level. Thus, they were of interest to and approached by those demonic elements that seek to disrupt the Work. This is clearly demonstrated by the betrayal of Judas, perhaps the cleverest of the disciples, whom the text says the devil entered, although an esoteric view of the relationship between Jesus and this apparently evil student, is that Judas consciously took on the responsibility of the betrayal, because no one else would carry out the necessary role. Ethics are spiritual conduct especially under adverse conditions. Thus a person on the Path is tested by Satan to see if his being is sound and his faith true. This occasionally involves some strange situations in which a person must sometimes act out the reverse of a commonly understood code, as many mystics have done.

The approach of real evil usually only occurs when the soul is awakened to its potential of free will. Prior to this, most of us behave according to our code of upbringing or acquired reflex actions, as any intense course of self-observation will reveal. However, when you are in a situation in which you can actually influence events by your inner knowledge, then a conflict can arise between what you would like and what you ought to do. To complicate things further as a test, the issue is often projected onto the external situation or people by the shadow side of our psyche, which can block out the light of honesty with subtle ploys like blame and justification. This is the work of our interior Satan. In matters of the spirit, the higher Luciferic element offers apparently well-considered advice that can be disarmingly convincing, like knowing best, if one does not check it against a simple spiritual truth, such as not interfering in another's life. Here is where the Ten Commandments and the Eightfold Path act as a bastion against the Luciferic distortion of reality which is witnessed in so many brilliant but deviant teachings about spiritual matters which do not free but imprison the soul. Many people mistake psychic charisma for the spirit. Real spirituality is simple and its essential principles are designed to support and protect. True ethics are self-evident truths that need no detailed explanation because they speak directly to the soul in any situation, no matter how complex it may seem on the surface. Conscience knows what is true and false. The soul possesses this capacity as a gift, unless it is seduced by evil. Kabbalistic ethics are concerned with inner morality, but they also relate to conduct in the world. Thus your integrity becomes a living expression of the root meaning of the word 'integration' between that which is below and above, within and without.

The practice of integrity is vital to a spiritual tradition, for it not only safeguards the individual, but the Work. Over the last few centuries Kabbalistic ideas have been stolen and adulterated by those who only sought magical powers, with the result that an image of dangerous hotchpotch has overlaid the real purpose of Kabbalah. Because of this, the tradition has fallen into disrepute amongst Jews who see it as a degenerate form of occultism. Thus, by the last century the reputation of Kabbalah had fallen from high respect during its most original period in Medieval times to a superstitious repetititon of magical formulae. This happened because the Work was not protected in the right way. It is not secrecy that guards the tradition, but correct conduct, and if this is not present, then people do not find the door to the inner path which is their birthright. The lack of real spirituality today amongst clergy has made many Jews and Christians turn to the Eastern religions for their esoteric instruction. This is sad because they have within their own Western traditions all the higher knowledge and methods they need for the development of the Occidental psyche and spirituality.

Not all ignorance and immorality is to be found in the outer world. There are those on the fringe of the Work who are referred to as noted as "Wolves in sheep's clothing!" They can be people of relatively high inner development who have all the appearance of being on the Path, but in fact have left its narrow way. Many such gurus gather around them students who seek similar powers themselves; those who come are under the spell of other-worldliness or those looking for real knowledge. The characteristics of such dark teachers are their preoccupation with superiority, exclusiveness, their own mastery, absolute obedience and with keeping up the mystery. If their position is ever doubted then there is inevitably a crisis in which they apply psychic and social pressure. Their word is law. They are usually fiercely supported without question by those dependent on them.

Sometimes it takes much experience to separate the genuine teacher from the false, because the latter often possess fragments of Truth. One test is the level of ethics applied. A sound but strict instructor will acknowledge a student's right to disagree and allow him to depart with goodwill and perhaps a recommendation to another school. A false instructor will assert that his is the only way and seek to discredit any other tradition. This clearly is not the esoteric view which recognises that all truly spiritual ways lead to God. Often such a leader is the idol of his students and stands in the way of their progress. Sometimes it is 'the teaching' that is held up to be the sole mode of enlightenment. This is another Luciferic device to lead inexperienced aspirants into a gilded cage. Such 'teachings' cause psychological blindness and spiritual pride. One hallmark of this kind of school is the lack of humility and personal conscience. Often there is a strange collective sterility and conformity about the manner, dress and lives of the teacher and students. The converse is a real company of seekers in the presence of intelligent direction, love, discipline and integrity which allows for group and individual progress. Here we have the qualities of the soul and the mark of Companions of the Light.

35. Companions

When going on a long, arduous and dangerous journey, it is always wise to have good companions. However, such people are not easily found. Normally, we feel that our closest relationships are with our blood family and in ordinary life this is true for most people. Certainly up until recent times, even members of a family who did not get on personally still retained a strong relationship. The social and economic revolutions of the twentieth century have changed much of this pattern in the Western world, and so people do not always remain in their families, or even the social groups they were brought up in. Many, because of education, opportunity and travel leave what was in effect their village, be it in the countryside or in the city, never to return, except on visits to the old home. This is particularly true of those of the post-1960 generations who wandered throughout the world looking for a spiritual alternative to the materialistic solution that has brought much physical comfort, but with it many social and psychological problems.

Seen on a large scale, mankind is on the move. It has, in the more economically advanced countries tried both the extremes of a political ideal as a way of life and found them wanting. Young and not so young Americans, for example, are no longer convinced that the possession of wealth brings happiness, and nor do the deeper thinking Russians believe that the Soviet system is the answer to life's dilemmas; hence the dissident movement. After a long search, many sensitive and intelligent people give up because they find no alternative to the rat race and immerse themselves in passing the time in many games that range from the infantile to the various sophisticated forms of amusement that avoid the obscure thoughts of ageing and death.

A few seekers still keep looking. They follow different trails trying to find the rainbow's end. They read of it in books of which there are now legion, and they hear about it through hearsay, but rarely do they make direct contact with anyone who is actually working on the spiritual path. There are many who believe they are walking the Way, but it is soon clear from the style they live their lives that this is not so, and that their driving motivation is ego. This can manifest in personal power or the need to be special, the wish to be led, or the desire for the unusual. It can even be fashionable to be seen in spiritual work, as it was with many, like the 'Flower Children' and guru movements of the last two decades. The residue of this period is still with us, in that many people who are no longer young and idealistic are now deeply enmeshed in the realities of life. Most have families and pursue professions, and many have forgotten the promise of that epoch of awakening. A few, however, still yearn for the inner life, even though they have lost faith in charismatic leaders and suspect that many so-called spiritual organisations are either power- or money-orientated. This creates a profound loneliness and sometimes a deep despair.

If one does contact a true tradition, it is usually the result of much work and the fact that Providence will respond and help the genuine seeker. A book turning up at a critical moment, an apparently chance meeting or the realisation that a certain acquaintance has an esoteric connection brings a sense of surprise and wonder. Such moments are momentous, because they can only happen when the individual is ready. At any other time the book would not be seen, the meeting missed and the casual hint by the old friend go unnoticed. However, when the person is awake enough to spot and take up the lead, many new things begin to happen.

After the initial stages of confusion and conflict, as you extract yourself from your old life, which sometimes means separating yourself psychologically, if not physically, from your family and friends, you enter into a companionship of the spirit. This does not mean that you reject your relatives or cut off from old friendships, although this does occasionally happen, but that you form a completely new set of relationships with yourself as the intermediary between your various worlds. This echoes the actual situation at a higher level. The effect, if properly carried out, and not used as an excuse to escape worldly responsibility, is to act as a mediator between Earth and Heaven to help raise the level of the society or circle you live in, as you impart, often unseen, the spirit you have received from what are sometimes called the Companions of the Light.

The notion of the *Havarim* or Companions is an ancient one and is recognised in every tradition. In Kabbalah they have been called by various names down the centuries. At one time such groups were called 'Those who Know'; at another 'The Wise-Hearted'; at another 'Masters of Service'. They have been named 'The Ones of Understanding' and 'Those who Reap the Field'. This last title perhaps gives us a clear picture of their aim, in that they work in the world, even though their orientation is heavenward. However, before one enters fully into such a company there are several stages.

The first is the probationary period. This may last a few weeks or many years, depending on the commitment and quality of the work done by the individual. This is monitored by the next level whose members are not yet initiates, but who are deeply involved in the Work. What constitutes an initiate has often been debated, but the truth of the matter is that when a person is prepared to devote the whole of life unconditionally to the Work, he can be considered an initiate. No part-time Kabbalist exists. It must come first. Everything is centred round the Work. Personal and public crises may come and go, but the Work must be continued. Nothing can take precedence over it. This has been said by many spiritual masters, and not a few have died for the sake of the Work. It is a hard line of demarcation, but humanity has benefited from such commitments, as the life's work and death of both Jesus and Socrates bear witness. Such constancy is vital to hold the chain of a tradition and keep the flow between the upper and lower worlds. When going on a long, arduous and dangerous journey it is reassuring to have such reliable companions. One's life may depend on them at some time.

The companionship of the Spirit begins with the first contact of someone on the Way. From here, it develops into a deep friendship that no ordinary link or relationship can match. For example, people may not see each other for years, and yet they will talk, when they meet, as if they had parted only yesterday, because the level they communicate upon does not belong to ordinary time. Over the years such relationships develop to a point that there has to be no immediate contact. Indeed, some grow deeper in distance. Gradually, there emerges a network of companions who are not only good company, but act as mutual watchers over the progress of oneself, other individuals and groups. United, several such people can form not only a greater vessel of receptivity to the higher worlds, but act as a bastion against any onslaughts from evil, at either the physical or subtler levels. Such support is occasionally vital in certain crises.

Usually a group is centred round a tutor or teacher. The first focus is the most common, because a tutor is often a senior student who just transmits the theory of the tradition and shows how to carry out its practices. A teacher is another matter. This is an advanced person who actually has the power to make a living connection for the group between those below and those above. The rest of the group is usually divided into beginners, who are learning how to learn, those who are translating the study into reality, those who are aware of what is involved, those who know but have not yet committed themselves fully and those who have formed an interior core within the main group. Thus, there is an internal hierarchy that has the possibility of every rung of the ladder of spiritual evolution from the probationer to the Messiah, if one were fortunate enough to be in the right place at the right time. There are, of course, the sub-divisions of personal resonance and things shared. Thus, the usual social and professional affinities generate fellowship, love affairs and even marriage, although like all human activities, such relationships can create the usual complications. These, however, should be handled by the Kabbalist with a deeper understanding and be put to use for self-development and service to the Work.

The presence of a group of companions is vital in spiritual work, because it brings a sense of scale and balance. Many an individual has been saved from slipping off the Path by the check rope of their companions. To be alone is sad enough, but to climb the Holy Mountain without a guide, or at least a friend is to tempt trouble. Therefore, you learn to cherish your spiritual companions, even though you may sometimes be in conflict with them, which occasionally happens, for even groups have their crisis as they undergo changes from time to time. Here, we begin to consider the wider and deeper implications of our study, for while we will not deal in detail with the work of a school (that is another book), we will go on to look at the next stage of contacting the Companions of the Light in the upper worlds, who gather round and watch over any serious enterprise that is being carried out below on Earth. This will give us an insight into the connection and continuity of the kabbalistic tradition through time and space.

36. Upper Room

A kabbalistic meeting is a place where a working group comes together to discuss or practise Kabbalah. It usually occurs in a space especially prepared for the occasion. This may be no more than the slight alteration of a domestic room to make it into a sacred spot or a special chamber specifically designed for the purpose that is used for nothing else. There is no general rule, except there be a focus of attention upon either an altar or a symbol of the tradition. The chair of the tutor is secondary and must never be more than that. Seen in Tree terms, the tutor sits at *Tiferet* with the point of aim at *Keter*, the Crown of the group Tree. In this way there is no identification with even a teacher as anything more than a place of interconnection, because each student must make his or her own interior communication to the Crown.

The form of the meeting, like the setting, can be varied. This depends on the time and place and the conditions prevailing. In one period there may be no more than a brief format, in another time and place a complex ritual to meet the needs and possibilities of the age. For example, the service in the Temple of Jerusalem was highly formal, with prayers, music and sacrifices, while, no doubt, the meetings in the small apartment rooms of Gerona in medieval Spain, were probably more like university seminars. Some meetings in 16th-century Galilee closely resembled a seance.

Every age has its particular work to do, and every group its own peculiar task. Thus, no two groups are ever the same, although they may be branches of the same line. However, there are certain things they do share. The first is the reason why they gather together. If they are not convened in order to serve God, then they are not kabbalistic groups. Anything less reduces them to low magic or worse, if they seek only to exploit the forces they invoke. Another thing that is shared is the high degree of honesty that is to be expected. This level of integrity should be the norm; indeed any deception will automatically separate an individual from the group. This does not have to be implemented by anyone but occurs spontaneously according to inner laws. Without openness nothing can flow up or down or between the members. This does not mean discretion cannot be exercised; that is quite different, although it requires maturity and some conscious development to discern and practise the difference.

Many groups meet once a week. This is a natural rhythm. Some members might contact each other on other days, but that is according to necessity and inclination. Once a month a group might meet just to meditate or perform some ceremony that cannot be carried out during an ordinary workshop meeting. What is about to be described can be executed during a weekly occasion. Let it be a model that can be adapted to local conditions.

Let us assume that a group meeting has started off with a silent coming together. After this comes the evocation of the Tree and the Names of God. By the time the petition for the Holy Presence to manifest during the meeting has been asked for, everyone should have moved out of the ego state into the consciousness of the self. After a moment's pause in silence, the working session can begin with a discussion of the current exercise. Let us assume that the week's study has been the detection of help from above that often goes unnoticed. One person might speak about being directed out of his usual way in order to meet, by apparent accident, an old friend in need. Another may tell the story of how she was aware of a softening hand on her shoulder while writing a particularly severe letter—it was not sent. Yet another might describe how he came into possession of a much needed book which was out of print. A secondhand copy had been found in a junk shop where he had been looking for a mirror. A discussion could develop out of these examples, and slowly as other incidents are collected, a pattern begins to emerge. It might seem that in many cases a specific need is met or a certain danger warded off. All the events pivot upon a moment in time when the juxtaposition of spiritual, pyschological and physical conditions are adjusted to achieve a definite effect. Out of this come many questions. These are collected and collated until they are formulated into a concise set of enquiries. The group is now ready to approach the Companions in the upper room.

Tradition has it that whenever two or more are gathered together in the name of the Holy Spirit, then there will be a corresponding gathering above to listen and assist those below. Sometimes members of a group who are in a higher state actually hear and see these beings quite spontaneously. In this operation, an attempt consciously to perceive them will be made. Drawing everyone in the room into full attention, the leader then proceeds to raise the communal level. This is done by taking the group into an awareness of the body, up through the preoccupation of the ego and into consciousness of the self. Then, working in concert, they hover above the roof of the house, before rising up into a high and Holy Place of meeting. There each person is asked to visualise all those present in a domed chamber with a hole in the ceiling. After this scene is established, everyone is requested to look around with his mind's eye and see who else is there besides those they are acquainted with.

Many people discover that there are persons present that they do not know sitting next to them, and then again sometimes they catch the face or voice of their spiritual teacher who greets them with a characteristic remark. While this phenomenon is interesting in itself, of greater importance is the discussion going on between the individuals at the centre of the circle. They sit directly under the aperture in the ceiling, through which can be seen the firmament of stars. A light percolates down into the room to illuminate the inner group, who conduct a discussion on the questions posed. The group just listens. In Kabbalah the inner circle are sometimes called 'Members of the Academy on High'. The particular rank of those involved in the discussion, however, would depend on the calibre of the group.

After listening to the various reflections, which usually develop from what has been talked about below, the upper meeting is thrown open for questions. Here, the earthly tutor invites each person to ask his questions, and others that might arise. A period of silence is observed to allow the answers to be given, although not everyone in the group below will receive a reply. People can lose the contact. When the process is complete, and the heightened consciousness can no longer be held, the tutor will sense that it is time to close the session. After thanking the Companions above for their help, the tutor then slowly brings the group down by stages to the house and back into the room. All present stamp their feet to earth themselves after opening their eyes.

When everyone has fully re-entered his body, observations are called for by the tutor. Different people report on the answers they received. These are silently pondered for a few minutes before any discussion should begin. The analysis should generate more questions which leads to the development of the theme that is being explored. In some cases an enormous amount of material, say about the nature of the soul, may have been received, and this is shared with those who could not see or hear so clearly. Indeed, there may be some present who did not even get off the ground and sat in frustrated silence wondering if the others were just fantasising. This situation can happen for many reasons. A person may not be physically well, under psychological duress; he may not yet have learnt the technique of lètting go of sensual experience, or he may have been blocked from ascending because he was not in a suitable state. After the group has explored the experience to its full, new conclusions may emerge. Occasionally, if the company is in a particularly good state, they may return to the upper chamber and have a second and deeper session with their normally unseen instructors. This exercise must not, however, be carried out too often lest it lose its potency by over familiarity.

At the end of the meeting the Tree is descended, finishing with an appropriate prayer or text.

After the candles have been blown out and the various duties, such as who will buy the next week's bread and wine, who will write up the evening's notes and who will make the coffee and wash up, have been dealt with, the formal meeting is dissolved. From this point on, until all go home, the talk can be personal so as to allow individuals to enter the earthly world and relate socially. This is carried out whilst still retaining the inner mood of the meeting, which will be taken afterwards into ordinary life. Thus, each person always keeps an inner connection with the other members of the group, and the Companions of the upper room.

This exercise like the others described, is one of many used in Kabbalah. Obviously such operations must be executed with great care, with checks made on those who participate in them, to make sure they can cope with such experiences. An epileptic fit, for example, can be triggered by such a high intake of energy. Generally speaking people are only allowed to take part in these excursions when there is adequate precaution below and protection from above. This is one of the tutor's responsibilities, besides watching over individual development, co-ordinating the group and acting as liaison officer between the worlds. In the next chapter we examine the long-term effect of this kind of work.

37. Chariot

Over a period of time the accumulative effect of kabbalistic work brings about a transformation within a group. One of the products of this change is the formation of a vehicle that can carry consciousness out of the ordinary state and into realms that are beyond the capability of most individuals. This is because the processes of inner development that co-ordinate the aspects of the psyche in the individual also form a collective organism within the group. This subtle chariot, as it was called, is a yetziratic vehicle that can bring back something of the higher worlds as well as take people there. Let us look at its structure and dynamics so as to perceive its nature and substance.

Taking the group as the material and model of the chariot we can see, for example, how its *Malkhut*, or physical base is established by meeting in the same place at the same time. Over the years the fabric of the house, used for study and practice becomes saturated with the kabbalistic actions, emotions and thoughts generated and experienced there. It also builds up a reservoir of psychological energy that forms a detectable field in the room. This strengthens each time a meeting or operation is carried out, and thus, the chamber begins to become a vessel for the fine residue of the upper worlds, which gradually accumulates and creates a distinct atmosphere of a sanctuary. This phenomenon will deepen over time to produce a remarkable effect in that whoever enters the room will be, unless he is sick or spiritually dead, inwardly lifted by a concentrated presence of Spirit such as sacred places have. Hence, the elemental structure is refined to such a degree that it is no longer just an ordinary room, but a physical connection to the levels above.

The *Yesod* of the chariot is made up by the ordinary ego level of the group. After a time group members, like any other collection of people, will begin to relate. At first there will be individual connections; then associations through shared interests. Later as deeper personal and spiritual relationships develop, the group will

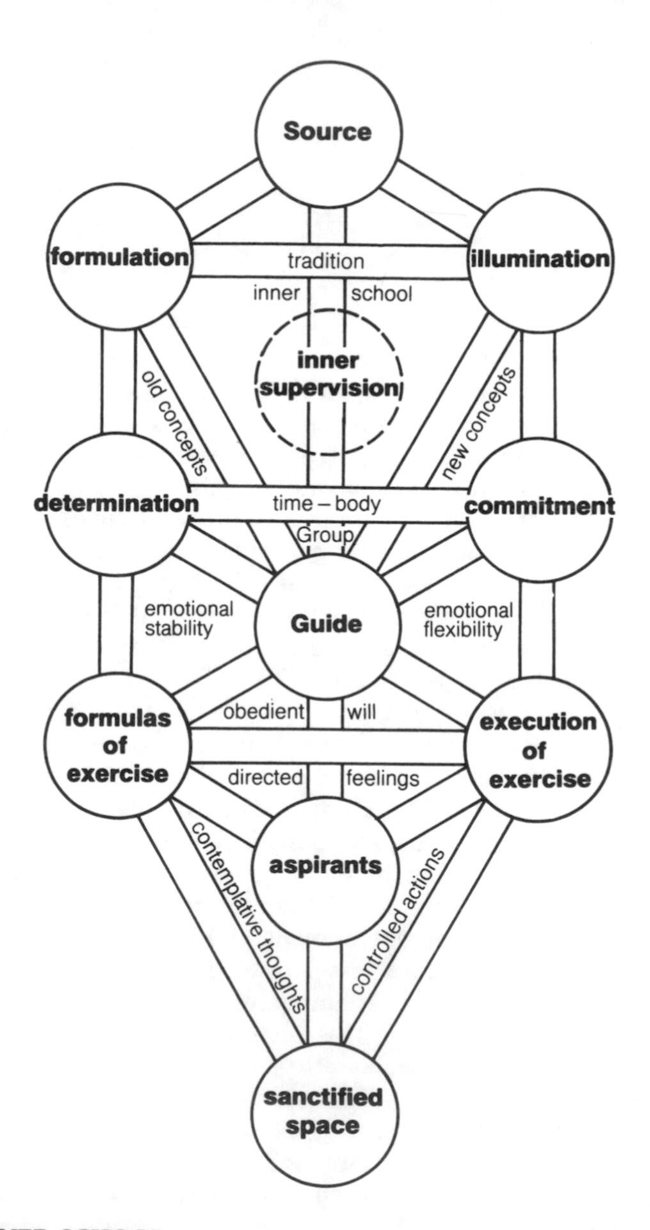

11. **INNER SCHOOL**

Here is the group Tree in action as the structure is invested with consciousness during an exercise. As the triads of the Lower Face are held and raised by directed effort, so access to the higher levels becomes possible. This opens contact through the central sefirah with all members of the group – past, present and absent – and the level of inner supervision that links the school to the whole Kabbalistic tradition.

slowly divide itself into the doers, feelers and thinkers. Moreover, within these three sub-triads, there will be those who always tend to take the initiative and those who will hold back, making up the extrovert and introvert division of the lower face of the group chariot. As the organism begins to emerge, the phenomenon of group identification will appear as each member integrates with the others, in memory, when they are not together. In time this will generate a comradeship such as is found on board a ship; and this analogue is not so far removed, if one considers a group as an ark floating on the waters of life.

As the lower face of the chariot Tree is slowly riveted together by shared experience to form the central *Yesod* of the company, so there begins the emergence of the different levels. The first is quite easily recognised when a stranger comes to a meeting. Initially, there is the tribal sense of the outsider, even though the much welcomed person might be from another group or spiritual discipline. This reveals the yesodic image of the group and its particular character, and limitations. Without guidance this collective ego could become an exclusive sect clique. A kabbalistic group is expected to avoid this pitfall and raise a quite natural communal feeling up to the level of spirituality. This is done by applying the group consciousness to reflective observation about itself and its performance regarding the Work. This is not a mutual therapy, but a process in which everything discussed is related to the principles of the Tree. Thus, there is built up an objective working method and trust that holds the personal tendencies of all the individual egos in obedience to principles. Under this discipline, the *Yesod* of the group becomes a stable foundation and reflection of whatever might be going on collectively.

The gradual education of the group's *Yesod* by the techniques of ritual, devotion and contemplation produces, with diligent effort, a highly sensitive instrument which registers every action, feeling and thought in the group, so that the doer begins to comprehend the thinker, and the feeler the thinker and doer, and *vice versa*. This creates possibilities denied to the individual on his own, for it grants insight into other types of experience, and enables even the newest student a glimpse of what it is like further along the path and what qualities might be needed. A group *Yesod*, moreover, facilitates a greater resolution of what is seen in the Worlds above and below. Its wider image, like that of a great telescope, gives a larger view than that of which most, if not all, members of the group are capable.

The next level to be developed is that which lies beyond the threshold defined by hodian theory and netzahian practice. It grants access to a higher level of consciousness than the ordinary mind. This is often noted, in that people who come to the group in a depressed state or with some mundane preoccupation, are usually elevated out of it. Indeed, some soon realise after a meeting has begun that they were just immersed in ego problems. The level of awakening is the weekly meeting itself, and is the place that most of the members should be, at least once, during the session. Alas, many oscillate between *Yesod* and *Tiferet*, so that when the majority are below the *Hod-Netzah* line, the level of the group is noticeably low. This is usually the point when the tutor introduces some stimulus to bring the group back into the triad of awakening again, that is *Hod, Netzah* and *Tiferet*.

At any given moment, a member of the group may be in one of three distinct levels. For example, a person's attention may be absent, as they consider some worldly problem. Such a state almost excludes them from the group because they are there only physically. The second condition is to be so yesodically involved in discussion that one is quite unaware of what is actually happening. This can only be observed by those in an awakened state who are really present and in touch with whatever is flowing down into it from above. The fourth level of the soul constitutes what is called the 'time-body' of the group. By this is meant, the subtle organism that has evolved over the years, which joins all its members, past and present, near and absent, in a union of love, discipline and truth; that is the three sefirot of the soul triad. This organism is the delicate chariot-cum-vessel a group can make, form and create for itself by conscious effort to collect, fuse and integrate their Work into a tangible form. Here is the group's upper room where it may meet with and welcome its Inner Teacher, as well as contact others who are absent or dead.

In kabbalistic terms the soul level is the gateway into the higher Worlds, because it is not attached to the physical realm, except by its connection with the place where the three lower Worlds meet. This triad is the *Merkabah* or vehicle in which all that has been acquired by the group is held in yetziratic form ready for use each week. Such a chariot can exist for decades, even though a group may have long dispersed. Indeed, when a group that has not met for some years is reconvened, it usually finds that nothing has changed, despite their physical ageing, and that all can enter the collective chariot as before and make use of its facilities. Of course, in time such vehicles, like their physical counterparts do become redundant, so that over the centuries the form that was applicable during, say the eleventh century, is no longer as efficient as a new model. That is why Kabbalah periodically changes its mode of presentation, as in the twelve-hundreds, when the Babylonian system was remodelled in Gerona to meet the crisis between faith and reason in Spain and France. Every culture and epoch has its own problems and solutions.

The development of such vehicles is essential not only for a group, but also for the Tradition, because through it the Teaching is passed on. By this I mean that actual experience of the higher worlds transforms theory and practice into reality. Thus, there can be moments when everyone present at a meeting is lifted up and enters a higher state. This is possible because they are carried by the momentum of the group's chariot. Many novices have perceived for themselves, if only for an instant, the cosmic insights that they have read about. This can only happen within the safety of a group with its disciplined structure and support. One such example was when a group, which was composed of newcomers as well as senior students, was shown a shaft of golden light falling vertically through a ceiling from a great height out of a deep blue vault of sky and into a small crowded room to leave an indelible impression of the existence of Grace. At another time, a probationer, not given to visions, saw a great eagle floating high over the meeting place. This is a symbol of the Holy Spirit. Whilst on another evening some members of a group became suddenly aware of other beings in the room, who were watching over the meeting as if from another dimension.

The development of the inner vehicle of a kabbalistic group requires great effort on everyone's part. For instance, each member can act as a changing element within the meeting and take up various roles in the structure and dynamics of its Tree. Sometimes, one can actually perceive who are the pillars, and which triads or sefirot are being occupied or acted out by those present. Occasionally, the whole working scheme can come into view and one can know at what level the group is, at that moment, as it holds a position, according to its centre of spiritual gravity. If a group can develop and maintain a high degree of conscious interaction, then even more can be given and received from above. This kind of work requires a commitment in which no member ever falls below the level of the soul triad during a meeting. Such a standard can only be achieved after many years, when each individual has developed within him or herself a stable and receptive personal vehicle to act as a conscious instrument between the Worlds. This is the theme of our next chapter.

38. Instrument

We have seen how a group develops and integrates its various levels, so it is with an individual. The chief difference, however, is that the group works on a different scale and operates from a less refined base to begin with. Like the group, an individual seeks to become a vessel that can receive and impart what is brought into its range. This is contingent on how far and deep the person is prepared to go in Kabbalah. Everyone has his limits, although there are some whose ambition exceeds their capacity at a given time. To develop the higher levels before the lower, and so skip in-between stages, is to court disaster. Every step must be filled before the influence of the higher worlds can be transmitted consistently. Indeed, to maintain a constant link between Heaven and Earth, without a graduated connection, would burn one out. Only those who have made, formed and created these inner bridges can carry a heavy spiritual charge for any period of time. To try is to strain those connections that have been made and so impair the levels that are operational. This is the warning of the tragic Talmudic story of the four rabbis who entered Paradise. One died, one went mad and one lost faith. Only the last returned safely.

In order to proceed with a degree of security, all the theories and practices given must be carefully learnt and carried out over a long period under wise supervision. In time the seven lower halls, as they are traditionally called, are systematically entered and a balanced position is established in each. This process follows the ascent up the Tree of the psyche, and though you may touch and even have a tentative hold on one level, there will be many moments when you have to drop level, so as to correct a function or dissolve some habit that has crept in to distort a lower triad. A watch over the whole inner Tree has to be constantly maintained, so that a balanced progression in the refinement of the inner chariot can continue safely. When a certain degree of development has been obtained, there begins the connection and building of the

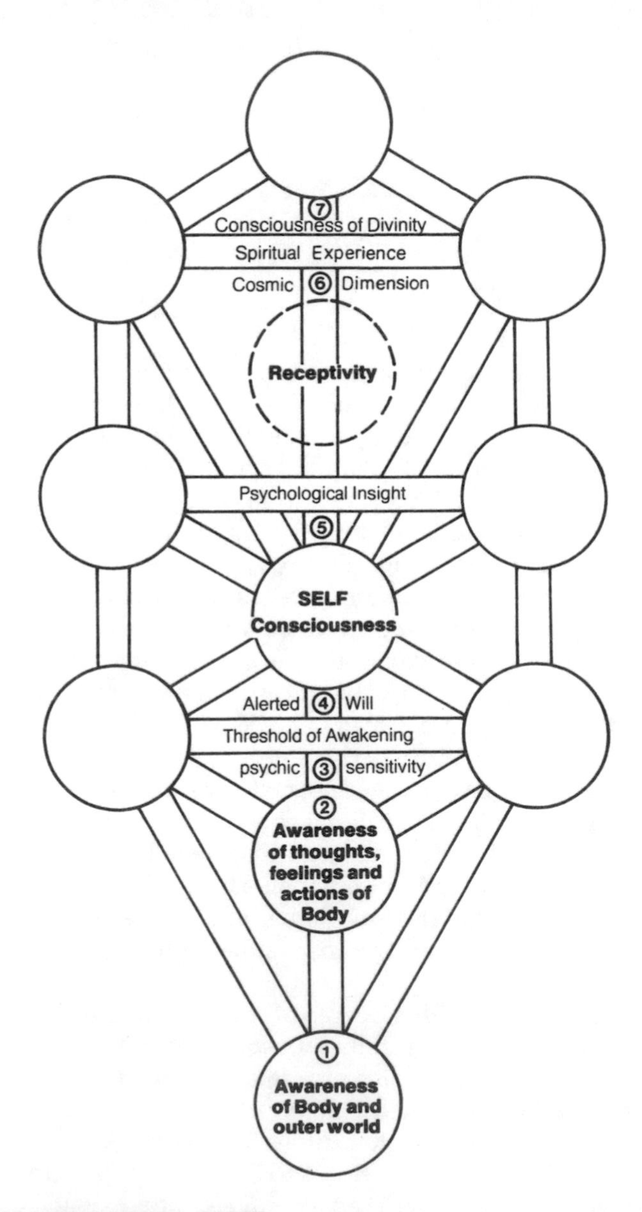

12. PSYCHOLOGICAL STEPS

The tuning of the psyche follows the laws of the Tree. Thus as each level is progressively aroused from its optimum state into a greater consciousness, the whole psyche begins to resonate and become more receptive than the mere sum of its parts. This enables the instrument to be sensitive to both inner and outer phenomena and to great and small events simultaneously, and thus to give a deep picture of the World of Formation that acts as a bridge between the physical and spiritual.

next chariot of the spiritual body. However, before this can occur certain stages must be passed through.

We have seen how an increased physical awareness reveals the four elements at work in our bodies, and how through their intelligence we may become conscious of the elemental world about us. We may also, through this elemental connection, gain access to our organic bodies, and so receive insights into the mechanical, organic, chemical and electronic realms that operate beneath our skin. Observations of these levels are of immense use, because by analogy, we can ascertain the nature and state of our psychological functions. The ability to switch worlds by conscious will is a vital skill in the Work, and much effort should be devoted to shifting levels between body and psyche. In time we should be able to pinpoint and relate parallel levels in each body, like the organs reflecting feelings and *vice versa*, or the ego working off the habits programmed by the autonomous nervous system.

The next stage is to integrate the ego and its adjacent triads of thinking, feeling and action. If well trained, then *Yesod* will function like a first class manager watching over the various functions and balancing them with great skill. The yesodic ego shares the same point of cognition with the body's *Daat* or Knowledge, and so co-operation between these two will be valuable practice for the similar, but higher communication between the *Daat* of the psyche and the *Yesod* of the Spirit. The third level is that of the feeling triad which doubles as the place of willingness. Here a high degree of sensitivity enables the psyche's functions to operate and so help in the general co-ordination of the lower face of the psyche, which is completed by the fourth level of awakening. When all the triads involved are within the range of an alert ego, then their combined power fuses into a concerted capability that ordinary fragmented consciousness knows nothing of, except in a crisis or a moment of Grace. The lucidity associated with this state of gadlut alertness should become the norm for the Kabbalist. Buddhists call it mindfulness.

The extending range of interior awareness brings into the light of the self at *Tiferet*, all the triads of emotional and intellectual complexes. These psychological aggregates of memories, reactions and stimuli, after a period of Work, become increasingly interrelated instead of being randomly triggered and associated by circumstance. As such they operate more like a well-organised company rather than a rabble. This allows for the accomplishment of things impossible to the undisciplined psyche. Interior or exterior problems can be handled with greater ease, because the resources that can deal with them are not only more readily available, but can work with increased power. Thus, like an integrated group of people, the psyche develops its capacity to act and be receptive in the wider range made available by the improved communication between its normally divided parts. Some call this state 'being together'.

The soul triad which hovers above the centre of the Tree becomes, with the increased integration of the surrounding triads, more directly involved with everyday life instead of just being an unconscious conscience. It can actively participate in the lower face by working through the self of *Tiferet*. This means it can transmit what it has received at its level, and inform the yesodic ego. An example of this is when a man picks up that something is wrong in a situation. If it is correct, he can generate conscience in others by the presence of soul consciousness, without interfering in the process that is going on. In this way he may create conditions for self realisation without anyone, but those on the same level, knowing. In some cases people just start behaving decently because the person is near them. For obvious reasons this exercise can only be executed properly by someone who has no personal desire for power. It will be remembered that the soul triad is the place of testing and temptation.

The sixth level of the psychological chariot is the triad of the Spirit. This cannot be fully developed without passing through an awareness and integration of all the lower levels. Its unconscious presence is sometimes perceived in children and simple people. To possess a conscious spirituality is quite another matter. To operate at this level requires that person voluntarily to submit to the deepest kind of Work. However, this signifies more than just effort. It means that the ego is quiescent so that all that is personal no longer matters. This does not, in Kabbalah, suggest that the self is without will, but that one does what one is told in obedience, although to whom or what is important. In this tradition only God's Will counts; the rest is but advice. When a true spiritual submission is made, then the dark glass of *Daat*, the sefirah of Knowledge, begins to clear and the way to the Divine opens. Such a breakthrough can come because of long or intense work, or through an act of Grace. Its quality is cosmic, in that the soul is seen set against a celestial background rather than in an earthly context. One begins to shift worlds, and so the *Daat* of psychological Knowledge becomes the spiritual *Yesod* of Creation. The man who suddenly saw all the lives of the people in a supermarket as patterns was perceiving through this level.

This conversion of state in the sixth hall is the prelude to the seventh, which completes the psychological organism. Here, we are told, one comes in direct contact with the Divine Presence as one touches at the *Keter* of Formation, the *Tiferet* of Creation and the *Malkhut* of Emanation. [See diagram 4]. At this point where the three upper Worlds meet, another transformation occurs, as the whole of the psychological Tree becomes not only integrated, but suffused with Divine Light and the Wind of the Spirit. In such a state the psychological organism becomes unified and so no longer split in sections by its functions and levels. Like a perfectly healthy physical body, it can, in this state carry out unearthly manoeuvres, such as exploring history or observing distant places. However, while these powers and others come with the maturity of the psychological body, their prime purpose is to be agents between the upper and lower worlds, so as to serve events in either. Clearly the possession of such a vehicle demands the highest integrity of the individual, but then that is what is meant by the word. If this is lost then the unity of being is broken and a shattering occurs, often with tragic consequences. This is a crucial point of development, for here is where Lucifer especially seeks to tempt people to fall, like himself, from Grace. Thus, the greater the height, the more the individual is tested so as to be proved that he or she is able to use their gifts responsibly.

As we have seen, the development of the psychological organism is a long and arduous matter. It may take many lifetimes to accomplish completion, although it is possible in one, if the commitment is there and it serves Providence's purpose. For most of us who slowly plod up on the Way, it is the gradual acquisition of an instrument that is of enormous potential. A fully developed psyche can fly higher than any rocket and penetrate deeper into the nether regions than any bore hole. Its range extends beyond the most powerful microscope and largest telescope. In vision, it can wander around the solar system and perceive, through imagination, the smallest processes in matter. However, of greater importance is the fact that it is possible to enter Paradise or even Heaven while still on the Earth. Mystics have known and exploited this reality over the centuries, and not a few Kabbalists have experienced during life what most of mankind only glimpses at the moments of birth and death.

Such a possibility is open to anyone who works along a path of self-development, but few unfortunately know what they see or hear when these moments of vision occur as the dark glass brightens just enough to allow a flash of the upper worlds. It is one thing to visit a higher realm and another to realise what has been revealed, as many students discover when they read the writings of the mystics or go there themselves. The visionary must also possess knowledge.

39. Vision

In order to understand visions we must first be clear about illusions, so as to be able to tell the difference. As a general definition, it could be said that illusions are subjective projections of our own or of others, while visions are objective and are impressions of things that exist in their own right. A simple example of this would be an imaginary anxiety that something bad has happened to someone, only to find it was a projection of our own anger or fear, as against the sense that something odd has occurred at home, and later to discover that it has been burnt down. The latter is only too real in concrete terms, while the former may be no more than a fantasy.

Another characteristic of illusion is that it often has no order, in that whilst it may have its own kind of pattern, it has no relation to what is really going on or connection with any kind of integrated reality. By this is meant that it does not fit into the general scheme of creation, except as one of the elements of chaos or separation that seek to make a universe of their own, at the centre of which lies the ego of the maker. Many people live out their lives in this manner. Taken to its extreme, are insanity and criminality because there is no relationship to the laws of reality or society. When penetrating into the depths of our own psyches or into the lower heights of the universe, encounters with these elements in ourselves and those beings who live on these levels are to be expected. Therefore, one must check what is experienced against the criterion of "Does it take one closer to, or further away from the Presence of God?"

In Kabbalah, order is implicit, and this is a sign that whatever is seen is part of the general plan of Creation. Thus, whatever is shown should fall into the recognisable scheme of the Tree and its various divisions. It is taught that there are seven levels in everything that exists, even visions. These are usually divided into the literal, allegorical, metaphysical and mystical at the earthly level; and the soul, spiritual and Divine in the heavenly level. Seen practically, these levels represent different ranges of cognition, so that any event has the possibility of being a key to illumination. A vision is a situation where the emphasis is centred in the celestial rather than the terrestial realm.

The reason why the Bible is so remarkable is because much of its material contains all seven levels. For example, the story of the fall of Jericho before Joshua and the Israelites illustrates many principles. First, let us consider the background. Now the Children of Israel, that is the as yet unintegrated aspects of the psyche under the Spirit, represented by Israel, have escaped the bondage of Egypt, that is slavery to the body, and crossed the wilderness. This desert represents a stage only too well known as the purging of useless aspects of the psyche. During this period all but two of those who originally left Egypt died. That is, all the old habits have gone, and a new generation born out of the time in the wilderness have arisen, led by the only original and constant psychological element that was fit to enter the Promised Land. This is symbolised by Joshua [the name means 'Deliverer'], who takes the freeborn Israelites across the river Jordan, which marks, like the crossing of the Red Sea, a major breakthrough into another dimension. Here, the situation may be seen as the entering into the zone between the psyche and the Spirit where many of the old collective concepts, represented by the Canaanites, have to be destroyed by Israel. This process, begun with the conquest of Jericho by help from above, came to be called the Wars of the Lord that were to clean out the land and make it Holy, for it had become degenerate since Jacob had left there.

Thus, we have in Joshua, chapter VI, the falling wall episode which may be seen literally as history or allegorically as a symbol of the first confrontation with a corrupt set of ideas represented by the city, and metaphysically as a description of an esoteric approach to a psycho-spiritual problem with detailed instructions. This process involved circuiting the town six times, once each day in silence, and then seven times on the last day, with the mass shouting of the host backing the blasts of the priestly trumpets. At this point the walls of Jericho collapsed and the army entered to destroy everything that lived in the town. Seen as a complex of concepts this event may be considered as an account of the defence system around some redundant beliefs dissolving, whilst at the level of the soul, the direction that "the people shall ascend up, every man straight before him" speaks of the rising up and occupation of the vacated complex. This is verified by a moral test in the injunction that no one should take the treasure found for himself, lest he be accursed by it, but that it should be consecrated unto the Lord. That is, the spiritual wealth that Jericho did possess should be purified and rededicated to the Divine. A minor incident in this chapter, the saving of Rahab, the prostitute and her family who had earlier helped the Israelite spies, is typical of the fine detail to be observed in scripture and visions, for they imply much to be pondered on besides the main story.

Strangely enough, when reading more directly visionary literature, like the Books of Enoch and the Merkabah texts, we find the material less easy to understand. This is because it is not earthed as are the scriptures, which are designed to blend mystical principles with historic events, so that untrained people could sense that there is a relationship between the upper and lower worlds. In the case of the Hekalot literature of old Judea and the Babylonian rabbinical schools, accounts of heavenly journeys were only for private circulation. This was because the mystical side of Judaism could easily be misunderstood. It was therefore restricted to the most learned or pious. Indeed, to speak openly about, for example, the three aspects of Divinity, could be seen as heretical in an essentially monotheistic religion. Thus, much of the material was made deliberately obscure in order to confuse anyone but those who had a foot on the ladder of vision.

Records tell us that the ancient rabbis would form groups in which a master would go into a deep meditation after all the procedures of ablution and preparation had been completed. As he rose from level to level, he would report back what he saw, which would be noted down to be discussed later. Sometimes, a question would be asked through the master, if he had not lost contact with the incarnate level. Indeed, once a teacher was brought back by being touched by a piece of soiled cloth, so as to get an important observation clarified. For obvious reasons such exercises were carried out under strict supervision, and certainly no one who was unqualified to be present was allowed into such a session.

The reason that such things can be written about now is that what was exclusive knowledge then is now general esoteric information. For example, you can go into any good bookshop on comparative religion, and purchase texts that have been secreted for centuries. Unfortunately, many of the ancient techniques of ascension have been adopted by people who do not understand the full implication of what is being done, and thus avoid the responsibility of what goes with these processes. Therefore, books have to be written in order to give some idea of what is involved when these methods are used. To recapitulate: before going on such a journey, there must be a solid background of discipline, theory and practice, and a reliable instructor, as well as good company on hand. It is vital that an aspirant realises that there are great dangers in this Work, but if a correct and diligent path is followed, then these obstacles become useful tests of inner development.

In the book of Enoch there are varied and detailed descriptions of the heavens and their inhabitants. These accounts were naturally influenced by the culture that the visionary lived in. Here, we have the blend of the subjective and the objective in as much that the world of Creation has no form, being primarily a realm of pure energy. However, in order to be able to perceive that world, it is necessary to clothe these patterns of force and archangelic entities in an intelligible image for the psyche. Thus, the consciousness of the visionary uses what is already available in the memory which has an enormous bank of personal and collective imagery to draw upon. This is why each age and every mystic has a slightly different version of the upper worlds. What is essential remains the same, if we can discern what lies beyond the face of the description. In the technique that follows, the process is reversed, in that an ascension journey is set out in a series of images which the student can enter, be guided up and through the various levels until he perceives behind the scenes evoked, the reality they represent. There will be moments and places when illusion may intrude, but these can be quickly identified after some practice. The method used is a reliable one because it does not allow the mystic to wander, but holds the attention to the path like, as one rabbi said, "A ladder in the midst of one's house by which one may ascend to and descend from Heaven".

40. Chariot Rider

After the appropriate preparations have been completed, the Tree erected and permission and blessing requested from the Most High, the chariot rider moves from the state of being acutely aware of the body and the mood of the ordinary mind, into the position of hovering above the place where the operation is being carried out. From there the earthly terrain is surveyed as if from a great height, in ascending in imagination, until the world below, as previously suggested, looks like the bottom of a great ocean. At this point the scene is transformed, so that the rider shifts worlds from the level of elements and action into the watery realm of Formation, or the purely psychological world.

Continuing to rise, looking neither to left nor right, the ascent takes the rider to the top of the waters from where the light filters down into the depths from which the rider is emerging. As the surface of the great sea is broken, the vision expands to that level where a deep blue sky containing a myriad of stars shimmers overhead. Looking up from the turbulent waves, a sense of the universe is experienced with extraordinary clarity, and as the rider swims ashore, the impression of cosmic power touches the face in the form of a great but gentle wind.

On gaining the shore the rider walks upon sand that is not of the Earth, for each grain is an exquisite pearl of perfect symmetry and purity. Nor is the landscape like the terrestrial world, for the rocks are composed of the clearest refined crystal. The forms of the flora to be seen are also quite unlike any earthly foliage, their colours are deeper, yet more subtle, and the texture and design of each plant quite different, although strangely familiar. It is as if the plants were the archetypal essence of each species, in that their appearance is a continuous cycle of manifestation from seed to fruit, so that one perceives in their ever repeating patterns a whole season in every moment. The same could be said of whatever creatures come into the view of the rider. They also are continuous in their composition, having not only the life span of their species

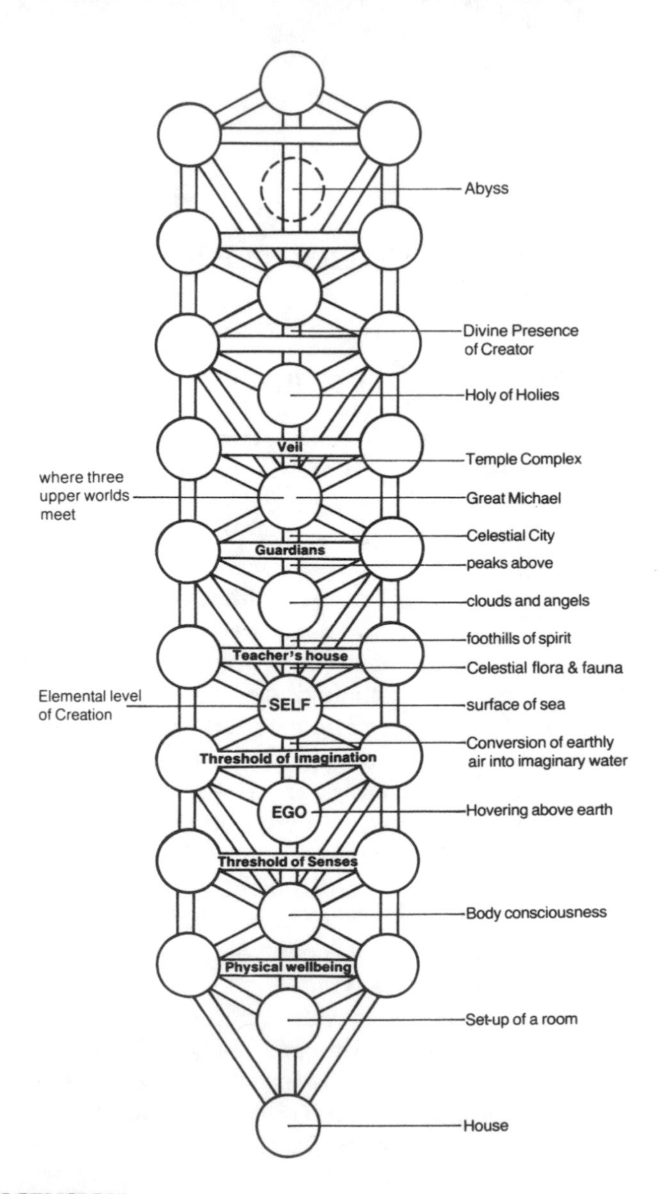

13. ASCENSION

Here there are various stages of ascent set out on the great Ladder. In the exercise the consciousness is raised up from the earthly and out of the senses to enter into imagination and the watery realm of the psyche. From the contact point of Self the journey moves on into the airy World of Creation before climbing the celestial mountains to reach the Heavenly Jerusalem. Here the fiery Kingdom of Emanation is approached via the Temple of Light in which resides the dark Holy of Holies that shields the aspirant from the Face of the Divinity.

played out in each instant, but the greater rhythm of evolution unfolding its manifestation. These creatures, like the plants, are cosmic in scale, so that the rider only perceives a fraction of their archangelic function.

Moving on, the rider, as in previous journeys, climbs the foothills of the huge mountain range that towers above the ocean. Far away on the horizon, the Holy City glitters on the crest of the tallest mountain. This distant goal has been observed each time the rider has ascended to the Beriatic shore. It is glimpsed through a gap in the high cloud that cloaks the peaks of the range. The rider notes how the clouds always part, at this point, if only for a moment, to reveal the City. The rider can just make out the shimmering walls and towers before the cloud closes again. This act of Grace is encouraging, for the City is where the rider hopes to go if permission is granted.

The rider proceeds up a by now well-known path. Taking care over dangerous crevices and ignoring the voices that call from gulleys to draw him aside, the rider eventually reaches the high hill upon which the Inner Teacher lives. As the gate is approached the Teacher is seen at the window waiting. The beloved and wise face smiles and nods. The door is reached and opened. The Teacher extends hands in a loving welcome. After taking some refreshment in the Teacher's study, the rider is asked to make ready. While the rider waits, he reflects upon that which is done and that which is yet to come. The front door has been left ajar, so there is still the opportunity for turning back.

Beckoning the rider to an inner room the Teacher, dressed for travel, stands before an altar and asks for safe passage to and from where they are about to go. If no omen or event occurs to deter them from departing, the Teacher then takes a staff and leads the way out of the back door of the house and up the mountain.

The first part of the journey is easy, but as height is gained, so it becomes more difficult to breathe. As the climb becomes more steep and dangerous so the Teacher's stamina and skill becomes more apparent while the rider becomes weary and unsure and has to be helped. When they have mounted the lesser peaks they look down to see an extraordinary sight; for the world below is now perceived floating like a vast galaxy in space with endless depth in all directions. Turning back, the rider sees that the Teacher has gone on, and is about to enter the cloudy mass that hovers overhead. The Teacher awaits the rider, and then stretching out the staff, instructs him to hold on to it no matter what happens. Going before the rider, the Teacher takes him into the cloud. The rider loses sight of the figure in front and becomes fearful as all about thunder and lightning crackles and splits the misty darkness. Enormous creatures fly round them. The wind of their great wings almost tears the staff from the rider's grasp. It is only the gentle upward pull of the Teacher that enables the rider to go on through this awesome zone.

When the Teacher and rider emerge from the top of the cloud, the celestial city is seen in all its glory. Its walls and towers sparkle like a frozen fountain that emanates light at every angle. As the couple draw near to the gates, great figures of mist with swords of fire step forward and demand identification. The Teacher speaks a Holy Name and the beings withdraw to allow them to enter the gates. The rider follows the Teacher along one of the great avenues that radiate out from the centre of the city. The streets are full of beings that are human and yet far more refined and perfect than those seen on Earth. Their faces and bodies are translucent, and their eyes luminous with a profound intelligence. They are all conscious of who and what they are all the time. The awe-filled rider observes everything and takes note.

On reaching the focus of all the roads the rider sees that the Teacher has brought them to a vast Temple. It is a magnificent building constructed of variegated lights. Its substance is not of the world they are moving in. They approach its outer court and enter, to be met by a company of radiant entities whose faces are strangely familiar to the rider. Famous and revered names and titles come into consciousness, but the rider is not given time to identify anyone, for the second and inner court is opened to the Teacher, the rider following. They come to the sanctuary area of the Temple. There a huge angelic being stands in scintillating armour with a fierce sword of fire. The Teacher bows and presents the rider. Great Michael, Captain of Hosts, Priest of the Heavenly Jerusalem, acknowledges them and the great Temple door opens into the sanctuary. The Teacher takes the rider to the entrance and indicates that he should go on alone. The rider hesitates to enter the sanctuary but his name is called and he enters and sees the Holy of Holies. It is an indescribable building of beauty, simplicity and pure light. A veil is drawn across its face. Nothing can be perceived, except an utter silence and stillness. After a moment's

Grace, in which a profound sense of the Presence of the Divine is experienced, the rider's name is called again, but from behind.

Walking backwards, he withdraws from the sanctuary and into the inner court where the Teacher awaits. From there, the Teacher gently leads the awestruck rider out of the Temple complex. They pass once more along the great avenue thronged with shining beings to the city gates as the rider slowly enters the relative universe again. After a pause in which to reorientate, they depart from the Holy City and descend into the cloud below. Having passed through this hazardous zone they come out onto the lower slopes of the mountain and make their own way down to the home of the Teacher. Here they rest and reflect on what has happened with questions and comments noted down for later consultation. The rider then takes leave of the Teacher and follows the solitary path back to the shore. Before re-entering the Sea of Yetzirah, there is a glance towards the Celestial City which may be revealed through the clouds. The rider then walks into the waves quickly sinking down into its swirling depths. Holding firm against the current he approaches the bottom of the ocean and converts, by imagination, the psychological waters into terrestrial air, so that he ends the journey hovering over the house where his body is. On entering the room he fuses the psyche into the elemental vehicle and terminates the operation with a prayer of thanksgiving. Coming down the Tree, the exercise is earthed by a stamping of the feet, so that the mundane is touched and connection with the physical senses re-established. After a pause the debriefing should begin and a report be written up. Later, notes should be added if any forgotten detail has not yet been included. Such personal visions should only be discussed with *'Ha yode 'im'*, or 'those who know' as the old chariot riders used to be called.

41. Interpretation

In order to gain a deeper comprehension of our journey to the inner Jerusalem, let us look at the exercise described in the last chapter from the point of view of kabbalistic theory and interpretation. In this way, we may begin to differentiate between the levels and their qualities.

Starting at the body, at the *Malkhut* or Kingdom of the psyche, we begin with the first stage of the seven lower halls. Here, we become aware of the four elements, before rising to the second stage of the ego to perceive the lower psyche's mood. We then shifted from the level of the ordinary sensual mind into that of the imagination, that is, we converted the *Daat* of the body into the *Yesod* of the psyche. From here, we rose out of the body up through the willing triad into the awakened state from where we viewed the world below our gaze, as if from a great height. This level is the *Keter* or Crown of the World of Action and Elements, which is to be perceived in its physical form as the earth, the sea and the atmosphere, with the light of the sun as fire. Here we transformed the *Keter* of the physical world into the *Tiferet* of the psychological or the World of Forms.

At such a moment our normal view of the universe is changed; for example, we perceive how the physical world is much denser. Indeed, this is so much so that the atmosphere through which we are ascending is easily converted to a watery consistency, as we switch our frame of reference. Thus, by altering our state and scale, we no longer fly but swim, because we ourselves have become sufficiently light to float in the fluidic World of Yetzirah. As we break the surface of the atmospheric ocean we enter another dimension. Here we experience the upper levels of the World of Formation, which present themselves in symbolic form as the mountains, sea, sky, and fire of another plane. If we examine the substance and dynamics of these higher elements, they will be seen to be of quite a different order to their earthly counterparts. At this point we stand where the three lower Worlds meet, that is the *Keter* of Assiyah, the *Tiferet* of Yetzirah and the *Malkhut* of Beriah, although we may not as yet be able to perceive all of them, or be able to differentiate one from another. This takes time and much practice.

On gaining the shore our rider then saw some flora and fauna. These revealed both the pattern and dynamics that lie behind the plants and animals we see manifest in the physical world. Here we witness how the creative energy of Heaven unfolds in a multiplicity of forms to reveal the total cycle of each entity as it is seen in Paradise. We also glimpse what the Garden of Eden might be like. Every possible colour, texture and line can be observed in an ever changing scene. Everything is in motion as its potential is momentarily realised in the ebbs and flows of Yetzirah. It is only on earth that the cyclic forces and shapes are held in substance, and decelerated in their rhythms to concur with the slower and gradual evolutionary process going on at the cutting edge of the universe in fully manifest matter.

Moving on, the rider then climbed the foothills to the mountain range. These represent the climb up to the place of the Inner Teacher and mark a separation from the physical realm, but not before one is accosted by both friendly and hostile inhabitants of the intermediate zone. Safe in the House of the Soul, we meet and greet our mentor, whilst still holding the providential sight of the Heavenly City in the heart. This is the objective of our journey, but first we must prepare to pass through the *Daat*-veil of the Spirit, the layer of cloud, before reaching the place where the three upper worlds meet. While resting in the room of self-consciousness, we pause and reflect a while. If we make use of the time the Teacher is preparing for the journey, we can look about us at the things in the room and learn something about our souls. The way the chamber is arranged and its state will tell us much. Some people find it simple, others complex. Yet others see it as very old or new, whilst some are surprised to discover it ordinary, primitive or exotic. Each of these images reflect our inner world. The garb of the Teacher is extremely informative. Some mentors wear oriental clothes, whilst others occult or religious raiment. This outfit is usually matched to the archetypal image associated with the self at the *Tiferet* of the psychological Tree. In one individual it might be a wise old person, in another a soldier or nun, or even just a non-visible being. The relationship between the rider and the Teacher is very revealing as there are the various degrees of the child—parent—peer interconnections. Sometimes, for example, the face of the Teacher is often an older or younger version of oneself, although it may be, at other times someone quite different, a separate entity, if contact with one's own *Tiferet* is not yet established.

The inner chamber of the Teacher's home is the place where permission and entrance into the next world is gained. This is the *Malkhut Ha Shamaim*, the Kingdom of Heaven, which opens the door into the sixth stage that lies behind the triad of the soul. Here the rider and Teacher begin the steep climb up through the spiritual peaks and into the cloudy levels where the creative and chaotic forces work amidst the cosmic weather system of the universe. Here we see the difference between the individual level of the soul, as represented by the intimacy of the Teacher's house, and the vast and transpersonal dimensions of the great mountains and their airy inhabitants who cannot be seen but only sensed as they thunder by amid the clouds. The tenacious connection of the staff between the rider and mentor in the mist is the axis of conscious attention that holds one to the path through that *Daat*-veiled zone. On emerging from the cloud, the seventh triad of the yetziratic Crown, Wisdom and Understanding is reached. This is marked by the calmness of the fine air, and the light emanating from the Celestial City, which represents the *Keter* of the Psyche, the *Tiferet* of the Spirit and the *Malkhut* of the Divine. The Heavenly Jerusalem is within sight, although again its approach is not without risk for it is well protected for our own sakes.

The beings to be encountered before the City gates are the guardians of these higher thresholds and may be seen, according to one's level, as archetypes within the psyche, or objective creatures protecting one from being burnt by the light of Divinity. If entrance is not granted, then one is not ready for the moment to be experienced in the Holy Temple. In the case of our vision, passage is made possible under the aegis of the Inner Teacher. Thus we enter by proxy, and so glimpse symbolically the interior of the Celestial City and its inhabitants. The sights to be seen there may be only in the projections of imagination, but what the images portray can reveal something about the higher worlds. Take, for example, the layout of the avenues and the Temple. Their geometry is loaded with meaning and a great source of information for the contemplative. The construction of the Temple out of pure light, however faintly perceived, usually creates a deep awe, as the rider realises that this is the entrance to the Divine World of Emanation. Such a moment is not the stuff of dreams but of vision and leaves a deep impression upon the psyche.

After passing through the outer and inner courts, which represent the Yetziratic *Keter* and the Beriatic *Tiferet*, the sanctuary is entered, that is the *Malkhut* of Azilut. Here great Michael, whose name means 'Like unto God', presides as the guardian and High Priest in the Heavenly Jerusalem. Beyond is the veil before the Holy of Holies that leads into the Divine Presence of the Creator. This is the deepest part of oneself that is accessible by vision. To go further is only possible to those who have the prerequisite of Holiness, for it involves leaving the body, and this is obviously highly dangerous for the unevolved. Therefore, the veil is not drawn, and we are called back by name to symbolise our limited individuality in relation to the Absolute of the Holy One. The return from the Temple to join the Teacher is to begin the descent. Here we come down from the highest level of the seven lesser halls, which correspond to the fourth stage of the Spirit and the first of the Divine. Working primarily from the yetziratic side of the experience, we only catch a flavour of these higher worlds in the forms presented to us, but at this phase of development this might be more than enough.

To summarise, we left the physical world at the self and climbed up through the psyche to the mid-point of the Spirit, where we touched Eternity. Thus, on the way down, we will note a decrease of light, a loss of energy and an increase in density. What appeared before as brilliant, will now seem by contrast, dull. This is because as we descend from the City and into the clouds of the cosmos, we pass out of the serene influence of Divinity and are caught up in the great drama of manifestation in time and space. These events engulf us in the processes of becoming. We are no longer with the immortals. When we emerge out of the base of the cloud and look back, we hear the rushing of cosmic winds. This awareness can be retained even after we come down to Earth, when we recognise the buffeting of Providence. The return to the home of the Teacher and our departure to the lower depths should by now be a not too infrequent venture.

Set out on Jacob's Ladder, this brief analysis will show how to place the main elements of an inner journey. Once the levels have been established, subtle refinements will emerge, on reflection, to fill in the gaps. After some practice the operation will be seen as a continuum, with the details of the ascent and descent describing the interpenetration of the various levels, as each phase merges into the other, according to the laws of the extended Tree. Thus if we observe closely enough, we may see how, for example, reality changes according to which level we centre our consciousness in, as one does when shifting from a personal to an objective understanding of fate. The greater the precision of discernment, the finer the appreciation of the different worlds, and so one becomes a better instrument to receive and impart the exchange of influences. In the next chapter we will attempt a deeper penetration, but from another point of view, so as to experience perhaps with Grace, the seven great halls of the Spirit.

42. Meditation

Up to this point we have used techniques related to the physical and psychological worlds. These have the advantage of having substance and form to guide us on our inner journeys. What is about to be described takes the process much further, in that the Kabbalist begins to penetrate the dark glass of *Daat*, or Knowledge, where there are none of the familiar steps found in the lower World. However, because each world is based upon the same model, some notion of the spiritual realm is possible, as we theoretically climb Jacob's Ladder from the first Heaven, at the place of the self, to the seventh Heaven in the process of meditation.

To attain such a height and depth requires either long and diligent work, or an act of Grace. It cannot be obtained easily, because to exist at this altitude of the Spirit requires, as said, some kind of interior vehicle. This can only be evolved over time, although some people may incarnate with a highly developed spiritual chariot because of work done in a previous life. To possess such a well-developed spiritual body means that the lower half of the Beriatic organism of a person has evolved and become sufficiently stable for the paths between the Beriatic *Hod* and *Netzah* to emerge and convert the yetziratic *Daat* into the *Yesod* of the Spirit. When this has happened, then the person is said to have established a foundation in the World of Creation.

Let us assume that our Kabbalist has worked for many years upon the body and psyche, and that the balance and maturity of these two organisms is such that the spiritual body has evolved to some degree. If this is the case, then it is possible for the Kabbalist to begin the practice of deep meditation. By this is meant something quite different from what has been discussed up till now. Meditation in this context means to experience directly the levels of the Heavens, to rise through the seven states of the Spirit and to come into the Divine Presence, not by the agency of an image, but in intimate contact.

The procedure is begun like all other operations, although by now the Kabbalist should be able to reach an awareness of the self, at the centre of the psychological Tree, by just remembering who he is, and why he is on the Earth. Indeed, the preparation should be a simple act of conscious intensification of the *Gadlut* state, which is mindful of his inner and outer situation. However, meditation is a special occasion, and so space and time is set aside for its practice. It should be begun in the usual way by deliberately bringing the body and psyche into a receptive condition.

Having reached the place of the self, a shift should be made in which consciousness is moved from the Crown of the body and the centre Sefirah of the psyche, to the Kingdom of the Spirit, that is the *Malkhut* of Beriah. This is the Gate of Heaven which is traditionally called the *Vilon*, or Veil. Here the stage of Devotion is entered. This means that all the power of the soul triad is concentrated into an emotional amalgam of Truth, Mercy and Justice to make the person aware of both their vices and their virtues. These are impartially reviewed and considered. All imbalances are corrected, if possible, by conscious acknowledgement and scrupulous honesty mitigated by generosity. This allows progress, but holds the soul to account. When an equilibrium has been attained the veil may then be drawn back to reveal the second heaven which is called the Chamber of Purity. Here repentance can occur which cleanses the soul. This gives the consciousness a lucidity which may precipitate the window of the Spirit being opened through the *Daat—Yesod* conjunction that joins *Yetzirah* and *Beriah*.

The state of purity can be described as like the clean freshness of mountain air with the scale of wide vision to match. This is where all spiritual traditions meet and no conflict over outer forms can occur. Such an objectivity leads on into the third heaven of Sincerity. This virtue is rooted in the beriatic sefirot of *Hod*, *Netzah* and *Yesod*, and so constitutes the theory, practice and image of spiritual work in its true sense. Here a person operates from deep within, having the equivalent of willingness at the cosmic level. Thus, they will do whatever Providence requires, be it to live, work or even die, for the sake of the Holy One. Few people can hold this level of spiritual action, although many touch this plane of maturity, as it is traditionally called, in deep meditation. The dynamic calm that pulsates from this triad is the prerequisite for entering the next level.

As the meditator enters the spiritual triad of awareness it is said that they are 'with God', that is they are at the Crown of the psyche and in direct contact with Divinity in the Heavenly Jerusalem. They have come into the equivalent of the Temple complex or where the three upper worlds meet. Here consciousness of God is no longer a remote reflection of Light, but a direct coming into the radiance of *Azilut*. Some people actually perceive the rays of Emanation coming down into a deep inner space, but this is only a psychological image of something that has no form. The shift into the meeting place of the three upper worlds constitutes a major change in the person. In many cases, because the range of consciousness is still small, all contact with the Earth is lost. Moreover, the awareness of the psyche is diminished as individuality is reduced to a dot within cosmic space. However, the speck of 'I' responds to the Divine Presence, as the limited self within each of us experiences the SELF of the Unlimited. This takes the meditator out of the psyche and into the equivalent of the soul triad of the Spirit, that is universal Truth, Justice and Mercy. Here, we are told, we move into the triad of Holiness, which means to experience a wholeness and healing of our beings. There it is possible, it is said, to perceive all we have ever been, even as the Buddha saw all his past lives in a cosmic moment.

From the place of Holiness one comes before the Azilutic sefirah of the Living Almighty and experiences the power of Divinity. This level, we are told, is where the great Archangels of the Face chorus the praises of the Holy One. Some people, we are told, actually hear their voices and even join in the universal choir that hovers in this vast Place of Sanctification, as it is called. Clearly no words can describe the ecstacy undergone in such a state, and we can only guess that to touch this level is to know what it is to be blessed. People who reach this level usually say nothing about it, although the shining of their faces often reveals where they have been. This extraordinary light sometimes remains for a while before fading, unless it is renewed by constant return to that level. The incident of Moses coming down the mountain with a blinding countenance is an example.

Penetration of the seventh heaven is a rare occurrence as a conscious action, although it is said that each person at some point in his life has a flash of what it is like to be in the Presence of YAHVEH ELOHIM, the Lord God, Creator of the Universe, at the Crown of Creation. Such an experience can be obtained, according to Kabbalah by inwardly repeating this Holy combination of Divine Names in a state of deep consciousness. This means it must only be done if a person fully realises whose Name he is calling. To reach the highest heaven is to be at the heart of the Divine and therefore mutual Love is the key to this meeting with the Holy One. Indeed it will be noted that as each step is taken, so one is met by Divine encouragement. Some say it is like being welcomed by a beloved. The Songs of Solomon describe well the yearning and union.

Anyone who comes into the *Arabot*, as the seventh heaven is called, enters the place beyond which lies the Great Abyss. By this is meant the point where total union occurs from where no one returns, because they have become one with the Godhead. Thus, unless one's work is done, there is no stepping into the highest place of Knowledge before the Three Great White Heads of the Holy Tree, for to go higher would be to meet God Face to Face, and so realise the highest Name I AM THAT I AM. This can only be done when the destiny of an individual has been completed or Grace allows such a return. The seventh heaven is the greatest height one can reach in the World of the Spirit. There at the limit of the universe a deep meditator must choose to go on, or turn back to fulfil the Work they were called forth, created, formed and made for.

To reach these depths in meditation requires total commitment. Moreover, one may wait perhaps for many years before achieving such a level, while others might reach there by Grace in an afternoon. There is no guarantee of what can happen. Each individual has a different timing. Meanwhile, what is important is to retain what has been received during meditation, whether it be an insight into some small problem or the afterglow of the Divine Light. Some people attain the higher levels by constant persistence, others by great but short bursts of sustained effort, whilst yet others, who do little work, achieve great results because they move at the right moment and go easily through the eye of the needle at *Tiferet*. A useful way of seeing the process is to imagine a hollow shaft running through all the worlds. Because of the ever-changing conditions, both within and without, the shaft is rarely in perfect alignment, although occasional conditions, created by Providence, sometimes allows, like the hole in the clouds, a person to pass right up the shaft, if only for an instant. The objective is to align the axis of the shaft within ourselves and so be ready to ascend or experience the Divine Light shining down, without impediment, through all our being. Such a possibility must be prepared for during each meditation, although it may not happen very often. When it does, it is not easily forgotten, for then one knows that what seemed so far away is in fact so near that it is difficult to distinguish between I and Thou. This brings us to the moment when the relationship between mine and Thine becomes a reality and a responsibility.

43. Self

It is the aim of all mystics to know The Holy One. In Kabbalah this is a primal objective. Such an experience often places the mystic apart from the main orthodox body of opinion and custom, because having tasted the reality of the Divine, he finds it difficult to be encumbered by ritual actions, devotional forms, or indeed even metaphysical ideas. However, while consciousness of God is possible without these modes, few mystics dispense with them, because they are necessary to help comprehend and express the experience to themselves and others in their tradition. This is why Kabbalah operates within the context of Judaism, although the degree of identification with time-honoured practices varies according to period, place and individual inclination. This fact may be difficult for the conventionally minded to accept, but one must differentiate between following ancient custom for its own sake and worshipping God.

The life and work of the Kabbalist set out in this book can be practised deep within the orthodoxy or on the margin between the religious way and the method of occultism, both of which are part of the traditional Judaism, as the line of Baal Shemie, or Masters of the Names, well illustrates. At the present time there are thousands of seekers of esoteric knowledge who hover somewhere between two apparent extremes. The difference, however, is only in the matter of method, provided the aim is the same. Thus, the unorthodox Kabbalist can have the same spiritual experience as the Hassidic rabbi because they share the same objectives as the mystics of Christianity, Islam and all the other great religious traditions. It cannot be any other way, or the Universal Teaching found everywhere makes no sense, and we have every reason to believe this is not so.

There can only be one pivot to every true and complete Teaching, one focus to all rituals, devotions and contemplations. There is only one reality that the mystic can contact, and that is the Absolute. Now the Name of God is known in every language spoken by the human race. It may be this and it may be that, or it might not be anything that can be named. The Holy One is and is not, is remote and yet at the heart of all. This is the mystery of God.

When the Kabbalist touches and is touched by the Divine, then it is said that he is known by name. The meaning of this is profound when you consider that a name is the acknowledgement of a particular being by themselves or others. To possess a name is to become individual, to be quite separate from others who might be quite similar to oneself. And yet this is another mystery: in this very uniqueness is an intimate solitude that can only be known by that self. This self is a spark of Divine consciousness. It is in this state of isolation because it was divided out from Adam Kadmon so that it might experience separation from the Divine and so be able to look back at its own reflection. Thus each self is a photon of Divine Light removed from its normal habitat in the World of Emanation and embodied in the lower Worlds of Creation, Formation and Action. When an individual comes to know and be known by the Holy One, then something Divine begins to manifest and this dissolves the sense of isolation that many people feel, but know not why. To be known by name is the prelude to acquaintanceship, then love, and eventually union.

The human self is an atom of Divinity. It is a miniature image containing in its nature the dynamics, structure and consciousness of the Divine SELF that permeates all Existence. Thus as an individual becomes increasingly aware of the mirrored relationship between the macrocosm and the microcosm, so a human atom's consciousness expands above and below, without and within. In this way, the Divine starts to see Itself in ITSELF. This process of acquaintanceship is the beginning of a long and complex courtship that extends over all the Days of Creation. Gradually every level of Existence is involved and every creature takes part in the process that leads up to the Holy Marriage of God beholding God. However, as said, only mankind, wherever it appears in the universe, can encompass the totality of what is involved, and even then only a few human beings at a time can climb the ladder of consciousness and file through the one place where each person realises Whose image they are.

Fortunately, such moments are not as rare as imagined, for when sufficient consciousness has been accumulated, then the Divine can manifest in the most unusual settings. For instance, it has not been unknown for Divine consciousness to become present in the consciousness of an individual sitting in a room or walking down the street. There are many cases of this type of experience. Those nearby the person may not be aware of what is going on, but this is because they are not conscious enough to perceive what is Self evident. The word 'Self-evident' is used because in such an instant only the SELF can be aware of ITSELF and *vice versa*. This is the ultimate moment of reflection as I AM THAT I AM beholds I AM THAT I AM within the confines of the flesh, soul and spirit. Such a moment is a turning point in anyone's life. After that nothing can be seen in the same way any more.

In Kabbalah, the term *Devekut* meaning 'to cleave unto' is used to describe a state of inward holding and communion with the Divine. This condition is not reserved just for the Sabbath or for the daily cycle of ritual, but is sought and performed in every moment of the day. In some traditions it is called "to be in constant recollection". Others call it "Self-remembering", but we have to remind ourselves Who it is remembering WHO. Such a realisation can change our whole relationship to life and the world at large, for we begin to perceive that the consciousness that looks out of and into our being is the same as that which looks down at us from the frontier of the universe and up from the edge of the atomic world. There is nowhere where God is not, and yet as the ancient rabbis noted, God is not the world, which is but a reflection.

The mystery of the Immanence and Transcendence of God has puzzled many for centuries, but for those who have experienced the *Shekhinah* or the Divine Presence, there is no problem. I AM THAT I AM is also that which has no Name and is therefore in Kabbalah called both EN SOF, which means 'without End' and EN, which means 'Nothing'. As all these Names are but forms, they themselves are no more than ciphers for human intelligence to grasp. However, when a person moves beyond the range of the senses, the sensitivity of the psyche and the scope of the spirit, then the 'I' of the self encounters the THOU of the Holy One.

When this relationship between the Creator and the creature becomes apparent, there emerges between what is in manifestation and that which is beyond, a profound dialogue which is continuous, as long as consciousness is sought. From this conversation is established a connection that many mystics have spoken of, if only by hint, for not a few have been persecuted by the orthodox of their religion who do not know what it means to have such an experience. This is because direct experience is always a threat to a priesthood that has no real spiritual connection and is only concerned with preserving the social form of a tradition and its own status.

Generally speaking Kabbalists never speak of these matters to anyone except those who know and even then such conversations are limited, because it is not possible to describe the indescribable. It has been said that the Holy One enjoys good company and especially yearns for intercourse with human beings, who are the only creatures capable of perceiving the grand design of Existence. This is because they can extend their being both below and above the level they are born into, which gives them a special place and particular access to the Divine. As yet most of the human race is insufficiently evolved to be able to recognise this possibility, and therefore those who have reached the stage where they recognise their potential bear a considerable burden. They must not only seek to communicate with the Divine and assist in the unfolding of the Cosmic Plan, but teach those who follow, as well as aid the millions of people who as yet do not even suspect what the universe is all about.

According to another kabbalistic tradition, the *Shekhinah* is in exile. This goes back to the fall of Adam and Eve, who descended from a state of Grace in the Garden of Yetzirah and put on coats of flesh, which we acquire on being born. The Lord-God having compassion upon us, tradition says, came with mankind into exile in order to be a comfort to those who realise they are imprisoned in matter. However the aim behind this act of Divine Love was also to assist these sparks of Adam embedded in the elemental world, and help them return to what they were, even before the Garden of Eden. Thus, as an individual comes into the awareness that he or she is not alone, so a hidden radiance awakens and seeks to unite with Itself. This concealed Light illuminates everything about it, although only those with a degree of SELF-awareness may detect it. The effect of this consciousness of SELF upon the Earth is crucial, because there is only a small amount of such knowledge at present on the planet. The implication of this is vast, because it reveals not only the starting point of the Earth's spiritual evolution, but the reason for the third of the four journeys through Existence. Thus, having made contact with the Crown of Creation, an evolving human being must turn back down Jacob's Ladder, in order to impart what has been received. This is vital for the universe for without everyone's consciousness parts of Existence will remain dark and unknown to Adam Kadmon. The Work of Unification is the concern of the Companions of the Light whatever their earthly tradition might be. In this Labour of Love there is no differentiation, even as there is no difference between the SELF in one human being and another. All is One, say the mystics, and the One is in All.

44. Universe

When a Kabbalist looks at the world, nothing is seen as separate. The universe is one piece, like the body; it is an interlocked system of levels and aspects that make up a whole. Further, the Kabbalist perceives that the invisible part of Existence is the greater component, and that this unseen dimension governs what

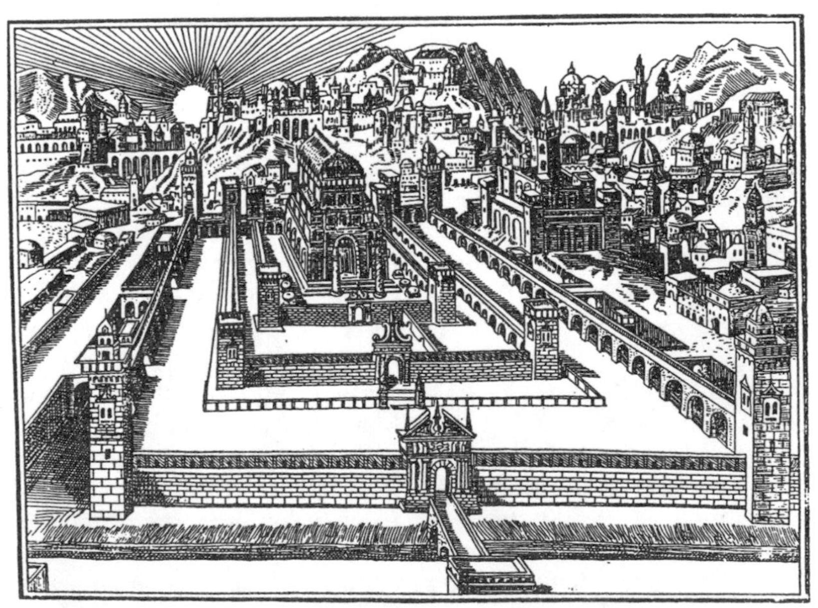

THE TEMPLE AT JERUSALEM.
(From a Passover Haggadah printed at Amsterdam, 1695.)

14. JERUSALEM
All is in the eye of the beholder. Here Jerusalem is seen as a 17th-century city by an artist of that time. But this Holy centre may be visualised according to whatever it means to the viewer, as it is a figment of belief rather than fact. The Kabbalist seeks to perceive all the levels of what is to be seen and so behold the seven other Jerusalems within the physical walls of the city, even as a stone contains form, creation and a spark of the Divine.

happens in its denser and more physical realms. This is quite the reverse of how most people see the world. Modern science tends to examine the end of the chain of causes, and assumes for example, that the chemical processes in the brain determine the quality of the mind that uses it. Indeed, for centuries, since the ancient world picture of a ladder of being was destroyed by the Age of Reason, the Western world has perceived the universe as a vast machine composed of elements and patterns with no explanation such as how it all might be designed by pure consciousness.

It is only in the last few decades that the notion that there is a remarkable order behind existence has re-emerged. The most advanced scientist now admits the chances of anything organising itself spontaneously into a monkey or a galaxy is very remote, and that clearly, by the way the mathematics of the universe have been worked out, there is a distinct suspicion that there is a remarkable intelligence behind it. Of course all mystical traditions have known this fact since such Work began, and there are many systems in the various lines from Vedanta to Kabbalah, which describe how the world began and how it will end. While this is a fascinating study in itself, perhaps more important to the mystic of today is what the situation is now.

The Kabbalist, belonging to a tradition that takes into account all the worlds, sees the universe as several interacting levels. For example, one looks at a landscape. Let us take the view of Jerusalem from the Mount of Olives. On the face of it, it appears to be like many other sun-bleached Middle Eastern cities. There are the hills and the buildings, the crowds and the markets, the communities and the holy places. Many artists and photographers have caught the image of it, and yet, if we probe below the surface, we may perceive worlds within worlds.

Beginning at the bottom of Jacob's Ladder, the Kabbalist becomes aware of the elemental strata of the city. It is built on limestone that was formed by water millions of years ago on an ocean bed. It has moved since then from its flat layered configuration into folds, then hills, which still continue to move and shudder in the occasional earthquake. The element of water flows continually through it as rain and snow, mist and frost, to percolate and wear away its substance. Likewise, air moves over its hills, and through its streets and houses, to raise dust and blow odours away, as well as give breath to all the creatures that live there. Fire comes with the sun, moon, planets and stars to illuminate and warm every nook and cranny, and so feed and nourish the living rock as well as plants, animals and human beings. These four elements interplay as rhythms in the seasons making the city cold, wet, dry and hot. Jerusalem has an elemental life that was begun with the first brick, grew with each new building, put out roots and leaves with its roads and walls, bore flowers in its palaces, and fruit within its temples; all to decay and die when the final trace of the city has gone as the last brick returns to dust.

The plant and animal levels may be observed at a glance, but there is more to them than may be seen in the olives and palms, the donkeys and goats that live in the city. A vast number of different species have bred and died in a great flow of life that passed through the fabric of the place. Every tree, bush, scrub and plant has its place in a long forest that has stretched through time to decorate, drop fruit, feed and shade Jerusalem. Above, below and among the ancient stones, a whole world of insects, birds and animals live out their existence in exactly the same way as they did when Solomon ruled. Only human beings change, and this we can see as our eyes wander over the many examples of architecture left by succeeding holders of the site.

As we enter the world of mankind there is a shift in dimension. Faint traces in the soil of the hill of Ophel reveal the work of long vanished Canaanites, as do fragments of the walls of King David's city. Houses and fortifications, now but ruins, speak of the Herodian epoch and a classic column, at a street corner, of the Roman period. A monk in ancient habit reminds one of Byzantium, and the Dome of the Rock, of the Arab conquest. The medieval church of St. Anne indicates the presence of the Crusaders and the scratched crosses in the walls the visit of pilgrims from all over Christendom. Mamluk and Ottoman Turk occupation of the city is revealed in the style of walls and windows, while the brief British mandate is perceived in a cast iron postbox. Throughout all these occupations by various conquerors, the Jewish population has retained continuous foothold in its capital despite periodic massacres and exiles. This natural and historical aspect of the city is the lower face of the Tree of Jerusalem.

If we shift our perception once more to that of the mid part of the Yetziratic Tree, we shall see how Jerusalem is also a city of the soul. It began at the time of King David when it became the political and the religious centre of the nation. Later, exiles in ancient Babylon saw it as the earthly focus of their spiritual home. This notion was developed after the destruction of the Second Temple and retained by Jews in the Roman and Persian Empires, the Moslem world and medieval Europe as a powerful symbol of identity. It is still held as such by Jews wherever they are. This Holy City has existed in the minds of people who have never seen it, for over two millennia, and if one can see with the inner eye, it is possible to perceive a subtle structure within the fabric of the decay and restoration of present-day Jerusalem. This same charismatic city exists for Christians and Moslems, although they see their own versions of it. This is because each Faith has its own Yetziratic form, with symbols and values that none of the others recognise. Indeed, even within the same tradition such divisions occur. The Armenian monk does not see the same Jerusalem as the Catholic, nor is the orthodox rabbi aware that his view of the city is quite unlike that of a Jewish tourist. Jerusalem contains many faces each dependent on the beliefs and projections of the beholder. This is the level of the psyche or the world of Formation.

At the level of the Spirit, where there is no form, all who can operate here would perceive quite another Jerusalem. They would see it as a vortex of spiritual power into which the energy of millions of hearts and minds is focused. These currents would arise from all over the world, ebbing and flowing as the Sabbaths of Islam, Judaism and Christianity come and go each week. They would also perceive the permanent canopy of a spirituality built up over centuries of worship that hovers like a crown above the city. Such a field force of Beriatic energy acts as a great lens to catch and direct the celestial dew that falls continuously from the upper worlds. This cleansing Grace enhances the city, and makes it a holy place despite all the conflict that has occurred there, so that all that come to it sense something sacred which is greater than a nation and wider than a civilisation. It is to millions the spiritual *Malkhut* of the World.

To those with yet deeper vision, the Temple Mount with its golden domed mosque set out upon the site of the Holy of Holies, has a sacred Presence. This is the trace of the Divine Light that once occupied that Place, for tradition says that the *Shekhinah* departed from the Temple just before it was destroyed. The afterglow of the Light may be seen as a reminder of the Eternal, in contrast to the drama of the city's history. Many souls have borne witness to the Divine dimension in Jerusalem. The memory of saints, sages, prophets and Anointed Ones, is still strongly felt, even though the sites of their tombs and memorials have long been replaced or decorated beyond recognition. To those aware of this level these holy human spirits are all one company, irrespective of their religion. Each carried in his or her own time a consciousness of Divinity as they strove to manifest Light amid the frequent bouts of darkness of ignorance and barbarity that possessed the city. Some were hidden and some were directly caught up in the battle between good and evil. Others were solitary and yet others deeply involved with society when religion became equated with political power. Jerusalem is a microcosm of the world and the mirror of mankind. Every human level is to be seen in its streets from the most indolent mineral, hungry vegetable and assertive animal kind of person, to those who are on various degrees of the spiritual path.

As we can see, it is possible to perceive the whole of Jacob's Ladder in Jerusalem. However we cannot all be there and so the Kabbalist seeks to apply the same criteria to wherever he or she might be. Such an application of knowledge requires constant practice so that the vision does not fade, but is continually enhanced as what is revealed is transformed into an expansion of being. In this way a quite ordinary street becomes the venue of the miraculous as things emerge about people and places in the eye of a conscious beholder. In such a moment, space and time become a kaleidoscope, as the height, depth and scale of everything merges to form a vision of what has been, is now, and will be. This is the insight of prophecy so often written about in kabbalistic literature. The possession of prophecy is one of the gifts of the Spirit. However, the responsibility that goes with it is not just to perceive the state of the universe and predict trends, but to actually help those living in it to adjust to each situation as Creation moves on its way towards perfection. This is the carrying out of the Work at all levels.

45. Work

It is not enough to be able to see all the levels of Existence, although this would be an asset, but to work within it. Despite its reputation of being concerned with the higher realms of the universe, Kabbalah has always been an essentially earth-related tradition. Indeed, Kabbalah has been divided into a speculative and a practical aspect, the latter sometimes being associated with magic. This is a misunderstanding of what the Work is really about. In its original and purest form, theurgy, to give it its more respectable name, was the art and science of adjusting situations from the higher realms so as to allow a process to proceed or to create conditions wherein a situation could develop that would aid Creation at large, or an individual to evolve, and so serve God. To manipulate forces for private gain or set up relationships between elements that are out of the normative order was considered improper, and indeed, no more than bad magic. Fortunately, only those with real knowledge of such principles could perform these acts. Those dealing with natural magic were called shamans and sorcerers, while those concerned with the psyche were known as magicians. Priests and high priests dealt with the Spirit. In Kabbalah, such individuals were known as Baal Shem, although they might be at any of the levels.

Baal Shem means 'Master of the Name'. By this title was meant that a person had the ability to call upon supernatural powers. This skill enabled the practitioner to rearrange the higher flow of forms and forces in order to accomplish some purpose on Earth, according to their own will. Here is another dimension to the commandment "Thou shalt not use My Name in vain", that is, for personal reasons. The most well-known individual to bear this title was the Baal Shem Tov, which means the 'Master of the Good Name', that is he performed such acts only under obedience to the Divine. The Baal Shem Tov lived in 18th-century Poland where the most important miracle he performed was to heal and revitalise a deeply shattered Jewish community and give many thousands of despairing people back their faith in God, after one of the most tragic massacres of their history. This is an example of the Work of Unification on a large scale. Out of this apparently unlearned man came a major religious movement that is still very alive today. This could only occur because the Baal Shem Tov was able to bridge the worlds and act as a channel for the Divine Radiance, so that Light could reach the mass level which had been isolated from the general stream of life by the grim shells of persecution, depression and poverty. From that time forth the simple and hard life of the Jewish peasant was converted into joy by everyday action being seen as a mode of worship and illumination of ignorance. Out of this came a completely new subculture of religious affirmation. The demonic grip of cynicism had been reversed and a whole community saved from going under in a loss of faith. Only the miraculous, working through a 'Master of the Name' could have obtained this result.

A miracle is when the laws of a higher world supersede those of a lower world. Thus, for example, human intelligence can override nature, and men fly to the moon and back. In Kabbalah the principle is simply taken further in that events are influenced from a higher and generally unrecognised dimension. Thus prophetic foresight will stimulate preparations many years ahead of the time when something is needed, like the building of the Ark for the preservation of the Teaching. In a more practical way, action taken at a higher level can open the door to possibilities denied by the usual mechanics of a situation which often repeat old patterns. An example of this is when the psychological climate of a district is altered by the spiritual charging of the atmosphere by a community of meditators. People in the vicinity start to sense a certain calm in that part of the town. Less crime occurs for instance. Sometimes, it takes a long period to build up such a force field, and at others times it might be achieved in a short while. This is due to the ebb and flow of Creation. Timing is one of the most crucial factors of the Work.

To understand when and when not to act is vital in Kabbalah. In order to be able to do this one has either to know the situation deeply or be able to sense when to move. Some people have an intuitive knack of knowing the moment. These we call lucky in petty matters. In the issues of history they are seen as symbols of an epoch like Napoleon or Hitler, who caught the tidal flow of their time, but did not recognise its ebb and therefore were destroyed along with millions of others who followed, or were caught in their wake. The Kabbalist cannot afford to make mistakes in matters of the Spirit, as did Shabbtai Zevi, the 17th-century mystic, who with thousands believed he was the Messiah, until he was discredited at the crucial moment, and so bitterly disillusioned his followers. Therefore, prior to any Kabbalistic operation one contemplates all aspects of a situation before taking action, if any. This is done according to a familiar set of criteria.

Any event may be set out on the Tree because it must have its various levels in order to exist. Thus a situation has the interaction of the pillars and upper and lower faces, as well as the reactions of the different triads and Sefirot that compose it. For example, if an event is waxing, then the right hand pillar is particularly active with all the processes of repetition [*Nezah*], expansion [*Hesed*] and inspiration [*Hokhmah*] in the initiative. If the opposite is true, then the process is the reverse. From this follows the principle of oscillation, as the Tree moves in a continually adjusting rhythm to the forces and forms at play within it. By this method the discerning Kabbalist can decide that it is not wise to move against the tide, but wait for the flow to turn and place an impulse in the ebb that will bear fruit when the active phase begins again. Such operations can modify a process so as to accelerate, or even stop it in its tracks, if required, as with the heroin taker whose addiction was neutralised by deep prayer which is more powerful than bodily desire. Here we see the upper face overruling the lower face, the Spirit commanding the flesh. Many of the Baal Shem Tov's miracles were of this order.

On a larger scale the timing of miraculous events is often extraordinary in that several things happen simultaneously. This is because Providence works towards a moment when all the pillars, Sefirot and triads of a situation are in near perfect equilibrium. At such a moment the miraculous occurs apparently spontaneously in the birth of a remarkable person, or an impulse that has an effect for many centuries. The Kabbalist watches for such moments on the lesser scale of his or her own life so that action can be taken in some local matter that could affect the future of a project related to the Work. This might be organising a lecture or the finding of a place for a group to meet. This is the day-to-day task of the Kabbalist. Larger operations, like the creation of a school of Kabbalah require sustained effort over many years. During this time the long term aim can be lost and the spiritual line broken due to missing critical moments. Modifications have to be made if a living esoteric tradition is to regenerate itself over the ages. An example of this is the operation that is designed to meet the need of both spiritual and secular communities like the rule book of St. Benedict upon which most monastic orders are based. These early monasteries spread out over Western Europe bringing light and civilisation into the areas that had become barbaric after the fall of the Roman Empire. Whilst we do not live in such obviously difficult times there is still much work to be done in the world where materialism is rampant and the old forms of religion have lost much of their spirituality. Nearly every esoteric tradition has now come out into the open to meet this situation.

To provide a place where people who are seeking out a spiritual life can be taught may be the main work of a Kabbalistic school. Many individuals wander about amid the conflict and confusion of ordinary existence with desperate questions that no one outside real spiritual work can answer. The priest and the rabbi will more often than not give a learned response rather than a reply from inner experience. This is not enough for the seeker who wishes to know the truth. It is vital to hear it from the mouth of someone who knows for him or herself. When the seeker makes a connection with a tradition it is the duty of the school to nourish their soul and cherish their spirit. This is done by the good company and genuine teaching given out by a reliable instructor. Thus everyone in the Work has the responsibility to look out for such people and bring them in, after they have proved that they are seriously committed to the spiritual path. In this way the line is continued from generation to generation and the knowledge of the higher worlds is transmitted down the ages.

Looking on a yet larger scale, a kabbalistic school is but part of a network spread around the world which not only operates in the present, but forms part of a vast chain stretching back through time. As the living manifestation of Kabbalah, all Kabbalists hold to the covenant that has been passed down from Abraham who received it from Malchizedek. This tradition of receiving and imparting has created a deep spiritual stratum in the cultures of Christendom and Islam, as well as Judaism. It is also the esoteric basis of the Western occult tradition which ranges from the early masons to the modern Rosicrucians. Because of their common root, all these lines are joined in the Work, although their areas of operation may be far apart. Thus communication between schools and respect for each other's way is essential to the unification process that is surging forward at the moment.

The impulse to unite and co-operate with other genuine spiritual traditions is not to be confined to those of the Malchizedek tradition, but also extends to those whose Way originates in the Far East, the Far West and the southern hemisphere. If these paths come from and lead back to the same Divine Source, they are our spiritual kindred. The process of unification, however, does not mean a uniformity of mode, as past missionary movements have sought by conversion and Inquisition, but the realisation that the Divine takes pleasure in all the manifestations of the Work which may be seen like different flowers in a field. Indeed we are led to believe that it is only in the upper realms, where form is no longer relevant, that religions lose their identity, as people move closer to unity.

The Work goes on all the time and at every level. It is carried out here below by the living and simultaneously above by the Celestial Council of the Spirit. These great Beings direct the operation according to their rank and watch over mankind as it moves between the mass unconscious unfoldment of evolution and the conscious development of individuals as they take up their places in the awakened part of humanity. To realise what is being done for us is not enough. We must be deeply grateful to those who have gone before and help those in the next generation who will take our place. These in turn will aid the ones who will follow them. This is the way the Work of Unification is carried on. It is our privilege and obligation to perform it.

46. Completion

The Work of the Kabbalist begins and ends with the highest Name of God, I AM THAT I AM. In this Divine Name is the sum of everything that has been, is, and shall be. It defines all Existence from the coming in, to the outgoing of Being. By this most Holy title the universe emerges from No-thingness into the full manifestation of matter, and returns in the reflection of the Name to the One Who holds everything in Existence by the Will to be.

On the level of the individual this same Name has its profoundest meaning in that as the self becomes conscious of the SELF, so the Name comes into realisation in the depths, as well as the heights of Existence. Thus, the macrocosm and the microcosm meet in the individual who is a cell of Adam Kadmon. Seen from the viewpoint of our position, an incarnate human being is placed exactly midway between the Crown of Crowns and the Kingdom of Kingdoms. Thus a person centred in the *Tiferet* of the psyche is also at the place of Beauty on the Great Line of sefirot that runs down from the top to the bottom of Jacob's Ladder. Here at the position where the three lower worlds meet, a human being can hold a consciousness that has a contact with the middle face of the Five Gardens, as they are sometimes called, that span the extended Tree. This middle face has the sefirah of the Holy Spirit at its centre and the place where the three upper worlds meet at its top. Thus, whoever holds their consciousness here has access to all the worlds.

So far we have outlined the journey down from the Divine Adam in a state of innocence and the climb back up in the process of experience. We have also given a glimpse of how, after some training one may become a vehicle to receive and impart what flows down from Heaven. While all this is important, the greatest effort eventually is, as stated, to be able to join all the worlds within one's being, so as to act as a liaison between the various levels. This means that one may also lift what is below to the attention of that above, as well as convey the Heavenly influx consciously to a specific place below. The implication of this is enormous, for it brings up the possibility of intercession.

Intercession is the work of indirectly helping a situation. This may bring assistance from above or below. Such work requires an impeccable motive and the certainty that it is right to intervene. In this way it is possible at least to ease a situation, or perhaps at best raise it from the mundane to the sublime and so effect a profound change, like a spontaneous healing. Most of these operations are appropriate when there is a situation that is clearly beyond the personal scope of the Kabbalist, but nevertheless, needs attention, because circumstance has indicated that something should be done. It is then that the procedure of intercession is applied.

Intercession is when the Kabbalist presents a problem, such as the difficulty of another person, to the higher worlds, so that something may perhaps be done about it from that level. This is permitted, in that Providence often brings about the circumstances, so that others involved may witness or experience the intervention of Heaven. In the case of the person for whom the intercession is being made, it can be manifested in a miraculous moment or a graduated resolution as the mundane situation is eased from the worlds above. This might take the form of some money turning up, or of someone going away which gives a respite that may be used to free or dissolve some old pattern and so allow everybody to move on. For the Kabbalist such an exercise will also be of benefit, if only to improve the contact points between Heaven and Earth as well as expand the range of possibility available at that stage of spiritual development. This is because such operations increase the scope of consciousness and refine the vehicles of body, psyche and spirit, so that they become more like the sacred robes of Aaron, the High Priest.

The symbolism of Aaron's raiment described in such detail in Exodus, reveals what ideal an individual must slowly work towards when making these 'inner garments' by conscious effort. To hold this aim is a continuous process, which begins with bringing the physical body into good health and goes on to organise and develop the psyche and spirit, which correspond to the chequered and blue vestments worn by Aaron. The golden ephod he had over the other garments represents the Divine factor, with the golden plate on the turban engraved with the Name of God as the ultimate Crown.† The making of these interior layers, however, was not enough in itself. There had to be, as described in Exodus, a ceremonial dedication before a priest could carry out his duties. It is the same for the Kabbalist. While formal ceremonies are performed, it is more often than not that Providence sets up an initiation procedure in real life situations which tests, checks and confirms one's degree of development at each stage, to make sure one is ready. As each inner garment is put on, so there can be no return to the values and ways of ordinary life, although one may well be in the midst of it.

To be a true Kabbalist is to be responsible for what one does. This means that whilst one operates under obedience, nevertheless, free will still operates. This can allow evil to have access, for there is the possibility of temptation and corruption at every level. Thus, without seeking it, one is in the middle of the battle between demons and angels who represent the forces of order and chaos that struggle within the vast travail of Creation. To stand on the great axis of consciousness that stretches between the top and bottom of Existence is not easy because any mistake could be crucial not only to oneself and others below, but also for the beings of the upper worlds.

The actions of a person at any level of spirituality are no less effective in the Heavens than they are on Earth. This is because the power focused in such an individual is greater on being grounded in the World of Action than any ethereal creature, which is limited to its own level. The potency of human will is more than ever imagined because we, unlike animals and angels, who dwell below and above, are potentially universal creatures. No other entity has this capacity for unity, for only the species of mankind is made in the complete Image of the Divine. All other beings are facets of this Image, that is, they can only operate within a limited context, so that however powerful or skilful they may be at one level, they are ineffective or cannot function at another. As one rabbi said, "Consider a shark out of its element or an angel confronted with a machine. Neither would know what to do." All other creatures, we are told, are incomplete aspects of Adam Kadmon. Every non-human type of life, above and below, is modelled on a particular attribute of the Divine Image. Thus each creature is a

†See the author's *Kabbalah and Exodus*. (Wellow, UK: Gateway, and York Beach, ME: Samuel Weiser).

highly specialised faculty, with this animal expressing the nose and that one the sight, whilst different angels reflect such principles as memory or death. Only a human being has all the aspects of Adam Kadmon and the ability to experience them. However, perhaps the most important possession given to mankind is free will which is unique to us alone.

The gift of free will is greatly misunderstood for while most people believe they have it, they seldom use it, preferring to be carried by habit and circumstance until fate confronts them with choice. When the option of true individuality is taken up, then there is an awakening of the soul, which allows people not only to act independently, but to be responsible for their own lives. If they come under spiritual discipline, then greater responsibilities are acquired. At the midpoint of development everyone stands upon the pivot of the inner and outer worlds. This is the kabbalistic meaning of "A righteous man is the foundation of the universe". To be in this position opens up the implication of the Biblical expression, "The Son of Man", for here is where the relationship between the individual and Adam Kadmon starts to operate.

Between the place of the self, where the three lower worlds meet, and the place where the three upper worlds meet, is the sefirah of the Holy Spirit. From here the Sacred Voice instructs the self and brings it up to that mysterious position on the Ladder where the Messiah, or the Anointed One resides at the place where the psyche, the Spirit and the Divine can mingle. Much has been said over the centuries about this enigmatic personage. I will repeat what I have learnt, and that is, that this being is the one perfect human incarnation of any moment in time. Thus, whilst the role is constant, the person filling it may change from instant to instant, as individuals on Earth reach this flowering of embodied realisation. As such they hold this role only as long as is needed, so that whoever fills this position may complete their earthly destiny. While most of these Anointed ones are unknown they are, nevertheless, the connection between all the worlds and the Divine. Thus according to this understanding there is a Messiah for every moment and generation. There always has been, is, and shall be as long as Mankind exists.

Beyond the Son of Man who is at this point the Way, the Truth, and the Light, lies the radiance of the Living Almighty, Who sits above the Great Heavenly Council that governs the universe. Hence the perfected individual ascends on the penultimate stage of the fourth and last journey, to stand among the Holy Spirits of the Face before entering into the Presence of YAHVEH-ELOHIM, at the *Keter* of Creation. Here, we are told, the Divine atom that has been separated from Adam Kadmon since leaving the World of Emanation speaks the highest Holy Name I AM THAT I AM in the full consciousness of its meaning. This act begins the final process of becoming united with the ONE at the Crown of Crowns. In this union the last vestage of separation dissolves and individuality disappears into the Divine Abyss of Holy Bliss, before passing out of all Existence and into God.

Until that time we on Earth must carry out the task assigned to us, living our each day as a witness to the Name of Names. In this way we fulfil our fate and so move another link in the chain of our destiny. When our task is finished, then we too shall return with the realisation of where we have come from, who we are, and where we are going. When this is done the Work of the Kabbalist will be complete.

ADONAI ECHAD: THE LORD IS ONE

Glossary of Terms

Arabot: Seventh heaven
Asiyyah: World of Making. Elemental and natural world.
Ayin: The No-Thingness of God.
Azilut: The World of Emanation: the sefirotic realm and Glory. Adam Kadmon.
Barakhah: Blessing or Grace.
Beriah: World of Creation and Pure Spirit. World of Archangels.
Binah: Sefirah of Understanding. Sometimes called Reason.
Daat: Sefirah of Knowledge.
Devekut: Communion.
Din: Judgement, alternative name for Gevurah.
En Sof: The Infinite or Endless. A Title of God.
Gadlut: The major conscious state.
Gevurah: Sefirah of Judgement. Literal translation Strength or Might.
Gilgulim: Cycle of rebirth. Transmigration of souls.
Hesed: Sefirah of Mercy. Sometimes called Gedulah.
Hod: Sefirah of Reverberation, Resounding Splendour.
Hokhmah: Sefirah of Wisdom and Revelation.
Katnut: The lesser conscious state.
Kavvanah: Prayer with conscious intent: plural Kavvanot or special prayers.
Kellippot: World of Shells and demons.
Keter: Sefirah of the Crown.
Malkhut: Sefirah of the Kingdom.
Merkabah: The Chariot of Yetzirah.
Nefesh: Animal or vital Soul.
Neshamah: Human Soul.
Nezah: Sefirah of Eternity, also called Victory and Endurance.
Pechad: Fear. Alternative name for Gevurah.
Qlipoth: Western Tradition spelling of Kellippot.
Ruah: Spirit.
Sefirah: Containers, Lights and Attributes of God: plural Sefirot.
Shekhinah: Indwelling Presence of God in Malkhut.
Shemittah: Great cosmic cycle.
Teshuvah: Repentance, redemption and conversion of a lower face into an upper face.
Talmud: Recorded commentaries on the Bible and Oral Tradition.
Tiferet: Sefirah of Beauty. Sometimes called Adornment.
Yesod: Sefirah of Foundation.
Yetzirah: World of Formation. Psychological and angelic World.
Zadek: A just man.
Zelem: Image.
Zimzum: Principle of Divine contraction before Universe comes into being.

Index